A
Tourist's Guide
to Murder

Books by V. M. Burns

Mystery Bookshop Mysteries
THE PLOT IS MURDER
READ HERRING HUNT
THE NOVEL ART OF MURDER
WED, READ & DEAD
BOOKMARKED FOR MURDER
A TOURIST'S GUIDE TO MURDER

Dog Club Mysteries
IN THE DOG HOUSE
THE PUPPY WHO KNEW TOO MUCH
BARK IF IT'S MURDER
PAW AND ORDER
SIT, STAY, SLAY

Published by Kensington Publishing Corp.

A
Tourist's Guide
to Murder

V. M. BURNS

KENSINGTON
PUBLISHING CORP.

www.kensingtonbooks.com

KENSINGTON BOOKS are published by

Kensington Publishing Corp.
119 West 40th Street
New York, NY 10018

All Kensington titles, imprints, and distributed lines are available at special quantity discounts for bulk purchases for sales promotion, premiums, fundraising, educational, or institutional use.

Special book excerpts or customized printings can also be created to fit specific needs. For details, write or phone the office of the Kensington Sales Manager: Kensington Publishing Corp., 119 West 40th Street, New York, NY 10018. Attn. Sales Department. Phone: 1-800-221-2647.

The K logo is a trademark of Kensington Publishing Corp.

ISBN-13: 978-1-4967-2896-8 (ebook)
ISBN-10: 1-4967-2896-3 (ebook)

ISBN-13: 978-1-4967-2895-1
ISBN-10: 1-4967-2895-5
First Kensington Trade Paperback Printing: February 2021

10 9 8 7 6 5 4 3 2 1

Printed in the United States of America

Acknowledgments

Thank you to Dawn Dowdle, Blue Ridge Literary Agency, and John Scognamiglio, Michelle Addo, and all of the wonderful people at Kensington.

I have been blessed to get to work with some amazing people. Thank you, Derrick, Eric, Jennifer, Amber, and Robin for being such a great team. I also want to thank Deborah, Grace, Jamie, and Tena for all you do to help promote and support me.

This book wouldn't have been finished without my good friend, Lana Hechtman Ayers, for the amazing gift and for acquainting me with Maine. Thank you, Eileen and Carl Robey, for the lovely food at 1802 House and the wonderful inspiration and peace. Special thanks to Alexia Gordon, and Cheyney McWilliams for the medical advice.

Love and gratitude to my family, Benjamin, Jacquelyn, Christopher, Carson, Crosby, Jillian, Drew, and Marcella. And, special love and thanks to Shelitha and Sophia.

Chapter 1

"Attention." I clinked my knife against my glass. "Attention." Unfortunately, no one listened, and the chatter got louder rather than softer.

My sister, Jenna Rutherford, leaned close and whispered into my ear, "Does the phrase 'herding cats' mean anything to you?"

I glanced down the table. My boyfriend, Frank Patterson, had reserved space for us in the upper level of his restaurant. Initially, I attributed the upper area seating to the fact that it was Friday night and the lower level of the restaurant and bar was full, so he was providing us space in the not-quite-open-to-the-public section to give us a quiet place to dine. However, after watching and listening, I suspected the seating arrangements had more to do with preserving the sanity of his paying customers.

The noise level had yet to reach DEFCON 1, but we were pretty close. I glanced down the table at my mom, Grace, and her new husband, Harold Robertson. They were newlyweds, only married for about six weeks, and were still at that sickeningly romantic stage that made people look at them and say "aww" or that made you want to barf from the sugar overload.

It was hard to believe that my mom, at five feet and barely one hundred pounds, was the child of my five-foot-ten and well over two-hundred-and-fifty-pound grandmother. Two more diametrically opposed humans would be difficult to find. My mom, petite and fragile, and my grandmother, large and highly capable, were an anomaly. Although, I was learning that my mom had a bit of spunk buried deep down inside that she could pull out from time to time.

Harold reached over and started slicing my mother's roast beef because she was obviously incapable of slicing her own meat. I swallowed hard to keep from losing my dinner.

My twin nephews, Christopher and Zaq, had both just turned twenty-one. Each had brought a date. Christopher's date was a very serious young woman with a short pixie cut hairstyle and wire-rimmed glasses. I think she said her name was Tiffany or Brittney or some other Nee. She seemed shy, except when it came to politics and then she became loud and opinionated. Unfortunately, she'd chosen to start a political discussion with my grandmother. Melanie or Stephanie, or whatever her name, was ultra conservative and unyielding in her opinions on everything from capital punishment to abortion to gun control. Everyone's entitled to their opinions; however, she would have fared better by not sharing her opinions quite so adamantly or by not calling her date's great-grandmother a liberal, left-wing commie, especially not to her face. Nana Jo didn't take kindly to that, and it had taken both my brother-in-law, Tony, and Nana Jo's boyfriend, Freddie Williams, a retired policeman, to restrain Nana Jo from karate chopping the unfortunate waif. Thankfully, Jenna had seen the rumbling and grabbed Nana Jo's purse, which she rightly guessed held Nana Jo's gun. Needless to say, we made sure

Nana Jo was seated far away from Daphne or Sydney or whatever her name was during the meal.

Zaq's date was Emma Lee, a petite Asian American with dark hair, almond-shaped eyes, and the loveliest southern accent. Next to Emma was my assistant, Dawson Alexander, and his girlfriend, Jillian Clark. Jillian was a tall, young woman with dark, frizzy hair and the slender body of a ballet dancer. She was also the granddaughter of one of Nana Jo's closest friends, Dorothy Clark. Dorothy, like Nana Jo, was a vibrant older woman who was just shy of six feet tall and teetering toward three hundred pounds. Dorothy was an attractive woman and an incurable flirt with a black belt in aikido and a deep sexy voice that men found irresistible.

Ruby Mae Stevenson and Irma Starczewski rounded out the party. Ruby Mae was the youngest of Nana Jo's friends from Shady Acres Retirement Village. In her mid-sixties, Ruby Mae was an African American woman with skin the color of coffee with a touch of cream and salt-and-pepper hair that she wore pulled back in a bun. Nana Jo said when Ruby Mae let her hair down, it was so long she could sit on it, but I had never been fortunate enough to see it. Ruby Mae was from Alabama and had a lovely southern drawl, which she hadn't lost despite spending more than forty years in the Midwest.

Irma was the oldest of Nana Jo's friends. In her mid-eighties, she dyed her hair jet black and pulled it up into a beehive. Years of heavy smoking had left Irma with a raspy voice. At only five feet tall and less than one hundred pounds, Irma looked more like my mom than my grandmother. However, Irma was what my grandmother called a "man-crazed strumpet."

"I can't believe you're going to England with that crazy bunch," Jenna said, sipping her Moscato. "You'll be lucky if you're not arrested or kicked out of the country."

"It'll be fine. Besides, it's just one week. What could possibly go wrong?"

Jenna glanced over her wineglass and gave me her "you poor pitiful thing" look.

Like my mom and my grandmother, I didn't think my sister and I were anything alike, despite the fact we were both five foot four and roughly the same weight with dark hair and dark eyes. My sister was a highly successful attorney with a reputation as a pit bull, which she relished. If I were compared to a dog, it would probably be more of a Chihuahua or a poodle.

My boyfriend, Frank Patterson, sidled up next to me and whispered in my ear, "Irma just grabbed my butt."

Not normally a wine drinker, it was never a problem for me to be the designated driver whenever I went out with Nana Jo and the girls. However, tonight, I wished there was more than Diet Coke in my glass. I sipped it anyway and tried to steady my nerves and repeated my mantra. "It's just one week." This was going to be one heck of a trip.

Frank leaned close and whispered, "I'm going to miss you."

"I'll miss you too." I could feel his warm breath on my neck, and my pulse raised. "It's just one week."

He gave me a kiss behind my ear. "I'll be waiting."

I could feel the heat rise up my neck, but before I could say or do anything, Nana Jo took her knife and clanged her glass. "Now, listen up. Sam has something to say."

Just like the stock brokerage commercials for EF Hutton from my childhood, when Nana Jo talked, people listened. The room quieted down and all eyes turned toward me.

I cleared my throat and stood up. "Thank you all for coming to wish us well as Nana Jo and the girls and I prepare to leave for London tomorrow. I want to thank my assistant,

Dawson, and my nephews, Christopher and Zaq, for agreeing to use their mid-winter break to work at the bookstore."

Everyone applauded my nephews, who nodded their acknowledgement.

"Jillian and I will help too," Emma said. "We have a light schedule, and I think it'll be fun."

"Remember, Frank is just a few doors down the street if you need anything." I smiled at Frank.

He grinned. "I'll make sure they don't starve while you're gone."

"You better watch what you're saying," Tony joked. "Those boys will bankrupt you."

Everyone laughed.

When the laughter died down, I continued, "I also want to thank my brother-in-law, Tony, and my sister, Jenna, for looking after my babies, Snickers and Oreo, while I'm gone."

Jenna shook her head. "That's all Tony's doing."

Snickers and Oreo were my toy poodles, and I knew I'd miss them more than anyone. I reached down and pulled the folder from my bag. I passed out envelopes to Dorothy, Irma, Ruby Mae, and Nana Jo. "Inside these envelopes is your itinerary, the information for the tour, and all of our flight and hotel information. Please make sure you have your passports and all required documents."

"We got this," Nana Jo said. "I know you're only going so you can do research for your next book, but we intend to have fun."

"Research *is* fun," I muttered.

"I'd like to research one of those British royals," Irma said.

"They're all either married or too young for you," Nana Jo said.

Irma laughed. "No such thing as too young." She took a

drink. "I'll bet I could teach that Prince Charles a thing or two."

Nana Jo rolled her eyes, and I made the mistake of glancing at my sister. She didn't say a word, but her silent smirk spoke volumes.

I sat down and took a sip of Diet Coke. "It's only one week. What could possibly go wrong?"

Chapter 2

I spent a few more minutes trying to point out the important related items I had printed and placed in all their packets. Unfortunately, that's when the waitress arrived with another round of drinks, and if anyone heard my carefully rehearsed speech on the do's and don'ts of traveling abroad, it was purely by accident. Eventually, I gave up and sat down when I realized that not even my grandmother was listening. Frank gave my hand a squeeze but was beckoned by his new assistant manager to help with a problem downstairs and had to leave.

I passed Jenna the packet I had made for her with my itinerary, vet, emergency vet, and American Consulate information. She glanced through the envelope and then handed it to her husband and took another sip of wine. She didn't say it, but her eyebrows said, *You poor pitiful fool.*

After an hour, the party broke up and I looked around for my charges. It was my job to see the ladies made it home safely whenever we went anywhere where drinks were served. Ruby Mae and Nana Jo helped me drag Irma and Dorothy to the car. They had made their way downstairs. I found Irma draped around a man who appeared to be half her age, while Dorothy was doing shots at the bar with a group of young men having a bachelor party.

On the car ride back to Shady Acres Retirement Village, Dorothy lamented being taken away too soon.

"Five more minutes and I'd have wiped the floor with those lightweights."

Nana Jo glared at Dorothy in the rearview mirror. "It's not fair. You've got at least fifty years of drinking experience and more than fifty pounds on those boys."

I glanced in the mirror in time to see Dorothy stick out her tongue.

I tried one last time to remind the girls to make sure they reviewed the information on what could and could not be brought into the country as I pulled up outside the retirement village entrance.

Nana Jo was spending the night with me, so when the girls were securely inside, I drove the short distance to downtown North Harbor.

My bookstore, Market Street Mysteries, was located on a corner lot in North Harbor. The previous owners had built a garage at the back edge of the property line and then fenced in the area, creating a courtyard. I pulled into the garage and noticed the lights on in the apartment above. Dawson Alexander was home, and that light gave me a feeling of comfort.

Inside, I felt a pang of sadness when I was greeted by silence instead of the barks of my two toy poodles, Snickers and Oreo. Earlier, Tony had stopped by and picked up the poodles, their food, and all their gear. Not having to worry about the dogs was supposed to make things easier for me tomorrow, but tonight it definitely made my life lonelier.

"You go on upstairs," I said. "I'm going to take a look around and make sure everything is ready for tomorrow."

Nana Jo climbed the stairs, leaving me alone in the bookstore.

Opening a mystery bookstore had been a dream I'd shared with my late husband, Leon, for years. Before he died, he made me promise to move forward. I had no regrets about quitting my job as a high school English teacher to follow my dream. It had turned out to be a great decision. Nana Jo and I had always been close, but we had grown even closer these last few months. She shared my love of mysteries and had a knack for helping people find just the right type for them. I walked around the dark empty space and breathed in the smell of books, Murphy's Oil Soap, and coffee, which lingered in the building. It was a smell I loved, and one that now represented home. I enjoyed owning a bookstore even though I had less time to read now.

After making sure the store was secure and that everything was ready for my nephews, I engaged the alarm and climbed the stairs that led to my home.

When I bought the building, the upstairs had been one large loft space with hardwood floors, high ceilings with brick walls, and exposed ductwork. I had the space separated into two bedrooms, two bathrooms, and a large open great room and kitchen. The door to Nana Jo's room was closed, but a beam of light shone from underneath and told me she hadn't yet gone to sleep.

I took care of my nightly routine and went to bed. Unfortunately, sleep was elusive, and rather than fighting it, I got up and went to my computer.

Owning a mystery bookshop was only one of my dreams. My other dream involved writing British historic cozy mysteries. After Leon's death, I decided to tackle that dream too and had written a few stories. Writing mostly helped to occupy my mind and kept me busy so I didn't have quite so much time to sit around thinking about how much I missed my husband and wallowing in self-pity. However, over time, the stories had become more than a time filler, and I really enjoyed the fantasy world and the characters I'd created.

My e-mail flashed, and I realized that with all of the preparations for the trip, I hadn't checked it all day. I pulled it up and deleted the spam. There was one message from my agent, Pam Porter, from Big Apple Literary Agency. I could feel my heart rate increase as I double-clicked the message, even though I told myself it was probably just an update telling me the publisher who had previously expressed interest in reading the full manuscript wasn't interested after all.

As I read, my heart pounded even more, and I had to read and reread the e-mail at least three more times to make sure I read it properly. "Oh my God!" I shook my head to clear my vision and stared at the screen even harder. When I was sure my eyes weren't deceiving me, I screamed, "Nana Jo!"

For a woman in her eighties, my grandmother was still very spry, something she chalked up to yoga, aikido, and bourbon. Nana Jo ran into my room. She had large curlers sticking up out of the top of her head and was wearing a nightshirt with the snarky older lady from the Hallmark cards, Maxine, which read, *"Fool me once, shame on you. Fool me twice, you better have a good look at your insurance policy."* She also had a gun that I recognized as the weapon she usually kept in her purse.

She looked around the room frantically. "What's happened?"

"Nana Jo, put that gun down. I just got an e-mail and—"

She lowered her gun and narrowed her eyes. "You called me in here because of an e-mail?"

"It's from my agent. Listen." I turned back to my laptop. "'I'm excited to tell you that we have received an offer from Mysterious Books for your British historic cozy mystery. They're offering a three-book deal.'" I stared at my grandmother. "They want to publish my book."

Nana Jo gave a whoop, placed her gun on my desk, and then gave me a big hug. "Congratulations! I knew you could do it."

"I'm stunned."

"Well, I'm thirsty. Let's celebrate." Nana Jo hurried to the kitchen.

I followed her, still dazed. In the kitchen, she reached in the back of the pantry and pulled out a tall box.

She placed it on the counter.

I stared from the tall narrow box to my grandmother. "Where did that come from?"

Nana Jo grinned. "First, you have to open it."

I unwrapped the box, which contained a bottle of champagne with a label I recognized and knew was very expensive. I lifted the bottle out of the box and set it on the counter. "I don't understand?"

Nana Jo opened a drawer and rummaged until she found a corkscrew. "I bought this over a year ago. When I first read your book. I knew you'd get it published, so I wanted to be ready to celebrate when the big day came."

I wiped away a tear and gave my grandmother a hug. "Thank you. I just wish Leon . . ."

"Leon was always proud of you, and far as I can tell, nothing's changed." She sniffed. "Now, no more of that nonsense. This isn't a time for tears. This is a time for celebrating. You get the glasses."

I gave a giddy, slightly hysterical laugh and used my sleeve to wipe my eyes. Then, I swallowed any sad thoughts of Leon and the past, opened the cabinet, and took out two of my best fluted glasses and placed them on the counter.

Nana Jo uncorked the champagne with a loud pop and quickly poured the bubbling liquid into our glasses.

We each picked up a glass and held it aloft.

"To my beautiful granddaughter at the start of her new career. May you have as much success as Agatha Christie."

I giggled at the very idea of mentioning my name in the same sentence with my favorite mystery writer. However, I clinked my glass with hers and then took a sip.

We quickly finished our drinks, and Nana Jo refilled the glasses.

"The only thing better would be if we had something sweet to go with this."

I smiled. "I think I can help with that." I walked around to the freezer and reached in the back. I pulled out a frozen cheesecake. "I was saving this for a special occasion." I held up the box. "I guess this qualifies."

"You bet your bippy it does." Nana Jo smacked the counter. "Now, you nuke that puppy enough to get a fork in it, and I'll get the plates." She took two dessert plates from the cabinet, and I followed the directions on the box and microwaved the cheesecake just enough to soften it.

With cheesecake and champagne, we perched on barstools and enjoyed the late-night decadence.

Nana Jo took one bite and then hopped up and went to the refrigerator. She opened the door and glanced around. Not finding what she wanted, she sighed and closed the door. "The only thing that would make this better would have been a little dollop of whipped cream."

I smiled. "Oh, I can make some."

"Make it?" She stared at me. "Who died and made you Martha Stewart?"

I grabbed the heavy cream from the fridge and pulled out my new mini food chopper. "Dawson asked for one of these for Christmas, and they were so cute, I got one for myself too." I poured the cream into the chopper along with a tablespoon of sugar and a splash of vanilla. Then, I pulsed the chopper for ten seconds. I took off the lid and smiled. I took a spoon and placed a generous amount of the whipped cream on both of our plates.

Nana Jo gazed at the fluffy white clouds of sugary goodness and took a tentative bite.

I watched her face anxiously while she tasted it. When she closed her eyes and moaned in pleasure, I released the breath I'd been holding and giggled. "Good stuff, isn't it?"

"Hmm. That's delicious. How did you know how to make it?"

I took a bite and allowed the cheesecake and whipped cream to dissolve on my tongue before I chewed and swallowed. "When I went to the store to buy it, the sales rep was doing a demonstration. It was amazing. I couldn't believe how fast and easy it was."

We sat and enjoyed our treats in silence.

"I wonder what happens now?" Nana Jo asked.

I shrugged. "Pam's e-mail said she knew I was leaving for England, but she wanted to give me the good news now rather than waiting until I come back." I scraped the last bits of cheesecake and graham cracker crust with my fork and licked it like a popsicle until I'd gotten every crumb. "She said she'd give me the details when I got back."

Nana Jo took our empty plates to the dishwasher and placed the leftover cheesecake in the refrigerator. "Christopher and Zaq will finish that off while we're gone."

I sipped my champagne. "I'm glad she didn't wait until I got back to tell me."

Nana Jo smiled. "Me too." She grabbed the bottle of champagne. "Let's finish this bottle off and then we better get some sleep. We've got an early day tomorrow."

We sat up for an hour talking and sipping champagne. Eventually, Nana Jo headed off to bed and I went to my room. It was early Saturday morning, but between the excitement of the trip and the news about my book, I still wasn't sleepy. So, I decided to spend a little bit of time writing to help settle my nerves.

⁕

Wickfield Lodge, English country home of Lord William Marsh
January 1939

"What an incredible boor." Lady Penelope paced the floor of the Marsh family drawing room. "I don't think he's ever going to leave."

Victor Carlston sat with his legs stretched out in front of the fireplace. "Darling, you really shouldn't upset yourself."

Lady Elizabeth sat on the sofa and pulled out her knitting bag. She smiled to herself as she removed the soft, fluffy yellow yarn. She loved knitting and often found it helped her think clearly and eased her mind. All of the Marshes had sweaters, socks, and scarves that kept them warm through the cold, damp winter months in the British countryside. Nothing gave Lady Elizabeth more pleasure than knitting for her family and those she loved; however, this pram set for her niece's expected arrival was by far the item that gave her the greatest joy.

Lady Penelope walked over to her aunt. "Oh, that's absolutely lovely." She fingered the soft fluffy wool.

Lady Elizabeth smiled. "I'm glad you like it, dear." She pulled the pattern out of her bag and passed it to her niece. "I saw this beehive pattern at Harrods along with the softest wool, and

I just had to get it." She watched her niece carefully. "You do like it, don't you?"

"Oh, yes." She hugged her aunt. "I love it."

Lady Elizabeth smiled. "Good, then I'd better get busy."

Lord William shoved tobacco into his pipe. "You'll spoil the young fellow. Not even here yet."

The women exchanged a glance and held back smiles.

The door to the drawing room opened, and Lady Clara Trewellen-Harper floated into the room and flopped down on the sofa next to her cousin. "Gawd, what a ghastly man." She looked around at Victor Carlston, and her cheeks took on a rosy color. "Oh, Victor. I'm so sorry."

After a brief pause, everyone in the room chuckled.

Lady Elizabeth was torn between wanting to ease her young cousin's discomfort and the need to convey a message. She chose comfort and patted her hand. "It's all right, dear."

"We were just saying much the same thing before you came in," Lady Penelope said with a smile.

Lady Clara leaned back against the sofa. "Glad I'm not the only one who finds Captain Jessup irritating."

Lady Penelope looked around. "Where is the brute?"

Lady Clara waved a hand in the air. "Arguing with Peter . . . ah, I mean Detective Inspector Covington." She glanced away, but not before another flush spread to her cheeks.

The drawing room door opened again, and a

tall, lean, gangly man with thick, curly hair entered.

Lady Elizabeth noted the flush in Lady Clara's cheeks deepened as she looked up and the object of their conversation entered.

Lady Elizabeth smiled warmly. "Detective Inspector Covington, we're so glad you could join us."

The detective had a red patch on his neck, and his ears were aflame. He marched into the room and took out a handkerchief and wiped his neck.

"Why, you look positively furious," Victor Carlston said. He rose with concern and approached the detective. "What's happened?"

"That . . . man . . . Captain Jessup." He searched for the words. "He's a self-righteous, opinionated, overbearing . . ." He looked around at the women and softened his tone. "I'm terribly sorry. I shouldn't say such things, especially in the presence of ladies."

Lady Clara, calm, cool, and collected with her emotions fully in hand, whirled around and faced the young detective. "Why not? I've just been expressing similar sentiments about the Neanderthal." She folded her hands across her chest.

"She's right," Lady Penelope said. She waved a hand toward an empty seat. "You might as well come in and join the party."

The Scotland Yard detective sat down in a chair near the fireplace. "I've honestly not met anyone quite so . . . objectionable."

"And this from a man who spends all of his

days with criminals," Lady Clara said and marched back to sit next to Lady Elizabeth.

Detective Inspector Covington grinned. "Well, I do get out of the nick on occasion."

"You know what I mean." Lady Clara leaned across to speak to her cousin. "Can't we toss him out?"

Lady Elizabeth continued to knit. "All of the other guests from the wedding are gone, and I'm sure Captain Jessup will be on his way soon." She sighed. "Although, I must admit, he has managed to upset most of the household staff too."

Victor turned. "I'm sorry, this is all my fault. If it hadn't been for the darned plumbing problems, we could go home to Bidwell Cottage, and you wouldn't be subjected to all of this."

Lady Elizabeth shook her head. "Nonsense. You and Penelope are family. There's no way you could think of entertaining anyone until you can get the plumbing fixed, and I don't want to hear anything more about the subject."

Lord William Marsh chomped on the stem of his pipe. "Agreed."

"Thank you, all." Victor bowed.

Lady Clara tilted her head and stared at Victor. "I have to admit, I don't really see a resemblance between you both, and he certainly lacks your charm and manners."

Victor smiled. "Thank you . . . I think."

Lady Elizabeth turned to Victor. "How are you two related?"

Victor scratched his temple. "To be completely honest, I'm not really sure. He claims to be related to my uncle Percival, but Uncle Percy died before I was born, so . . . I'm not exactly sure." He shook his head. "I have to say, I wish he wouldn't talk about his political views."

Lady Clara stood up, stuck her nose in the air, and glanced down with a sour expression as though she just got a whiff of a foul odor. She spoke in a mocking voice, "I was chatting with my good friends, Joachim von Ribbentrop, the Foreign Minister, and the American Ambassador, Joseph Kennedy." She put her hands behind her back and paced the floor in a cocky manner. "We are all agreed that England would do well to listen to Neville Chamberlain. Britain isn't ready for war, and Americans don't have the stomach for another war. Americans are weak and more concerned with jazz and having fun than they are with world affairs, especially when those affairs are in Europe and not in her own backyard. Ha ha ha."

Everyone chuckled, but there was something sad behind the laughter.

Lord William huffed. "Bloody fool."

"Britain will be ready for war when the time comes," Victor said.

Lady Penelope choked back a sob. She quickly turned and took out a handkerchief and dabbed her eyes.

Lady Clara's face drooped. "I'm sorry. I shouldn't make light of the situation, but that man just makes me so angry."

"I know, dear." Lady Elizabeth smiled at her young cousin.

Just then, the door flew open and a young girl with dark curls raced into the room and flung herself into the arms of Lady Elizabeth, who managed to move her knitting needles out of the way just in time to avoid injuring the small child.

"Rivka, what are you doing awake at this time of night?" Lady Elizabeth feigned a tone of reproach but was unable to sustain it in the face of the vivacious child. She smiled and gave her a hug. "Where are your—"

Two thin, pale young boys of twelve with dark hair and eyes rushed into the room and halted quickly when they saw the crowd assembled.

"Brothers?" Lady Elizabeth finished.

Despite their expensive, well-made clothes, which Lady Elizabeth had purchased from Harrods on her recent trip into town, there was something about the children that marked them as being foreigners before they even opened their mouths to speak, whether it was the hungry desperate look that Lady Elizabeth sometimes noted or the fear that flashed in their eyes when they saw men in uniform. The children had arrived a few months earlier as part of the Kindertransport, a program that rescued Jewish children from Germany, Poland, and other Eastern European nations to the United Kingdom. The children hadn't been at Wickfield Lodge long, but in the short time, they had managed to endear themselves to Lady Elizabeth and the rest of the Marsh household.

At age two, Rivka was the youngest. Her twin brothers, Josiah and Johan, were her protectors. Although they had gained weight and their eyes were brighter, there was still a hunger that looked from their eyes that had nothing to do with food.

Penelope's eyes softened as she looked at the children, and she unconsciously placed a hand to her stomach.

Lady Elizabeth beckoned for the boys to enter and then patted the sofa. She had been working on her German so she could communicate with the children better, but she had quite a long way to go. In the meantime, gestures worked fairly well.

The boys hurried to the sofa and then jostled to see who would sit closest to Lady Elizabeth. The end result was Lady Elizabeth sitting on the end of the sofa with Rivka on her lap. One of the twins, she thought it was Johan, sat to her right, and Josiah perched on the sofa arm.

"Have you washed?" Lady Elizabeth said slowly. "Washed?" She made a circular motion around her face.

Victor chuckled. "Let me try." He turned to the boys. "Hast du dich gewaschen?"

Josiah and Johan nodded vigorously. "Ja. Ja."

Rivka giggled and shook her head. "Nein."

Lady Elizabeth glanced down at the little waif and gave her a hug. "Then you will need a bath and then off to bed you go."

She started to rise when the door opened and a tall, thin, stiff man with dark hair, which he slicked down with pomade to hide an unruly cowlick, piercing blue eyes, and a curl to his lip limped into the room. "Ah, here. I was just about to ask your butler where everyone had gotten to when I heard the commotion." He looked down his nose at the boys.

The atmosphere in the room changed, and Lady Elizabeth shivered.

A heavy sigh escaped from Lady Penelope, and she turned her back and walked to the window.

Lady Clara folded her arms across her chest and glared.

Lord William stuffed his pipe in his mouth and clamped down.

Detective Inspector Covington and Victor exchanged glances and struggled to find something to say to ease the tension.

Rivka leaned in closer to Lady Elizabeth and hid her face.

Josiah and Johan became stiff, and Lady Elizabeth noticed the fear that was always just under the surface had risen to the top.

Lady Elizabeth snuggled Rivka tighter. "Captain Jessup, you caught us enjoying a moment of family time before the children went up to bed."

"Looks like I arrived just in time." His lips twisted into what he must have assumed was a smile but looked more like a grimace. He sauntered over to Lady Clara and stood closer than propriety allowed. "Seeing as Victor and I are cousins, and he's now married into this lovely family . . ." He caressed Lady Clara's cheek with his finger.

She swiped away his hand as though swatting an annoying fly and glared at the ill-mannered visitor.

Lady Elizabeth saw Detective Inspector Covington's hands tighten into fists as he abruptly rose from his seat.

"As I was saying," Captain Jessup said, "now that Victor has married into this lovely family, that makes me a member of the family." He gave a sly glance toward the Scotland Yard detective, which seemed to say, *I'm part of this family and you are not.*

Detective Inspector Covington read the glance, and a red flush rose from his neck.

Captain Jessup threw back his head and laughed.

Victor stood from his chair. "Now, see here, I—"

Just as things were getting heated, the door opened and a small man with curly, dark hair, glasses, and a moustache appeared. "Ah, there you are."

Lady Elizabeth smiled warmly. "Joseph, please come in. I think you know everyone else here." She glanced around the room. "Except perhaps Captain Jessup." She extended an arm in the direction of the visitor. "He's a new *acquaintance.*"

A slight hint of color on the Captain's ears indicated he recognized the slight.

Lady Elizabeth turned to the captain. "Captain Jessup, let me introduce you to Joseph Mueller. Joseph is a brilliant scientist at the University of Cambridge and is married to Thompkins's daughter, Mary."

Joseph Mueller smiled broadly, stepped forward, and extended a hand. "Pleased to make your acquaintance."

Captain Jessup sneered and stared at the young man. After a tense pause, he asked, "Mueller, is that Jewish?"

Joseph lowered his hand. "Yes, it is."

Lady Elizabeth rose, still holding Rivka. Her back was straight and solid as steel. Her face was stone, her eyes cold. She took two steps and stood in front of the captain. "Do you have a problem with the fact that Joseph is Jewish?" She waited for an answer. Her posture, the set of her chin, and the glint in her eyes screamed that the answer to this question was of vital importance.

The silence was intense, and based on the expressions on their faces, everyone in the room felt it.

After a brief moment, Captain Jessup gave a fake laugh. "Not in the least." With an effort, he extended his hand.

Joseph Mueller hesitated a half second and then briefly shook.

When the men released hands, Captain Jessup turned and waltzed toward the window. He took a handkerchief from his pocket and, with his back turned, wiped his hands.

Lady Clara seethed and took a step toward the captain but was restrained by Detective Inspector Covington.

Joseph turned to Lady Elizabeth and bowed slightly. Then, he glanced at the boys. "Kommen sie."

The boys hurried, with Rivka, out of the room.

Lady Clara looked as though she was going to

speak but halted when Lady Penelope gasped. "Oh my."

Victor hurried to his wife's side. "Are you okay?"

Everyone stared at Lady Penelope, who stared back with a shocked expression. Suddenly, she looked up. "I think I just felt the baby move."

Chapter 3

I woke up Saturday morning at you-have-got-to-be-kidding-o-clock with drool running down the side of my mouth, the imprint of my keyboard on the side of my face, 517 pages of gibberish, and Nana Jo shaking my shoulder and yelling in my ear.

"Wake up!" Nana Jo lifted my eyelid open. "I've been calling you for fifteen minutes."

I swatted away her hand and sat up.

"You better shake a leg if we're going to make the shuttle." She turned and walked out.

I looked around to get my bearings. My alarm was buzzing, but I had ignored it.

One glance at the time sent my heart racing. I was thirty minutes late, which only left me thirty minutes to get dressed and finish packing before it was time to leave. I took several minutes to delete 510 pages of garbage, save what was left of my manuscript, and toss my laptop into a bag.

I showered, dressed, and shoved clothes into my suitcase in a mad frenzy. In less than thirty minutes, I was backing the car out of the garage and headed toward Shady Acres. I hadn't had time to style my hair, so it was stuffed under a baseball cap, and I wasn't wearing makeup. I comforted myself by repeating that I didn't know anyone in Chicago or England, so it shouldn't matter that I looked like a homeless person.

When I pulled into the Shady Acres parking lot, the girls were waiting in the lobby with their luggage. I popped the back hatch of my Ford Escape and got out to assist Larry, the front desk security guard, whom the girls had managed to corral into helping them.

Between Larry and I, we managed to shift, adjust, rearrange, and cram all the luggage into the back of the car *and* get the hatch closed after only four restarts. Apparently, the luggage needs for five women traveling overseas for a week is huge. Thankfully, Larry must have been a Tetris wizard in his youth. I couldn't see out of the rear window, but that was a minor point. We high-fived, fist bumped, and called it a day.

By the time all the luggage was loaded along with the four passengers, I was exhausted and dripping with sweat. One glance at the time and I put the car in gear, put the pedal to the metal, and burned rubber. Normally, I was much more of a conservative driver, but the shuttle that would take us to the airport in Chicago was forty-five minutes away in River Bend, Indiana, and according to the clock, we had thirty minutes to get there.

I was fortunate and didn't encounter any police on my way to River Bend. However, just as we pulled into the parking lot, I saw a large bus driving away, and my heart sank.

I skidded to a stop, leapt out of the car, and raced after the bus, but he didn't stop. I muttered a few choice words that might have even surprised Irma and slunk back to the car.

Nana Jo stared at me. "Are you going to be okay?"

"We just missed our shuttle to the airport. I'm hot. I'm tired, and I don't want to miss my flight to England."

She patted my leg. "You need to eat."

If I didn't know for a fact that my grandmother could drop kick me like a football, I might have been tempted to use some of my swear words. Instead, I merely stared at her.

"And you can stop glaring at me, or I'll take you over my knee and spank you."

The fact that I knew she was serious was probably the only thing that could have kept me from crying.

After a brief pause, she continued, "You're so upset and flustered that you're not thinking. Our flight doesn't leave for hours."

I stared at her for a few seconds and then shook my head. "So?"

She sighed.

Ruby Mae chimed in from the backseat. "Sam, Chicago is on central time, so they're an hour behind us."

"Chicago is only ninety miles from River Bend," Dorothy said.

They were right.

"You're sleep deprived from staying up all night writing," Nana Jo said. "Plus, you didn't eat breakfast, and your brain isn't firing on all cylinders."

"The shuttle has to stop for pickups," Dorothy said. "That's why we had to be here so early."

I took a few deep breaths. "You're right. I'm sorry."

I put the car in drive and headed out of the parking lot.

"Besides, if you drive to Chicago the way you drove from North Harbor, we'll beat that shuttle. You were hauling a—"

"Irma!" we all shouted.

Irma coughed. "Sorry."

I couldn't fix my lack of sleep, not yet anyway. Nor could I fix the fact that I'd missed the shuttle that was to take us to the airport. However, I was able to fix my lack of caffeine. My first stop was to a fast food drive-through, where I ordered a large hot coffee and a large iced coffee for good measure. Nana

Jo insisted I eat a sausage biscuit, which I normally wouldn't have touched, especially when there was bacon available, but her threat to spank me still rang in my head. Given my mental state, I ate what I was told to eat, and it tasted pretty good. Nourished and well caffeinated, I hit the interstate and headed to Chicago. It was still early, and the traffic into the city wasn't bad. Ruby Mae was right; Chicago was an hour behind us, so we would definitely make it in plenty of time, even if we hit construction, always a problem in the Windy City, or grid-locked traffic. I wasn't prepared to test my luck in not getting stopped by the police, so I eased up on the gas until I got in the city. I graduated from college in one of the Chicago sub-urbs and learned how to drive on the interstate by traveling home to North Harbor on weekends. My best tricks for navigating Chicago traffic were to maintain your speed and don't look to the left or the right. A glance to the side would show a semi traveling at breakneck speeds about to crush your vehicle like a bug on a windshield. In my youth, that semi would cause me to swerve and end up either swiping another vehicle or causing a near miss with blaring horns, hand gestures, and a lot of swearing. I maintained my speed and whipped through the city and to the airport in less than two hours.

I parked in one of the covered garages at O'Hare, which only cost a small fortune but was close to the security guard. I got out and said a silent prayer that my radio, hubcaps, and tires would still be there when we returned, and then I left the safety of my car in the hands of providence.

We unloaded the luggage and rolled our mountain of bags toward our terminal.

Between not having to make the extra stops like the air-port shuttle, the time zone difference, and the fact I wasn't hindered by a bus full of strangers forcing me to adhere to the speed limit, we arrived at the airport hours before our flight was scheduled to leave.

Inside the terminal, we stopped and glanced around.

Nana Jo patted me on the shoulder. "See, I told you there was no need to panic."

"Actually, you never said don't panic. You threatened to put me over your knee and spank me."

She shrugged. "Tomayto, tomahto. Same thing."

I shook my head. "I have a nagging feeling that something is going to go wrong."

"Don't borrow trouble. We're at the airport. We have plenty of time." She looked down her nose at me. "What could possibly go wrong?"

Those words ricocheted around inside my gut like a small metal ball inside a pinball machine.

By the time we got to the counter, the metal ball had lodged itself in my throat.

"What do you mean you don't have your passport?" Nana Jo said. "You coordinated this trip! You sent us a mile-long list with reminders on every page not to forget our passports. How is it that you don't have yours?" She snatched my purse and turned it upside down on the counter, dumping out the contents.

I was too devastated to be embarrassed even while strangers were handing me lipsticks and personal hygiene products that had fallen to the floor. Instead, I simply collapsed and cried.

Nana Jo glanced at me once but continued rifling through my personal belongings while I had a mental breakdown. When she had satisfied herself that I was indeed correct and did not have my passport, she looked down at me. "You're right. It's not in here."

"I'm going to need you all to step aside," the airline representative said. "I've got other passengers—"

Still seated on the floor with my back against the counter while Ruby Mae tried to coax me to stand, I couldn't see her face, but I recognized the sudden silence. I'd experienced it before. The frost in my grandmother's voice confirmed that the poor airline worker had just encountered the wrath of Nana Jo.

"Now, you listen here. We've waited patiently in line for our turn at this counter, and we won't be pushed aside like yesterday's garbage. We're human beings, and we expect to be treated like it. Do you hear me?"

"Yes, ma'am."

"Now, I'm sure we're not the first passengers who have ever had this problem. So, I'm going to need you to call your supervisor, manager, or someone who can help us resolve this matter."

"Yes, ma'am."

Nana Jo glanced down at me. "Sam, this is not the time to fall apart. There'll be time enough for that later. Now, get up here."

Her previous threat of placing me over her knee and spanking my bottom flashed through my brain. "Yes, ma'am." I scrambled to my feet.

Nana Jo handed her phone to Dorothy. "Get Jenna on the phone. She's a lawyer. She's bound to know what we can do."

Dorothy swiped through Nana Jo's contacts until she found the number, stepped away from the counter so she could hear, and started talking.

Nana Jo turned into an army drill sergeant and started spewing orders at the speed of sound. She then glanced at me. "You call Frank. He's got connections. If nothing else, he may be able to pull some strings."

I don't know if my brain was even capable of independent thought, but I followed orders and dialed.

The supervisor arrived behind the counter. He was a tall, dark-skinned African American man who looked like the Incredible Hulk. His shirt stretched across his muscular chest, and the buttons looked like they were ready to burst at any moment. "What's the problem?"

The counter attendant gave Nana Jo a smirk and raised her hand to beckon for the next person in line.

Ruby Mae stepped forward. "Bucky?"

The large man pulled his gaze from Nana Jo and looked at Ruby Mae for the first time. Then, his face, which had been cold and hard as granite, cracked, and a huge smile spread across his face. "Grammy Tee Tee." He climbed over the luggage scale. Arms spread wide, he gave Ruby Mae a big bear hug, lifting her off the ground.

Nana Jo gave the counter attendant a smirk.

Ruby Mae's family was huge. She had nine children and was part of a large extended network. She had a battalion of cousins, nieces, nephews, great nephews, and all manner of adopted relatives. Everywhere we went, her relatives popped up and showered her with hugs, kisses, and food. As her friends, we often benefitted from her connections.

When she finished greeting the Hulk, Ruby Mae turned to introduce us.

"Y'all, this is my great nephew, Bucky . . . ah, I mean Dave Junior." She smiled and turned to her nephew. "These are my friends." She pointed to Nana Jo. "The loud bossy one is Josephine Thomas."

Dave Jr. and Nana Jo shook hands.

"That's Dorothy over there on the phone."

Dorothy must have reached Jenna because she seemed engrossed. She was scribbling notes on the back of an envelope while talking. She nodded to acknowledge the introduction but kept writing.

Ruby Mae looked around and spotted Irma flirting with a man traveling alone, who looked like an accountant and was young enough to be her son. "That's Irma over there." She turned to me. "This is Samantha. We're on our way to England." She smiled. "Sam's an author, and we're going to help her research her next book, but she forgot her passport."

I had Frank on the phone and smiled. We shook hands, and I tried to look sympathetic without appearing too pitiful.

Nana Jo turned to glare at the woman behind the desk. "And this . . . person is not being helpful."

The worker gave Nana Jo a look that would have crippled a weaker soul. Nana Jo gave the woman a syrupy smirk.

"Well, I'm sure we can figure something out," Dave Jr. said. "Let's go have a seat and see what we can come up with." He grinned and picked up my luggage and placed it behind the counter. He then escorted us to a private office.

The office was cramped, but he managed to find five extra chairs so we could all sit. Apparently, arriving at the airport without proper identification wasn't uncommon, and the airport had a process for dealing with such cases. I would have to provide other forms of identification and submit to an interview with TSA.

Dorothy waved the envelope with her notes on it. "That's what Jenna told me."

I watched Nana Jo release a heavy sigh and realized how nervous my grandmother had been for me. I reached over and patted her hand.

My cell phone vibrated, and I read the message from Frank. Tears started to run down my cheeks.

"What's the matter now?" Nana Jo said. "It's going to be okay. You heard what he said."

I passed Nana Jo my phone so she could read the message. She looked up. "Frank found her passport on the steps leading to the bookstore. It must have fallen out of your purse. He's driving to the airport with it now."

Everyone cheered.

Nana Jo returned my phone. "You should marry that man."

Irma patted her beehive. "If you don't, I will."

I was too relieved to think much about Nana Jo's comment. When my nerves were back to a normal state, I would remind my body to be embarrassed and protest. It's taken a while for me to get to the point where I could date after Leon's death. Then, it took months before the guilt went away because I was dating and enjoying my life with another man in it who wasn't my late husband. I was finally ready to start a new future, but marriage? That word wasn't even in my vocabulary yet. I shook those thoughts out of my head. For now, I just allowed the tension to release through my tears and thanked God for sending such a kind, helpful, generous person into my life.

Dave Jr. smiled. "Great, having your passport will definitely make things a lot easier, especially when you're traveling internationally. How about some appetizers and drinks while we wait?"

He escorted us to the airline VIP Club Room and then provided vouchers for drinks and food while we waited.

The ninety-mile drive took Frank a little more than an hour. He texted me when he arrived, and Dave Jr. accompanied me downstairs to meet him.

Frank Patterson was five foot ten with a salt-and-pepper beard and hair that he wore cut short like most of the men I knew who used to work in the military. I caught sight of him standing in the terminal and flung myself into his arms.

We hugged, and I kissed him hard and long. Dave Jr. wandered off to give us some privacy.

When we finally pulled apart, we were both breathing hard.

He shook his head and laughed. "If that's how you greet me after you leave the state, I can't wait to see what will happen after you actually leave the country."

I snuggled close. "I owe you big for this." I glanced up into his soft brown eyes. "You are a lifesaver."

He grinned and handed over my passport. "Glad I could help."

"What do you want me to bring you back from England?"

He whispered his response, and I felt heat rise up my neck and giggled like a schoolgirl. Eventually, I gave him a playful tap. "I'm serious."

He gave me a hard stare. "So am I."

I waited a few moments. Eventually, he said, "I don't really want anything but you. However, when you're in Devon, if you happen across a painted rock, then bring that."

I must have looked confused.

"Look it up on Facebook," he said. "People paint rocks and leave them around Devon. You'll know one when you see it."

We took a few extra minutes to say goodbye and then he left to move his car, which was illegally parked near the curb.

I glanced around until I found Dave Jr. waving at me behind the counter. He completed my check-in, placed my luggage, which was still behind the counter, on the conveyer belt, and handed me my all-important boarding passes.

The desk attendant was still behind the counter. She smirked but said nothing.

I joined the others, and we headed back to TSA to complete our screening in preparation for our flight, which was now close to boarding.

The lines for international travel were long and slow, but I felt like I could endure anything now.

I passed my passport and boarding pass to the TSA agent with a smile and answered all questions with more exuberance than the situation required. I grabbed a bunch of plastic bins and removed my laptop, cell phone, shoes, keys, and pretty much everything else that I imagined would set off the sensor and waited my turn to walk through the screening device.

"Samantha, help."

I turned at the sound of my name and saw Irma being escorted around the scanning devices.

"What in the name of God is going on now?" Nana Jo said.

Two burly female TSA officers approached us. "Are you with that lady?" They pointed at Irma.

"Yes," I said quietly, "we're all traveling together."

"You're going to need to come with us," one of the women said.

"But what about . . ." I glanced at the bins with my personal belongings.

"Bring them with you," the woman said.

I grabbed my bins and walked barefooted around the screenings and followed the women to a TSA screening room, where Dorothy and Ruby Mae were waiting along with Irma.

"What's going on?" Nana Jo asked.

"Your friend here mentioned she had an explosive device on her body. Now, we're going to need to search all of you."

We glared at Irma.

Irma shrugged. "How was I supposed to know that hunky TSA officer I was flirting with couldn't take a joke."

Chapter 4

"Holy invasive procedures," Dorothy said, straightening her clothes as she entered the waiting room with the rest of us. "The least they could have done was buy me dinner first."

No one was in the mood for jokes, but I gave Dorothy a half smile.

"My last gynecology exam wasn't that thorough," Ruby Mae mumbled.

Dorothy was the last of the group to finish the examination, so we were all waiting. Irma had been the first to finish and was closest to the door. Nana Jo was uncharacteristically quiet, but periodically she cast a look in Irma's direction that would have withered a less self-absorbed person.

Ruby Mae tossed her yarn in the trash. Apparently, the TSA was afraid she was hiding something dangerous in her yarn and had unraveled the entire skein and left a tangled mess of bright yellow wool.

Nana Jo glanced at her watch. "We've got to run if we're going to make our flight."

The search took longer than I would have thought possible, and I had an overwhelming desire to shower, but it was finally over, and I was ready to push this episode to the back of my brain.

We took one last glance at our boarding passes to confirm the departure gate and off we raced. Because the cosmos wasn't done torturing me, our gate was at the farthest point from the TSA screening office as possible. In addition to racing through the airport, we had to take a shuttle, an escalator, and then run another stretch, dodging people, luggage, strollers, wheel-chairs, and carts. I didn't have time to think about the fact that my grandmother and her friends from the retirement village were in better shape than me and had passed me like I was standing still. Even Irma, who was the least athletic of the group, ran like a gazelle in spite of the six-inch hooker heels she wore. I decided to chalk her athletic prowess up to the fact that she weighed less than one hundred pounds and lumbered along.

I didn't stop to look at the gate signs. I merely followed my ears.

"You listen here, I don't give two flying figs about your schedule," Nano Jo said. "If you close that door before my granddaughter gets here, I'll scream bloody murder and sue your airline for discrimination against the elderly."

"I'm coming, Nana Jo," I yelled as I turned the corner and caught sight of my grandmother standing in the jet bridge. One foot on the plane and the other on the bridge, she had both arms extended and was blocking the door from closing and the bridge from being removed.

I flung my boarding pass to the attendant standing at the entrance, who reluctantly scanned it and passed it back.

Only when I had checked in did Nana Jo move to allow the bridge to be removed. As I entered the plane, I saw two armed security guards, who I suspected had been called to physically remove my grandmother.

Nana Jo and I sidled past the spacious first-class passengers, who were sipping champagne, and the slightly less spacious business class seats down to the cramped economy seats. We arrived only to find that our seats were already taken.

The flight attendant hurried down the aisle to help. One glance at all of the boarding passes indicated that because we were late arriving, the airline had given our seats away.

This was my last straw. My nerves were gone, and I had nothing left. I opened my mouth to ask the flight attendant if there were any other seats available. However, what came out was a wail and then more tears. I'm not one of those women who can cry cute. Nor am I a woman who can have an intelligent conversation while crying. I could tell by the stricken look on the flight attendant's face that the words that were in my head bore no resemblance to the ones coming out of my mouth. When one of the pilots came down the aisle to find out what the delay was, I cried even harder.

A third attendant who walked and talked with the authority of leadership came, assessed the situation, and took charge. She picked up my bags. "Follow me."

Nana Jo and I followed her back down the aisle to the front of the plane. However, rather than ordering us off, she pushed aside the curtain that separated first-class from the rest of the plane and pointed to two seats.

The relief made me cry harder, but Nana Jo pushed me down into a seat and fastened my seatbelt. "She'll be fine, now. Thank you."

I tried to say, "thank you," but I'm sure it was merely a gobbled mess.

The attendant leaned down and whispered to Nana Jo, "Does she have any medication?"

"No, but I think a glass of champagne might help to steady both of our nerves."

The woman nodded and hurried to get our drinks.

When she returned, I had calmed down enough to thank her. "I'm sorry, it's just been such a horrible day."

She nodded. "Well, you can sit back and relax now. We'll be taking off shortly."

Indeed, the plane started to back away from the gate as she spoke.

Nana Jo turned to me. "You all right now?"

I took a sip of champagne and hiccupped. "I'm sorry. I don't know what came over me."

"Stress and nerves." She leaned back. "Although, I have to admit, your nervous breakdown managed to get us some great seats."

"I didn't have a nervous breakdown." Even I could hear the petulant denial in my voice.

Nana Jo ignored it. She waved away my protests with her menu. "Whatever it was, I'm not complaining. Those appetizers in the VIP lounge have worn off, and I could eat a horse."

I rested my head on the seat back and gazed out the window as the plane sped down the runway and lifted into the air. In a few hours, I would be in England, researching my next book. A book that would one day be on the bookshelves at libraries and bookstores just like mine. I took a deep breath, said a prayer, and pulled the notebook from the bag near my feet.

～

"Dashed bad timing," Lord William said and puffed hard on his pipe.

The Marsh family listened intently, ears glued to the wireless of the BBC newscast.

Lady Penelope sat on the sofa. She dabbed

at her eyes with a handkerchief in one hand, while the other hand clasped tightly to her cousin, Lady Clara.

Lady Elizabeth, who was a fast knitter, was knitting much more slowly than normal, as she stopped frequently and gazed around the room.

The only person unaffected by the broadcast was Captain Jessup, who sat smoking in a chair near the window, legs crossed and smiling as though he didn't have a care in the world.

When the announcer finished, Lady Penelope let out a gasp and cried softly.

"Darling, please don't upset yourself," Victor said and hurried to his wife's side. "It doesn't sound as though anyone was injured."

Lady Penelope sniffed. "It's just so awful. I don't understand why anyone would deliberately set off a bomb in a tube station. Innocent people could have been hurt."

Captain Jessup chuckled. "That's the point."

Lady Penelope looked up. "What?"

"No point in setting off a bomb unless you intend to hurt people, is there?" Captain Jessup smiled.

"Barbarians." Lady Penelope hopped up and rushed from the room.

With clenched fists, Victor took a step toward Captain Jessup. "Was that really necessary? She shouldn't be upset in her condition."

Detective Inspector Covington placed a hand on his friend's chest to restrain him.

Captain Jessup threw back his head and laughed. "Sorry, old man. I had no idea your wife was so skittish."

Victor looked as though he would throttle the man with his bare hands. However, after a long pause, he turned and left the room.

Lady Clara seethed. "You really are an odious, ill-mannered oaf. Can't you see she's worried sick?"

Captain Jessup shrugged. "Actually, the bombs were left in the luggage office. If they'd really intended to harm people, they would have left them on the trains." He flicked imaginary ash from his pants and continued to smoke.

"Don't be daft." Lady Clara stood and paced in front of the fireplace. "It's not just the IRA bombs. It's the dreadful state of the world. First, that lunatic in Germany is running roughshod over a small independent nation like Austria and annexing lands from Czechoslovakia simply because there are German-speaking people there, and now we've got to worry about bombs within our own empire. It's got every *decent* person worried."

If Captain Jessup noticed the dig, he ignored it. He smoked with an amused smirk on his face. "That's why women shouldn't concern themselves with politics. You've got this all wrong."

Lady Clara stopped pacing. She folded her arms across her chest and stared at the captain. "Oh, have I indeed? Well, why don't you explain it to me then?"

He puffed on his cigarette. "You see, Hitler is simply fulfilling a plan that has been in the works for ages. It's the circle of life. These smaller nations have been given aid and allowed to create laws, which have made them believe they're in control, when in fact, they are mere puppets."

Lady Clara stared at the man as though he'd lost his mind. "Puppets?"

"Certainly, they're being used by the Jewish bankers and politicians who control their movements with their fat purse strings, but they were never intended to prosper and be independent, while the Aryan—" He broke off and took a few deep breaths. "Never mind, I doubt you would understand."

Lady Clara narrowed her eyes. "I understand a lot more than you could possibly think." She turned and marched out of the room.

Chapter 5

"Sam. Sam."

Nana Jo followed up her words with a slight shake.

I lifted my head and opened my eyes. When I focused, I saw the flight attendant standing nearby holding a tray with a steaming towel.

"Take one of these and wipe the drool from your face and get the sleepy crackers from your eyes," Nana Jo prodded.

I took the steaming towel and did as I was told. I'd learned over the years that resistance was futile anyway. When I finished, Nana Jo passed me one of the two cups of coffee she had on her seat tray—the one without lipstick around the rim.

"Coffee," I moaned and gulped the brew down, ignoring the heat as it coursed down my throat and seeped through my veins.

Nana Jo smiled. "Feeling more human?"

I nodded.

The flight attendant walked down the aisle carrying a coffeepot and topped our cups.

I raised an eyebrow and glanced at my grandmother. "Surprisingly perfect timing. You must have threatened her."

"I wouldn't call it a threat. I merely suggested her life would be much more pleasant if she kept the coffee flowing."

I had to admit it was great advice.

The pilot mumbled something over the speaker that sounded a lot like the teacher from the Charlie Brown television shows, except it was much more staticky. However, the flight attendants began collecting cups and other trash items, so I gathered we were close to landing. With just a slight hesitation, a flight attendant reached for Nana Jo's cup. Thankfully, the elixir had tamed the savage beast, and she leaned back and nodded. The attendant quickly gathered our cups and the now lukewarm towels.

I glanced at my watch. It was two in the morning in Michigan. After checking my cell phone, I adjusted my watch for the current time, which was six hours later. I expected to feel tired after only a couple of hours of sleep. However, the excitement of being in another country was enough to rejuvenate me.

Nana Jo and I left the plane and waited at the terminal for the others. After what felt like hours, Dorothy, Ruby Mae, and Irma all joined us.

"You three look exhausted," Nana Jo said without an ounce of tact.

"Oh, shut up," Dorothy griped.

"What's wrong with her?" Nana Jo asked Ruby Mae.

Ruby Mae grunted. "Normally, I'd stick up for you, but I'm siding with Dorothy on this one." She rubbed her back. "We weren't in those spacious first-class reclining seats."

"Well, don't blame me." Nana Jo glanced in my direction.

"It's not my fault. They gave away my seat and—"

Dorothy waved away my explanation as she bent over and stretched. "I'm not blaming you, Sam." She looked at Nana Jo. "It's just my nearly six-foot body has been crammed into a seat the size of a recycle bin for the past eight hours."

I heard a crack, and she smiled and stood up.

Ruby Mae, normally very congenial, fanned herself. "And I just spent the last eight hours with a three-hundred-and-fifty-pound man snoring like a buzz saw and practically lying in my lap." She shook her head. "How is it that those seats recline so far back in such a confined space."

No one had an answer, so we merely shook our heads.

Irma was the only one who seemed like her normal, flirtatious self. She smiled. "Well, I met the nicest man from Denver." She held up a scrap of paper. "Artie's going to call me when he's back in the States."

Nana Jo rolled her eyes. "Come on, I need to use the ladies' room, and then we have to get our luggage and make our way to Customs."

It was surprisingly comforting to see that the line for the ladies' room in London was as long as those in the United States.

Nana Jo sighed as she took her place. "Some things are universal."

By the time we made it to baggage claim, the majority of familiar faces from our flight had gathered around a luggage carousel. Like lemmings, we followed the herd to the carousel and waited. And waited. And waited. Slowly, all of the other passengers grabbed bags and wandered away, leaving us and a bleary-eyed businessman still staring at the carousel. The last bag, a large navy-blue roller, tumbled out. Dorothy and the businessman both reached for the bag, but Dorothy was faster. With one swing, she hoisted the bag off the carousel and placed her carry-on and purse over the handle.

Dorothy smiled. "Well, at least one of us will have clean clothes."

Nana Jo stuck out her tongue. Ruby Mae rolled her eyes, and Irma mumbled something that sounded like *jolly green witch*, but I couldn't be sure because she broke out into a coughing fit.

Dorothy pulled her bag along as we headed toward the Baggage Claims office. The businessman who had been standing nearby grabbed Dorothy by the arm.

He sputtered something that sounded like German. He waved his hands and then reached for the suitcase, which also now had Dorothy's purse and carry-on.

Dorothy swatted away his hand. "Watch it, bub."

The man's neck and face flushed red. His face became more animated, and his hand and arm movements expanded. He spoke faster, which didn't help.

"Listen, I don't know who you think you're messing with, but I want to warn you I'm not some old woman who you can push around."

The altercation was drawing a crowd, which included some uniformed men who looked like airport security. "What's the problem here?"

The businessman prattled on in German for about thirty seconds. His face deepened from rose to a deep merlot. His last gesture was to reach over and grab the suitcase.

"That's it." Dorothy squatted, reached over, and grabbed the man's arm. With a twist of her body and his arm, she hoisted the man over her shoulder and tossed him flat on his back. Still holding his arm, she dropped down and put her knee to his chest.

The man looked dazed and then squealed like a pig.

The security guard stood by in shocked amazement for a split second and then launched into action. "Steady on." He pulled out a radio and sent an SOS for help in baggage claim.

Within seconds, a group of uniformed men and women swarmed the area like locusts.

Several of the officers attempted to pull Dorothy off the now crying man.

Nana Jo and I pushed our way through the group.

"Wait. Please. Stop."

It took three men, but they managed to pull Dorothy to her feet. At close to three hundred pounds, she was a big woman. Years of martial arts training also meant that most of her weight was muscle rather than fat. When she stood, she continued to grip the man's arm. The man lay on the ground writhing in pain and then let out a blood-curdling scream. The officers tried to pry Dorothy's fingers loose, but she had a tight grip and clamped down like a vice.

Nana Jo shoved through the group and hauled back and slapped Dorothy. "Dorothy, snap out of it. Calm down and let go of that poor man's arm right this minute."

Dorothy's neck snapped back, and she glared at Nana Jo, whose hand had left a white imprint around the increasing red that rose up her neck. She blinked several times, and the haze seemed to clear from her eyes. She shook her head and then released the squirming man's arm.

The uniformed officers increased their hold on Dorothy.

"Now, what's going on?" Nana Jo asked.

For probably the first time in my life, I channeled my sister Jenna and went into full-blown pit bull lawyer mode. "Stop it. She's an American citizen, and I demand that you release her immediately." I couldn't have told you where I got the courage to demand anything from these security guards, but a lack of sleep and a rush of adrenaline had me on a high. "Release my friend immediately. She was merely defending herself. This man tried to steal her suitcase." I pointed down at the man, who was still lying on the floor grasping his arm.

The officers released Dorothy's arm and directed their attention to the man on the ground. Just as a paramedic arrived, a young college student wearing a St. Catherine's sweatshirt and leggings pulled a large backpack from the next carousel and then hurried over to us.

She raised a timid hand. "Excuse me, but do you need an interpreter?" She glanced down at the man on the ground, who was babbling. "I speak German."

The officers parted and made room for the woman to come forward.

The paramedics asked her to find out the extent of the man's injuries.

She squatted and had an intense but brief conversation, which resulted in a few sideways glances directed in Dorothy's direction. After a few moments, she stood. The man's injuries amounted to nothing more than a very sore arm. Nevertheless, the paramedics checked him over. By now, the man was sitting upright on the ground and sending laser beams in Dorothy's direction.

While the paramedics finished their examination, the girl directed her attention to the security officers. "He claims this woman stole his bag, and when he attempted to stop her, she attacked him."

"Why, the dirty, no-good lying weasel. I've never stolen anything in my life. This is my bag."

The security guards exchanged knowing glances and then most of them disbursed, leaving us with the original guard.

He ushered us and the now standing businessman into the Baggage Claims office and hoisted the bag onto the counter. He unzipped the bag and flung the top open. Inside were several men's suits, shirts, ties, and other garments.

Dorothy gasped, and a red river of molten lava rose from her neck and spread across her face. "I could have sworn that was my bag." She glanced from person to person like a drowning man grasping for a life preserver. She caught the gaze of the injured businessman. "I'm terribly sorry."

The man looked away.

Dorothy yelled and spoke slowly as though she were talking to a deaf child rather than an intelligent man who didn't speak English.

The businessman backed away.

The security guard closed the suitcase and handed it to the man, who babbled on in German and made his escape, making sure to leave a wide berth around Dorothy.

The student gave Dorothy a sideways glance, leaned forward, and whispered to the security guard, "I asked, but he doesn't want to press charges. He just wants to get . . ." She coughed. "As far away from the crazy American as possible."

Dorothy looked as though she would cry.

"Well, that's good news anyway," Ruby Mae said. "Maybe now we can *all* set about finding our luggage."

The security guard left us filling out forms in the Baggage Claims office. We filed reports with the airline and then made our way toward Customs. Just as we got to the line, Nana Jo turned and grabbed Irma by the arm. "Listen here, you love-obsessed harpy. If you thought TSA was rough, Customs has even less of a sense of humor. Answer the questions and cut out the crap or so help me God, I'll take this purse and shove it so far up your—"

"Next," the Customs officer yelled.

Nana Jo stepped forward.

There were multiple officials, and we each went to a different counter. Without luggage, there was little to discuss. *Yes, we are on vacation. No, we aren't bringing anything illegal into the country.* We barely had more than the clothes on our backs. I was thankful that I had my laptop as part of my carry-on.

As we each finished, we waited for the others. Irma was the last to join, but her Customs officer was a woman and she must have behaved herself because she too was allowed to enter the country.

Once we were set, we made our way outside and stood in the taxi queue. A long line of the classic black taxis idled by the curb, and the line went quickly. When we piled into a taxi, exhaustion faded to excitement. We raced away from the curb, and I smiled as I tried to adjust to the British manner of driving on the left rather than the right side of the road.

The cabby launched through the city. Red busses, Trafalgar Square, and monuments flashed by at the speed of sound. Far too quickly, we pulled in front of the hotel. It was hard to tell at first glance that it was a hotel, rather than a white town house, but a small, discreet sign and a liveried doorman indicated that we were indeed at the right place.

The doorman hurried to open the car door, and we piled out onto the pavement. He looked askance at us when there was no luggage, which meant there wasn't a need for the bell-boys, who hurried outside. Nevertheless, he smiled, opened the front door, and welcomed us graciously.

Located in the Kensington area of London, the hotel was a former town home of the Vanderbilt family. Converted from ten nineteenth-century town homes, the hotel had been refurbished but still maintained much of its original charm, including frescoes, decorated ceilings, stained-glass windows, and wood paneling. At least that's what I remembered from the brochures I'd scoured while planning this trip. However, now that I was here, I had to admit that much of the hotel's splendor was lost on me. The exhilaration I'd felt just a short time earlier had once again seeped out while I sat in the cab, and it had been replaced with exhaustion. The effects of being awake for more than twenty-four hours hit me. Unfortunately, that same wave of fatigue didn't hit Nana Jo and the girls.

"What do you think you're doing?" Nana Jo glared at me as I flopped down on one of the small twin beds that took up the majority of our room.

"Is that a rhetorical question?" I mustered up enough energy to turn my head, but after that great endeavor, I only had enough energy left to open one eye.

"Get up. You can't sleep now."

"Watch me." I closed my eye but was shocked awake when my butt was smacked. "What the—"

"Get up. You have to stay awake." She took two fingers and pried open one of my eyes.

"Why?" I swatted her hand away. Even without looking, I recognized the silence that followed. I squinted and opened both eyes to give her what I hoped was a scathing glare. I should have known it would be wasted on my grandmother.

"You're the one that sent all of those annoying tips every day for two weeks before this trip." She pulled out her cell phone and swiped several times before she found what she was looking for. " 'To avoid jet lag, force yourself to adhere to the time zone of your destination. England is six hours ahead of North Harbor, Michigan, so regardless of how tired you feel upon arrival, make yourself stay awake.' " She glanced down her nose at me with a self-satisfied smirk. After a full minute, she crossed her arms and tapped her foot. "Well?"

I have never come closer to throttling my grandmother than I did at that moment. Worse still was the fact that she was right. Actually, I was right, since it was my stupid tip. Nothing like being buffeted by your own words to bring your ego down a peg or two. I released a heavy sigh, dug deep, and forced one leg out of the bed and forced myself to sit up. It wasn't graceful, but it accomplished my objective.

Nana Jo nodded. "Great. Now, go splash some water on your face. We'll meet the girls in the lobby in ten minutes." She tapped a message into her phone and then turned and opened the door. "I'll wait for you downstairs."

With more effort than it had taken to move boxes of books in my bookstore, I hoisted my body up and stumbled to the bathroom, which was roughly the size of a postage stamp but had all of the necessities. I literally had to turn my legs to the side to close the door. I made a mental note to always close the door before sitting on the toilet, but smiled when I thought of Nana Jo's nearly six-foot frame using these facilities. The entire hotel room was small, but we really didn't need much space. We would only be here for one day. The itinerary for our trip included the option to add a day before and a day at the end of the tour, and today I was thankful.

When I was done, I washed my hands, splashed water on my face, and then stuck my head down to the basin and drank from the stream of water. I swished it around in my mouth in the hopes of getting rid of the carpet-like film that coated my tongue. I wasn't sure how excited I was for sightseeing, but I definitely needed to find a store where I could pick up a few toiletries and fresh underwear.

Downstairs, Nana Jo and the girls waited, although Irma had an elderly employee backed into a corner.

Ruby Mae shook her head. "I don't know where she finds the energy to flirt."

Nana Jo mumbled, "It's inbred in her, like a wolf bred for centuries into a domesticated house pet."

After a brief conversation with the concierge, we headed out in search of a chemist, which we learned was the British equivalent for a pharmacy or drugstore.

The chemist was just a block away. The only surprise was the prices. I knew the dollar wouldn't go far in Europe, but some of these prices were outrageous. However, nothing overcomes sticker shock faster than desperation. My need for a toothbrush, toothpaste, and deodorant overpowered all other emotions, and I plunked my credit card down with barely a whimper.

Encouraged by the idea of a shower, I hiked the two blocks to the tube station, where we were able to take a subway. Within a few blocks, we were at the stop for the hop-on, hop-off double decker tour buses. We took the bus past Buckingham Palace and several other attractions. However, when the bus pulled in front of Harrods Department Store, we hopped off, intent on picking up clean clothes in case the airline failed to locate our luggage quickly.

Even in my current state of exhaustion, I marveled at the magnificence that was Harrods.

Nana Jo whistled. "Wow! When they say Harrods sells everything, they mean it."

"They used to sell exotic animals too." I flipped through the brochure I'd picked up. "However, after the Endangered Species Act of 1976, they limited themselves to more traditional animals."

"They sell pets?" Dorothy asked.

"Not anymore. Apparently, they closed the pet shop after Mohamed Al-Fayed sold the store to new owners." I tried to figure out how I felt about that. I was a firm believer in buying pets from reputable breeders or animal rescue shelters, but when I'd come to Harrods before, the pets were one of the things I remembered.

"Well, we can't just stand here gawking all day." Nana Jo pulled out her cell phone. "Okay, let's divide and conquer. We'll meet in the tea shop in two hours."

We all nodded and headed off in various directions. I suspected we'd eventually all end up in the same places: lingerie, women's wear, and shoes. However, I was happy to have a few moments alone and headed off to shop.

It didn't take me long to pick up underwear, socks, jeans, pj's, and sweaters. I found a sales rack that didn't make my head spin when I glanced at the price tags. I grabbed a couple of dresses I could wear if any of the dinners required something a bit fancier than jeans. I even picked up a duffel bag to transport everything and was finished in less than an hour.

With another hour to spare, I decided to head to the tea room early.

I snagged a table for five, ordered tea, and pulled out my notepad to kill time until the others arrived.

* * *

Lady Clara was the last to enter the dining room for breakfast. Everyone except Lady Penelope was already seated and enjoying a full English breakfast. The dark circles under her eyes indicated she hadn't slept well, despite her artfully applied makeup.

Lady Elizabeth's eyes never left her young cousin as she filled a plate with bacon, eggs, toast, and beans. She smiled. Clearly a lack of sleep hadn't affected her cousin's appetite.

Thompkins stood quietly near the buffet, ready to assist at a moment's notice.

Captain Jessup finished a large plate and headed back to the buffet for seconds just as Gladys entered carrying a large container of beans.

Lady Elizabeth watched a frown crease Detective Inspector Covington's brow as he gripped his fork and stared as Captain Jessup moved behind Lady Clara.

"I like to see a woman with a healthy appetite," Captain Jessup said.

Lady Clara ignored the comment. She turned around to move to the table, but Captain Jessup blocked her path. After a few seconds, when it was clear the man had no intention of moving, Lady Clara sighed and stepped to the side to go around, but he moved so he remained in her path.

He ogled Lady Clara with a lecherous gleam in his eyes.

Lady Clara's cheeks flamed and her eyes flashed. After a split second, she gave the captain a smile and then stomped down hard on his foot.

"Oooph." Captain Jessup bent over in pain.

"Dear me, was that your foot?" Lady Clara said in a voice that oozed sweetness.

She took advantage of the captain's discomposure to sidle past him.

Lady Elizabeth noted the frown on the detective inspector's forehead had relaxed a bit, as had his grip on his utensil.

Gladys finished replenishing the buffet and had just turned to leave when Captain Jessup was able to stand. A flash of anger flew across his face but was quickly replaced with a grin.

"Excuse me, sir," Gladys mumbled, with her eyes down as she concentrated on the serving dishes.

With an elaborate flourish, the captain made a sudden move as Gladys tried to slide past. The maid let out a yelp.

She turned to look back at Captain Jessup, who had a sly grin on his face.

Unfortunately, the captain miscalculated Gladys's balance and grace. The shock resulted in her lurching to the side, and unable to balance the serving dishes, she splattered beans over the front of the captain's starched white shirt.

The captain let out an expletive.

Lord William bristled. "I say, there's no call for that kind of language, man. This isn't a brothel." His cheeks flushed. "I won't tolerate that type of language, especially in the presence of women."

Captain Jessup glared at Gladys, who looked like she was two seconds from bursting into tears.

Lady Elizabeth smiled at the maid. "That will be all, Gladys."

The maid managed a slight curtsey and then made a hasty retreat.

Lady Elizabeth turned to the offended guest. "Captain Jessup, I'm very sorry for the damage to your shirt, but our butler, Thompkins, is a magician at removing stains."

Thompkins gave a stiff bow.

"Removing stains?" he blustered. "My shirt is ruined. There's no way anyone will be able to get this shirt clean, and I shall hold you responsible for replacing it." He huffed. "Why, this is handmade and cost a small fortune."

Lord William's eyes narrowed, and his lips puckered as though he had eaten a lemon.

Lady Elizabeth raised a hand in a way that reminded all who saw her of her cousin King George. "Thompkins, please help Captain Jessup change."

The dismissal was clear and elegantly done.

Thompkins bowed. "M'lady." He turned and extended a hand for Captain Jessup to precede him from the room.

The captain paused and glanced uncertainly from Lady Elizabeth to Lord William and then

Lady Clara. He ignored the police inspector. Eventually, he turned and brushed past Thompkins as he left the dining room.

When the door closed behind them, the group released a collective sigh. After a split second, everyone started to speak.

Victor turned to Lady Elizabeth. "I'm sorry for the way my cousin behaved." He shook his head. "I feel horrible. If it weren't for the plumbing—"

Lady Elizabeth waved away his concerns. "It's fine. You're family, and I don't want to hear anything else about it."

"What a loathsome man," Lady Clara snapped. "The only reason Gladys dropped that platter was because that letch pinched her bottom."

"The cad," Lord William sputtered.

"Poor Gladys," Lady Elizabeth tsked. "I'll go down and check on her in a bit. However, first, I want to try an idea on you."

Everyone stared at Lady Elizabeth.

"I think Captain Jessup's . . . disposition may be a bit much for such a small group."

Lady Clara glanced around. "What do you mean?"

"I think if we had a larger group, it might help to . . . dilute his strong personality."

Lord William said, "You can't be serious." He stared at his wife. "You want to host a house party for that . . ." He searched for the right word.

"Well, I think it's an excellent idea," Lady Clara said before anyone else could object. "But who do we dislike enough to invite them here for an evening with him? We couldn't possibly invite people we like, so we'll have to invite our enemies."

"Now, do be serious," Lady Elizabeth rebuked.

"I am serious. Let's face it, he's so offensive that he'll offend everyone at the party, which is why we should only invite our enemies. Or, everyone will get so fed up by his pompous behavior, they'll kill him." She took a sip of her coffee and smiled. "Either way, I think it's a winning proposition."

Chapter 6

"Sam." Nana Jo jostled my arm, causing me to scratch a line through the last page I had written. This was beginning to be a problem.

The look on my face prompted a quick "Sorry." Then she flopped down in her seat and shoved a small mountain of shopping bags under the table. "I'm hungry enough to eat a bear."

The waitress hurried over and poured a cup of tea, which Nana Jo guzzled down like a skid row wino with a brand-new bottle of ripple.

Before the waitress could finish pouring Nana Jo's second cup of tea, we were overrun, as Irma, Ruby Mae, and Dorothy descended with enough bags to clothe a small third world nation. There were so many packages that they formed a border around our table. Eventually, the hostess wandered over and offered to take our bags and leave them in the luggage pickup area, where they wouldn't block the floor. We accepted the offer, although I doubt that we had much choice in the matter. After a few moments, she returned with claim checks and instructions on where to go to retrieve our bags.

Tea at Harrods was a wonderful experience with sandwiches, scones with clotted cream, pastries, and tarts. There was enough to fill all of us, and by the end of the meal, we were all feeling re-energized.

We left our bags and took another trip on the hop-on, hop-off bus. This time, we actually got on and off at several of the tourist attractions and took pictures with our cell phones. When we were worn out, we hopped on the bus and took it back to Harrods to retrieve our bags. One glance at our mound of bags, and we bypassed the bus and tube and called a taxi.

It took a few minutes and a bit of swearing, but the cabbie managed to cram most of the bags into the trunk. The others we put on our laps, as we squeezed into the cab. After a brief dash through the London traffic, we made it back to our hotel, and this time we were able to utilize the bellboys to get everything up to our rooms. After a few bag swaps, we got everything sorted out and were able to shower and dress in clean clothes.

Nana Jo was feeling generous and allowed me first dibs on the hot water. I overcame the desire to curl up in a ball in the bottom of the shower and just lay there while the hot water pelted my skin, and I quickly cleaned up and got dressed.

Nana Jo's shower was a bit longer than mine. When she came out, she declared, "I'll never underestimate the power of a hot shower again." She toweled off and quickly dressed.

With moments to spare, we hurried downstairs to the ballroom. As the elevator doors opened, Nana Jo looked around. "Right or left?"

I shrugged. "Let's try right."

We wandered down a hall to the right and stopped when we heard raised voices.

"You can't do this! You can't just sell the business. I'm your partner, Horace. Or, have you forgotten that?"

"I jolly well can sell the business, and I have done just that. We never had anything in writing, and you've been paid well for your time over the years."

We exchanged glances and then peeked around the corner. A tall, thin man with a large beaked nose was glaring down on a short, fat bald man with a small mustache who was backed up against the wall.

"Nothing in writing? I've devoted the last twenty years of my life to this business. I've become a specialist on British Crimes and dedicated myself to making this . . . enterprise successful. I've been the face and the voice of Peabody Mystery Lovers Tours."

The short man laughed. "That's just it, isn't it? It's *Peabody* Mystery Lovers Tours, and I'm Peabody, so I can do whatever I bloody well please."

"Why you . . ." Beak Nose grabbed the smaller man by the lapels and flung him into the wall, knocking over a tray that was left in the hall. "Don't forget who you're talking to, Horace. Don't forget that I know where all the skeletons are buried."

The tray crashed to the floor as the short man's head hit the wall. Nana Jo and I hurried around the corner.

"Hey, stop that!" Nana Jo yelled.

Her intervention provided just enough of a distraction to allow the beak-nosed aggressor time to collect himself.

Beak Nose released his hold on the smaller man. "Madam, everything is fine." He took several deep breaths and ran a hand over his head.

Rather than thanking us for saving his skin, Shorty took the opportunity to sneer at his attacker. "So common." He straightened his suit and adjusted his tie. "This display has confirmed that I was right about you all along. All you are and all you ever will be is a common laborer. How you could ever have thought yourself my equal astounds me," he snarled and strutted down the hallway, barely glancing at Nana Jo and me as he passed.

After a brief pause, Beak Nose took several deep breaths, turned, and bowed to us. "Ladies, I am terribly sorry for my behavior. I was . . ." He chuckled. "I was going to say provoked, but that's no excuse." He shook his head. "I behaved abominably, please forgive me." He bowed again.

We nodded and stepped aside as he walked down the hall.

"Interesting that the *common laborer* demonstrated better manners and more class than Mr. Hoity Toity." Nana Jo adjusted her collar. "Come on, this mystery tour is about to get really interesting."

Chapter 7

We retraced our steps back toward the elevator, and this time we turned left rather than right.

When we walked into the ballroom, we were greeted by Beak Nose. He had a printout with a list of names, which I assumed were all the passengers on our tour. We signed next to our printed names, as the others had done, and tried to escape without taking one of the bright blue *Hello, my name is* stickers, but this wasn't our guide's first tour. He smiled brightly. "Greetings, ladies. I'm Clive Green . . . I'll be your guide for the next seven days, as we explore the mysterious and murderous sites in and around the United Kingdom." He handed us a Sharpie and a sticker. "If you'll be so kind as to write your names on these, we'll get started shortly." A true veteran of the tour circuit, he waited until we obeyed orders before smiling and handing us a paper entitled, *Get Acquainted Reception.*

The room was decorated with overstuffed Edwardian furniture, and Ruby Mae had made herself comfortable on a sofa placed in front of an ornately carved fireplace. In true Ruby Mae fashion, she had her knitting lying across her lap but was eating a plate piled high with chicken and other delicious-looking items while chatting with one of the maids, a young, dark-skinned woman with a small afro and a bright smile.

Nana Jo shook her head. "I've got twenty bucks that's a third cousin twice removed."

I shook my head. "Only a fool would take that bet." I grinned. "Ruby Mae has the largest extended family on the planet."

Nana Jo pointed. "It looks like Dorothy and Irma have already acquainted themselves with Jim Beam and Johnnie Walker."

In a corner of the room was a bar. Irma had changed into a skintight leopard-print jumpsuit, which managed to be even more seductive than her typical bar attire of miniskirts and cleavage-boosting blouses. She had affixed herself to a white-haired gentleman with big teeth and a flushed face, who seemed quite content to be trapped.

Dorothy was also attached to a man. Close inspection identified her companion as none other than our German businessman from the airport.

I nudged Nana. "Isn't that the guy Dorothy decked in the airport?"

"Looks like the same guy." She shrugged. "Given the smile on his face, I'd say a peace pact has been achieved. It's either that or the two empty glasses and the bottle of Jim Beam have worked their magic. Either way, I think Dorothy will be happier."

"She has been pretty quiet since the airport incident. I just assumed she was tired." I stared at the two. "Although, I can't imagine how they're communicating. He doesn't speak English."

"Whiskey speaks everyone's language." Nana Jo wandered over to the bar and got a drink.

I smiled and glanced at the amber-colored liquid in their refilled glasses. She might have a point. I glanced around the room and noted the small cliques that had already formed. There was a couple standing by the window that looked very American. Both were blond-haired, blue-eyed, thin, and well-tanned. There was something about the two that screamed Florida to me. Although there was something about the woman that reminded me of a frightened rat. Perhaps it was the way she kept glancing around the room.

Our rude hallway brawler stood in a corner of the room. His nose was scrunched with a look like he'd just gotten a whiff of a foul odor, while a large-breasted woman in a dress covered in neon flowers, with an unfortunate hair color that was somewhere between Ronald McDonald and Little Orphan Annie, and an overabundance of gaudy jewelry pressed herself closer and closer.

Their animated conversation left me curious, so I sauntered nearby and eavesdropped on the conversation while gazing into a bowl of mixed nuts as though this was my first time seeing such things.

"Horace, you must remember," the woman said. "We were engaged . . . practically."

"I tell you, I have no memory of you, and I certainly have never had a relationship with you." He glanced down his nose at the woman. "What did you say your name was?"

A patch of red rose up her neck. "My name is Prudence Habersham." She waited for recognition before quickly adding, "Although, Habersham is my married name. Back when we were dating, my name was Pickelsimer. Prudence Pickelsimer."

"I can assure you that I never knew anyone with that name." He turned to walk away but Prudence would not be denied. She grabbed his arm. "You must remember me. It was a while ago, but I can't have changed that much." She gazed with desperation into the man's eyes and then gave a short deprecating laugh. "I'll admit I have put on a few pounds, but that was well over thirty years ago." She chuckled. "Everyone changes after that much time. Why, even you—"

"No one could have changed *that* much." He scowled. "You really must have me confused with someone else."

The woman's face grew redder and her chest heaved. "I don't make a habit of confusing the men with whom I've been intimate." She glared. "I'm not that type of woman."

The man smirked.

"If you think you can ignore me, then you've got another think coming. Remember, I knew you long before you were *Major* Peabody," Prudence sneered. "And, I'll get even with you for this . . . humiliation if it's the last thing I do."

Fear flashed across Major Peabody's face.

I glanced to the side and noticed an older gray-haired woman watching me as I watched the couple. Our eyes met. After an awkward moment, the woman shrugged and smiled.

Our eavesdropping was placed on hold when a glamorous couple entered the room. The couple stood in the middle of the room and looked around for all to admire. They were definitely attractive in a showy, overdone manner that seemed to shout, *We're part of the beautiful people.* They were both tall and thin. From afar, the woman looked stunningly gorgeous, but this ballroom was too small for that much ego. Up close, her makeup appeared to be applied with a paint roller. Her false eyelashes looked like spiders, and her perfume overpowered the room.

"Ah-choo!"

The kind gray-haired woman handed me a tissue.

"Thank you." I wiped my nose.

"Chanel Number 5." She smiled. "Normally, I like the scent, when it hasn't been applied with such a . . . heavy hand."

I sneezed again. "It is a bit overpowering."

The glamourous woman had a fur stole wrapped around

her neck, and she let the stole slip to her shoulders as she spied her quest. She extended her arms and walked over to Major Peabody. "Uncle Horace." She would have run over Prudence Habersham had the woman not stepped aside just as the scent descended on the major.

She engulfed the major in an embrace and then left two perfect copies of her lips on each cheek.

The major pulled out a handkerchief and wiped off the lipstick. "What are you doing here, Debra?"

The cool greeting didn't deter Debra. She merely laughed. "Uncle Horace, you are such a card." She chuckled. "You know I love your little games." She raised a hand to signal to the Mediterranean god she'd left standing in the middle of the room for all of the women to admire.

He caught the signal, flashed a smile like a toothpaste model, and strutted to her side.

She staked her claim by linking one arm through the demi-god's arm. "I couldn't wait to tell you the good news. Sebastian and I are engaged." She held up her left hand and wiggled her fingers. On her ring finger sat a rock slightly smaller than a tennis ball.

I was so engrossed in the drama playing out in the room, I didn't realize Nana Jo had moved beside me until she whispered, "It's a wonder she can lift her hand with that bowling ball on her finger."

The gray-haired woman leaned close. "It's a fake."

We turned and stared at the woman.

"How can you tell?" I asked.

She leaned close. "It's the way the light hits it. My father was a jeweler, and I know diamonds." She smiled and extended her hand. "Hannah Schneider."

Nana Jo shook. "Josephine Thomas." Then she turned to me. "This is my granddaughter, Samantha Washington."

We shook hands, and I gave her a sincere smile. I liked

Hannah Schneider, and I didn't even know her. Perhaps it was the way her eyes crinkled at the sides when she smiled or the intelligence that looked back at me out of her dark, sad eyes. There was an instant connection between us.

"Engaged?" Major Peabody shouted. "Engaged to do what? Live in squalor with some tanned gigolo?"

Momentarily shocked, Debra recovered well and laughed. She looked around. "Uncle, you are so hilariously amusing," she said with a slight edge to her voice. "Perhaps we can discuss this in private."

Major Peabody had had enough. "Private? What's to discuss? If you want to make a fool of yourself, go right ahead. You've certainly had enough practice," he sneered. "But, if you expect me to fund this unholy union, then you'd better think again, my dear."

"But, Uncle, really. I'm old enough to make my own decisions, and my mother—"

"Your mother was a fool." He shook his head. "She was just as headstrong and man crazed as you are. She married a no-good wastrel, and it looks like you're determined to do the same thing, but you're wrong if you think I'm going to sit back and allow this . . ." He looked the man up and down as though he were filth. ". . . this gigolo to have access to my money. You're both wrong."

Debra glared but then directed her attention to her fingernails, as though the conversation bored her to tears. "Well, blood is thicker than water. Like it or not, I'm your niece and only heir. Just how do you intend to stop me?"

Major Peabody's face grew red, and like the lid of a pressure cooker, he seemed ready to explode. However, within a few seconds, he flipped a switch and turned off the boiler. "As it turns out, my dear, I have already taken steps to disinherit you."

This shocked her, and she seemed ready to scream but was

halted when the major raised a hand. "I knew you would come up with some stupid idea like this, which is why I hired a private investigator to look into this . . . so-called model." He scoffed. "Sebastian Rothchild-Black, indeed. Even if he wasn't as bent as a nine-bob note, I'd never permit anyone remotely connected to me to marry someone with such a ridiculous name. *Sebastian Rothchild-Black,* indeed. You can't honestly believe I'd be associated with a Jew."

Hannah Schneider stood up and marched over to Major Peabody. "You are despicable. How dare you."

"I dare because it's my right as a gentleman as well as an Englishman."

"You should be hanged." Hannah's chest heaved in anger.

"And I would love to be the one holding the rope."

The tour guide was staring, openmouthed.

Debra turned to face him. "Better close your mouth, Clive, or you'll let the bees in and get stung."

Clive Green must have figured it wouldn't be good for the owner of the tour company to insult any more guests and stepped forward. "Ladies and gentleman, on behalf of Peabody Mystery Tours, I want to apologize for this unfortunate display."

A red-faced Major Peabody marched out of the room, followed quickly by his niece and her fiancé, the beautiful Sebastian.

Ruby Mae approached Hannah Schneider and comforted her while the woman collected herself.

Once the three purveyors of discord were gone, the tension relaxed in the room. Clive Green turned on the charm. Within minutes, he had everyone relaxed while we introduced ourselves. The tanned American couple introduced themselves as Dr. Vincent Blankenship and his wife, Tiffany, from Miami.

"Oh, you're a doctor?" Irma started to pull down the top of her blouse. "I've got this rash—"

"I'm on vacation!" the doctor shouted and turned away.

Irma shrugged and took a sip of her drink, completely unphased by the snub. When her red-faced companion with the big teeth identified himself as Dr. Albus Lavington, professor at the University of Saint Andrews, she fawned over him and all was once again right in her world.

A thin, sickly woman, who clutched a small suitcase, introduced herself as Lavender Habersham, Prudence's daughter.

Hannah Schneider apologized for her unseemly behavior, which was quickly waved away. She introduced herself as a housewife from Brighton and became weepy when she explained that this trip was supposed to have been an anniversary present. Unfortunately, her husband, Eli, had died just two months ago. Her children thought it would be good for her to go on the tour anyway, since she was an avid mystery lover. At that moment, I knew why I felt connected to Mrs. Schneider. We were both united in grief. It had been more than a year since my husband, Leon, died. However, there would always be a spot in my heart that nothing could ever fill.

The German businessman didn't seem to grasp much of what was being said but introduced himself as Oberst Senf. To everything else, he merely smiled and nodded.

"I wonder how he plans to learn anything on the tour if he can't speak or understand English?"

Nana Jo shrugged. "I guess he can try Google translate or something."

Clive Green finished by introducing himself as a twenty-year veteran of the Metropolitan Police, also known as Scotland Yard. When his position was made redundant, he took his years of knowledge of crime and the criminal underworld of Great Britain and joined forces with Major Horace Peabody in the Mystery Tours. He finished by reviewing the itinerary for the next day.

We were on our own for dinner and were told to meet downstairs tomorrow morning, promptly at nine for the start of our tour. However, to kick things off, Clive offered to lead the group on a Jack the Ripper walking tour to the sites where each of the victims from the grisly murders were discovered.

Tiffany Blankenship, the Florida doctor's wife, raised a timid hand. "Won't it be dark?"

Clive smiled and gave an evil laugh. "Precisely. The dark will be the best time to view the sites where the Ripper did his dirty work."

Most of the group chuckled nervously, but the American housewife didn't seem to enjoy the joke.

I was pleased when Nana Jo invited Hannah Schneider to join us for dinner. We spent a pleasant time eating, drinking, and talking in the hotel dining room. When we finished, we met Clive and the other members of the party in the lobby and headed out for our first guided tour to Whitechapel.

Clive Green was a knowledgeable and enthusiastic guide who milked the mystic and horror of the gruesome murders for every bit of theatrical drama he could.

Tiffany Blankenship shivered as we walked back to the tube station to head back to the hotel. "I could have done without all of the grisly details of those horrible murders."

"I'm not really a Ripper scholar, but I suspect he laid on the details a bit thicker than was necessary for dramatic effect."

She scowled. "Well, I could have done without the effect." She wrapped her arms around her body. "I think talking about that stuff just makes people want to do it . . . to re-create that horror."

"I don't know that talking about murders that happened over a century ago will inspire someone who isn't already deranged to that level of brutality, but I can assure you that you couldn't be safer than with this group of people."

She gave me a puzzled look.

I pointed to Nana Jo and Dorothy, who were walking in front of us asking Clive questions. "My grandmother and her friend are martial arts experts."

She looked skeptically at the older women and then her eyes asked, *Are you joking?*

"Trust me. I pity the fool who would try to attack you with either of them in the vicinity."

She gave Nana Jo and Dorothy another hard glance, but I noticed she dropped her arms as though she was no longer as cold as she was just moments earlier.

I smiled.

"Honestly, I'm not sure why Vince wanted to come on this tour," she mumbled. "I would have rather we went to a quiet beach."

"Not a mystery fan?"

She shrugged. "We came on this tour to get away from death and sickness and to . . . reconnect. I guess I don't find a tour focused on murder to be very romantic." She folded her arms again. "I wish we'd never come on this tour."

I wondered myself but decided it was better not to ask and walked along in silence.

Afterward, we returned to the hotel. Everyone decided to go back to the bar for complimentary drinks. I noticed Major Horace Peabody sitting alone in a large armchair. He had a large bottle of Scotch on a side table nearby and was making his way through the bottle. Tired from the day's activities, I decided to forego the drinks and went up to my room.

As tired as I was, I expected to fall asleep the moment my head hit the pillow. However, that's not what happened. Instead, I tossed for about an hour before I decided to get up and write to give my mind time to unwind.

Gladys sat at the large wood table with her head on her arms, facedown, and sobbed.

Mrs. McDuffie patted the maid on the back. "There, there, Gladys," she said softly. Then the stout, middle-aged woman narrowed her eyes. "I wish that little peacock woulda tried that on with me." She huffed. "I'd have shown him the power of a well-placed knee."

"I'm sorry, ma'am," Gladys mumbled in between her tears.

Frank McTavish, the footman, squatted next to the crying maid. "Don't cry, Gladys. I'm sure it'll be okay. Besides, if me and me mates ever get ahold of him in a pub one dark night, we'll teach him a lesson."

"Now, I don't want to be 'earing about none of that talk," Mrs. McDuffie said and sat up tall. "Although it breaks my 'eart to say it."

Thompkins entered the room with the stained shirt in his hands, which opened a new floodgate of tears for the maid.

"I'd like to get me 'ands around that bloke's neck and . . ." Mrs. McDuffie demonstrated with a tea towel exactly what she would like to do.

Rather than relieving the maid's distress, the demonstrations of support from her companions made Gladys sob even more.

Hyrum McTavish, the groundskeeper, poked his head around the corner. "What's going on?"

In a few short sentences, Frank filled in his father.

The groundskeeper squinted and stared at his son. Then he took his gnarled and knubby hands and sipped at the cup of tea the cook, Mrs. Anderson, had poured for him.

"Ta." He sipped his tea. The groundskeeper was never much of a talker, but his silence was deeper and more intense than usual. His expression was so serious, his son became agitated.

Frank nudged his father out of his reverie. "Da', what's the matter?"

"What did you say this bloke calls 'imself?" the groundskeeper asked.

"Captain Archibald bloody Jessup," Frank spat out.

To this point, Thompkins had listened in silence, but this type of language was too much for the prim and proper butler. He felt it was his responsibility to set an example of proper behavior befitting the servants of the Marsh family. He cleared his throat. "That's enough of that type of language. Regardless of any personal feelings on the matter, Captain Jessup is a guest of the Marshes and deserves to be treated with respect."

Applause.

Captain Jessup came around the corner and clapped. "Wonderful. I'm touched to come down here and hear such a touching speech."

Gladys and all the women hurried to their feet. Jim and Frank stood, but their postures were anything but reverential.

Thompkins glanced at the footmen with a look that indicated they would be dealt with later.

The only person who did not stand was

Hyrum McTavish. The groundskeeper stared at the former military man with a look that was just a shade short of disgust.

Captain Jessup sneered. "I guess I was correct in assuming the quality of servants isn't what it once was even in the great houses of the British aristocracy."

Mrs. McDuffie fumed. "Well, I never."

Thompkins bristled at the disparaging remark but maintained his perfect posture.

Hyrum McTavish looked around quizzically. His eyes landed on the captain. "Oh dear. Are you referring to me, sir?" He gazed up at the captain, and something like recognition passed between the two men.

Hyrum McTavish nodded and then used the table to hoist himself up from his seat with a lot more effort than he'd demonstrated earlier. He groaned as he stood. "Oh, some days me bones don't want to cooperate." He sighed. "Ever since Passchendaele, I've just been a shadow of my former self."

Captain Jessup gasped, and a look of fear flashed across his face.

The look wasn't lost on the groundskeeper. "Are you, by chance, a military man?"

Captain Jessup stared. "Did you say, Passchendaele?"

McTavish nodded. "Aye, I was just a private meself, but I served in the Battle of Passchendaele."

"I didn't know . . . I mean . . . reports were . . . there were heavy losses."

"Aye." McTavish shook his head, but he never took his eyes from the captain's face. "Far as I know, only two people survived that battle. Me and a sergeant. Funny man, that sergeant, he was terrified of bees. Allergic he was." He squinted. "I would recognize that sergeant anywhere."

There was a tense moment. After a few seconds, Captain Jessup backed up. "Yes, well, jolly good . . . I came down to talk to . . . Thompkins about my shirt, but . . . it can wait." He backed out of the room.

Everyone stood staring at the spot where the captain had stood just moments ago.

Mrs. McDuffie was the first to speak. "Well, what do you suppose that was about?"

Everyone stared.

The groundskeeper whispered, "What, indeed." After a few moments, he turned to leave.

Thompkins stared at the groundskeeper and recoiled at the look on McTavish's face. The groundskeeper had a look of pure hatred in his eyes.

I'm not sure what time Nana Jo came up to bed, but she was sound asleep when the alarm went off the next morning. The fact that she had fallen asleep without changing into her pajamas was probably a direct result of the amount of alcohol she'd consumed the night before. However, by the time I had showered and left the bathroom, she was at least awake.

"Good morning."

Nana Jo grunted and waddled into the bathroom.

By the time she came out, I was dressed. I'd packed all of my new clothes into my duffel. I had ordered two cups of coffee and had one waiting when Nana Jo came out of the bathroom. She walked to the table, picked up the cup, and downed the entire cup before she looked up. "Thank you."

I smiled. Nothing soothes the savage beast better or faster than caffeine.

Nana Jo dressed and consolidated her packages into one large bundle. Not having luggage certainly made packing easier.

In record time, we headed downstairs to get a more substantial breakfast, which I hoped would include bacon and a lot more coffee.

Our first stop was to the ballroom. I had left my brochure and wanted to pick up another one. I stuck my head in the room, which at first glance, appeared to be empty. I went in and looked around on the counter, where I found the brochures, and turned to go when I noticed Major Peabody. He was wearing the same clothes from the night before, but there was a strange tilt to his head.

Just then, Clive Green entered the room. He glanced in the direction of Major Peabody and slowly took a few steps toward him. "Major Peabody?" He waited. After a few seconds, he followed it up with a shake. When he got no response, he leaned over and felt the major's neck for a pulse. After a long pause, he stood and turned.

"He's dead."

Chapter 8

I didn't realize Dr. Vincent Blankenship had joined us in the ballroom until Nana Jo turned and said, "Dr. Blankenship, perhaps you should have a look at him?"

Dr. Blankenship frowned. "I'm on vacation."

Both Nana Jo and I stared at him, and he shrugged. "If he's dead, there's nothing I can do for him now."

Our silence must have shamed the doctor, who turned a slight shade of red and then huffed and took a few steps forward. He was halted by Clive.

"No. I think it would be best if we call a British doctor."

Dr. Blankenship's neck flushed. "I know there are a number of differences between the United Kingdom and the United States, but I assure you that I'm capable of determining whether or not a man is dead even in England."

Clive reassured the doctor that he meant no offense, while muttering words like "international incident," "red tape," and "the National Health Service rules." He insisted on calling a British doctor.

"Fine with me," Dr. Blankenship said.

"I'd better tell the hotel manager," I said. I rushed to the lobby. After a discreet word with the manager, he told me the hotel had a physician on call.

He dialed the doctor and asked him to make his way into the ballroom.

By the time the hotel manager and I got back into the ballroom, we were just in time to see two waiters carrying Major Peabody out of the room. I stopped. "Should they be doing that?"

The hotel manager said, "I'm sure the doctor would rather have the . . . ah . . . Major Peabody removed to one of our private guest rooms."

The hotel doctor entered and the manager quickly ushered him through the same doors where the major had just been carried.

"I may not know much about British law," Nana Jo said, "but it still seems odd to me to move a body before the police arrive."

Clive Green's return was so quiet, I didn't know he was behind us until he spoke. "The police! Why, there's no need to involve the police. Major Peabody died of natural causes. I assure you there's no need to call the police." He hurried off.

Nana Jo whispered, "Me thinks the *gentleman* doth protest too much."

Dr. Vincent Blankenship stared as the door closed. After a few moments, he glanced at me and Nana Jo. Perhaps he noticed the disapproval that was painted all over Nana Jo's face. He sighed. "Look, I've been working a lot of ungodly hours, and I finally get a week of vacation, and all I get is, *Can you take a look at this rash? Can you give me something for an upset stomach?*" He huffed. "Doctors deserve time off too."

Nana Jo raised an eyebrow but said nothing.

Clive Green hustled to round up the tour group and got everyone onto the bus. Once everyone was on board, he announced, "Ladies and gentlemen, as many of you may have heard, our tour owner, Major Horace Peabody, passed away quietly in his sleep last night."

The few guests who had yet to hear the news gasped in shock.

"Was the major ill?" Nana Jo yelled from her seat near the middle of the bus.

I nudged her with my elbow, but years of experience told me that my elbow would have little effect.

Clive cleared his throat. "Well, I believe the major had a bit of a dicky ticker."

The American couple were seated in front of us, and I overheard Tiffany ask, "What's a dicky ticker?"

Her husband shrugged.

Nana Jo leaned in over the seat and chimed in, "It's a bad heart."

"Oh."

Nana Jo sat back and frowned.

"What's the matter now?" I said.

"Usually people with a bad heart don't drink an entire bottle of Scotch."

"How do you know he drank the entire bottle?"

She glanced at me. "Surely, you noticed when we left him last night the bottle on the table next to him was almost full, and this morning the bottle was empty."

Professor Lavington was seated behind us. He must have been listening to our conversation because he stuck his head over the top of my seat. "I noticed that too."

Nana Jo fired back. "And did you notice there was a glass on the table near the major when he was sitting by the fire, but this morning, it was gone?"

Professor Lavington nodded. "Yes, and did you see how that niece glared at him last night? She looked like she would have loved to stab him right through the heart."

Nana Jo was bad enough without someone to egg her on.

I knew I needed to put a stop to this speculation. "Just because we are on a Murder Mystery Lovers Tour of England, doesn't mean there has to be a murder." I glanced up at our conversation hijacker, who merely gave me a skeptical glance and then sat back down in his seat.

I saw Ruby Mae was seated next to our new friend, Hannah Schneider, and I was happy to see the two of them hitting it off.

"Seems odd to continue on the tour while the owner is lying back there stiff as a board," Nana Jo whispered loud enough for everyone to hear.

Clive responded, "Major Peabody wouldn't want to upset your schedule." He pronounced schedule like "shed" and "yule" rather than the way Americans pronounced the word. "Major Peabody was a businessman as well as a Murder Mystery Lover, and I assure you nothing would have given him greater pleasure than knowing we're continuing his legacy."

"Fat chance," Nana Jo mumbled.

I gave my grandmother a hard glance, but it was wasted on her.

Within a few brief moments, our bus pulled away from the curb and we were on our way.

For about five minutes after our bus pulled away, I felt guilty about the idea of having fun while Major Peabody lay dead. However, I was on vacation; plus I didn't really know Major Peabody. It wasn't like we were old friends. So, I pushed aside all feelings of guilt and prepared to enjoy myself. In fact, I hated to admit it, but I was grateful Major Peabody's death occurred quickly. I hadn't had time to get to know him, so his death didn't affect me much.

Clive Green announced that the morning would be spent with a whirlwind tour through London. We made a quick stop at Buckingham Palace, primarily for photo opportunities. We were near but not close enough to the Royal Guard to embarrass ourselves too much. However, since this was a Murder Mystery Lovers Tour, Clive Green talked about some of the more ancient murders that had taken place in the past and even the attempted murder of Queen Victoria.

Our next stop took us to the Sherlock Holmes Museum at 221B Baker Street. I'll admit to being intrigued since Sherlock Holmes wasn't a real person. As we got off the bus, Hannah Schneider said, "I've been curious about this place ever since I saw it on the tour."

"How do you make a museum for a fictional place?" Ruby Mae asked the question that had been running through my mind.

Clive Green overheard us. "Ah, this is a question that many people have asked over the years. Sir Arthur Conan Doyle created the consulting detective who first appeared in print in 1881." The guide went into the history of Sherlock Holmes and his companion, Dr. John Watson. "As you all know, in the stories written about the detective, Sherlock Holmes and Dr. Watson shared a flat at 221B Baker Street from 1881 to 1904. In reality, there was no 221B Baker Street in 1881. Technically, there's still no 221B Baker Street. This building"—he waved his arm to encompass the structure— "was really 239 Baker Street. In the 1930s, this block of buildings was occupied by the Abbey National Building Society. From the moment the Abbey National moved in, they started receiving mail from all over the world for Mr. Sherlock Holmes. At one point, there was so much mail, they actually employed someone to respond to the urgent correspondence requesting the detective's help. In 1990, the Sherlock Holmes International Society opened a museum. We can't know for sure why Doyle chose to use this particular building for the detective, but Holmes's notoriety has made this address famous. The building is now listed with the British Trust in honor of the great detective and is decorated as it would have been in Victorian times with items mentioned in the stories."

We got off the bus and entered. The ground floor of the Victorian building was a shop peddling everything from deerstalker hats, pipes, and magnifying glasses to books, films, and all things Sherlockian. Tickets for the museum were included in our tour, so we were able to go upstairs to explore the three floors of the museum, which had been meticulously decorated to reflect the lives of the fictional detectives as written in the books. Nothing had been omitted from the experience, including the detective's pipe, violin, and armchair in front of the fireplace. On the second floor, there were rooms for not only Dr. Watson but for the detective's landlady, Mrs. Hudson, along with a life-sized model of Watson at his writing desk, supposedly penning one of the tales from their adventures. The third floor featured more models, including one of Sherlock's nemesis, Professor Moriarty.

Nana Jo sauntered up to me as I stood admiring the display. "Pretty amazing, isn't it?"

I turned away, hoping to hide the tears that had formed in my eyes, but I should have known better than to think I could hide anything from my grandmother.

"What's the matter?" She handed me a tissue. "And don't tell me nothing."

I wiped my eyes and blew my nose. "It's just so amazing," I whispered, careful not to be overheard. "He wasn't real. Yet he lived in the hearts of so many people." I shook my head. "I mean, Sir Arthur Conan Doyle was a writer. He created a character in his imagination, and he wrote about him. Now, here we are over a hundred years later, and we're still talking about him. People still care enough about this character to create a museum, and people, like us, pay money to come to see it." I stared at her. "I'm not explaining myself very well."

"I get it. You're thinking about it as a writer."

"I was just thinking, Leon and I were never blessed with children. When I'm gone . . ." I shrugged. "There may not be anyone who remembers me, but maybe . . . just maybe my books could be my legacy. Maybe when I'm gone, people will remember me."

She put an arm around my shoulders and gave me a hug. "Sam, you have so many friends and family who love you that you will be remembered, but I understand. I do. I hope your books will be as successful as Doyle's and that a hundred years later, people will build a museum in North Harbor to honor them."

I laughed. "I don't think I can even aspire to that type of fame. Right now, I'd be happy to see my book become a reality and maybe end up in a bookstore and a library."

Nana Jo tsked. "Nonsense. Your books are great. They'll sell a million copies."

I squeezed my grandmother. "You're biased, but I appreciate the vote of confidence."

We spent a few more moments admiring the level of detail put into creating the museum. I realized how important details are to a story. Without the details, readers wouldn't be able to visualize Sherlock's and Watson's lives. I made a mental note to include more details in my own writing and then went down to the ground floor and bought some gifts before we headed back onto the bus.

Once everyone was on board, Clive told us that he had received a call from the hotel. The hotel's doctor had examined Major Peabody and found nothing unusual. His death was attributed to natural causes. We were, therefore, free to move on with our tour.

Nana Jo squinted and gave me a sideways glance that indicated she didn't believe one word of what she was told.

I leaned close and whispered, "You have got to stop being so suspicious. Every person who dies hasn't been murdered."

"I don't believe every person who dies has been murdered. However, I grew up on a farm, and I know horse pucky when I smell it."

According to the itinerary, we were scheduled to have lunch at a pub, but Clive told us that we would be dining at the hotel instead. Back at the hotel, we ate together in the dining room rather than in the ballroom. After lunch, I was surprised to find Major Peabody's glamourous niece, who I learned was named Debra Holt, and her fiancé, Sebastian Rothchild-Black, would be joining the tour.

"What a hunk," Irma whispered as Sebastian walked past us to get on the bus.

Clive Green plastered a smile on his face and held out a hand to assist Debra aboard. "Glad you were able to alter your plans to join us."

She laughed. "Surely, you didn't think I'd leave you to run *my* business."

Clive stared. "Your business?"

"My uncle is gone, and I'm his only heir. I intend to make sure that his wishes are carried out and that the sale he was brokering goes forward." She smirked. "I love your little tour games, but this is business—*my* business. You should stick to your honey."

For a moment, Clive Green's face reflected shock and something else I couldn't name. However, within seconds, he had his mask back in place. But based on the laugh that Debra gave, it was clear she'd seen the crack and reveled in her victory.

Nana Jo nudged me. "She looks like the cat that got the cream."

"She certainly seems proud of herself."

We climbed on board and settled into the same seats we'd had earlier. I tried to contain my excitement, but it was a struggle. We were headed to Oxford. In the brochure, it had been described as a mystery lover's paradise. I wasn't sure if I would go quite that far, but the very name brought up memories of the British detective series *Lewis*, which I loved. I learned from research for this trip that Oxford has produced an abundance of crime writers, including Dorothy L. Sayers and P. D. James. Its academic ambiance, ancient towers, and hidden quads set the scene for an extensive list of mysteries. The reality was surprisingly much the same as what I'd imagined.

The ride took a little more than an hour. When we arrived, we stopped for a coffee break at a quaint shop to get a bit of refreshment. Once we were all revitalized by our caffeinated beverage of choice, we embarked on a guided walking tour of Oxford. Clive was knowledgeable and entertaining. He was able to speak intelligently not only about Oxford's colleges, chapels, and city haunts, like the iconic Christ Church College, but also places of interest to lovers of Lord Peter Wimsey, Prudence Vane, and Inspector Morse.

The brochures warned that there would be quite a bit of walking, so I was prepared with good sneakers. Nana Jo and the girls were all fit and well able to enjoy the exercise. Unfortunately, Prudence Habersham must have missed that part in the brochure and spent the majority of the trip complaining to her daughter, Lavender.

After the group was forced to stop to allow Prudence to catch her breath and rest for the fifth or sixth time in a little over one hour, Nana Jo voiced the frustration that the majority of the group felt.

"Why did you choose to come on the walking tour if you weren't prepared to walk?" Nana Jo asked.

Prudence bristled at the insult. "Well, I'm sorry. I've been ill, and I didn't realize that I would be such a burden." She dabbed at her eyes with a handkerchief.

"Don't try that passive-aggressive business with me," Nana Jo said. "You aren't sorry. If you've been ill, then you could have waited in the coffee shop when Clive over there gave you the option. Or, at the very least, you could have worn shoes that were fit for walking rather than pumps."

Prudence pointed to Irma. "Your friend there has on high heels."

"Irma's been wearing six-inch hooker heels since she hit puberty, and she could run a hundred-yard dash in those heels if she had to."

"Well, I never."

"Well, that's the problem, isn't it?"

Clive stepped in between the two women. "Now, ladies. I'm sure Mrs. Habersham is doing her very best." He smiled at the woman, whose face was now beet red. Then, he turned to Nana Jo. "Plus, we are doing great on time, and I promise we will see everything that Oxford has to offer. These little breaks are a great opportunity for photos."

Nana Jo huffed.

Prudence gave a simpering smile and fanned herself.

Debra Holt burst out laughing. She laughed for several moments and then turned to Clive. "You are the perfect stooge for this, aren't you?"

A vein on the side of his forehead pulsed, but he merely smiled and turned his back and addressed the group. "Now, I realize this isn't 'mystery' focused, but if we have any *Harry Potter* fans, you'll recognize that area as the place where Malfoy was transfigured into a ferret in *Harry Potter and the Goblet of Fire.*"

We all turned to observe the point, and several people took out their phones and snapped photos.

The tour progressed with fewer stops. Prudence walked

with a new determination. However, whenever Clive noticed her face was particularly red, he would pause near a bench and go into great detail about the history of a building or even a tree, which allowed a lot more time for rest.

When the tour finished, we were given a couple of hours of free time to explore on our own. Nana Jo and the girls decided a different type of refreshment was required, and we stepped into one of the honey-colored pubs to enjoy a traditional meal of fish and chips and a glass of the local ale before we had to head back on the bus.

I'm not a fan of beer regardless of its country of origin, but everything else was tasty. We were having a good time. Hannah Schneider fit in with our group well and told us stories about her children. It was only when she started to talk about her husband that she grew quiet or that a tear would form in her eyes. So, we steered the conversation away from the danger zone. There was only one dark cloud that marred our time. That occurred when Mrs. Habersham and her daughter entered the pub.

Nana Jo flushed. "I suppose I should apologize." She sighed. "I shouldn't have been rude, but that woman just gets under my skin."

"Why?" I looked at my grandmother. "I mean, I know she's out of shape, but I've never seen you so hard on anyone for that."

She shook her head. "It's not the fact that she's overweight or out of shape." She glanced toward the table where the two had settled. "I just don't like the way the woman gripes and complains all the time. I mean, if you can't walk long distances, no problem. She could stop any time. It's the way she complained and whined." She glanced down her nose at me. "You know I don't have any patience with whiners."

I nodded.

"I also don't like the way she uses her daughter like an indentured servant." Nana Jo tilted her head in the direction of the two women. "On the bus, Lavender suggested her mother leave that large carry-on bag on the bus, but oh no. Mama Habersham just had to have it. But she's not the one carrying two purses, hers and her mother's, along with that fifty-pound bag."

"I did think that was a bit much."

"That bag is pretty awkward," Dorothy said, leaning forward. "I offered to help carry the bag. I was going to carry it for a while to give the girl a break, but did you hear how the old lady snapped, 'Lavender can carry it.'"

"I wonder what she has in the thing," Ruby Mae said. "Have you noticed they take it everywhere and never let it out of their sight?"

Nana Jo sighed. "I guess I just let my frustration boil up, and I took it out on her for the wrong reason. I owe her an apology, and I might as well get it over with." She rose and headed toward the two women, but before she got to the table, Debra and her fiancé entered the bar.

When Prudence spotted Debra, she hopped up from her seat and hurried over to the woman. She grabbed her by the arm. "We need to talk."

Debra glared at the woman and then yanked her arm free. "I beg your pardon."

Prudence huffed and turned red. "I heard what you said earlier to that guide about you being the only heir to Horace's wealth, and I just want you to know that's not true."

Debra's expression of boredom and amusement vanished. "What did you say?"

Prudence noticed and took a moment to gloat. "You think you were Horace's closest relative, well, I'll have you know that you aren't. Horace and I were lovers."

Debra smiled. "Good for you. Who knew Uncle Horace

had it in him." She glanced up at Prudence as though she were a piece of meat and turned to leave.

Prudence's face turned purple with rage. "How dare you look at me like some tart."

"Well, you're the one that just announced to the world that you had an illicit affair with my uncle."

"It was a long time ago, after the war. I was a nurse, and he was injured."

Debra held up a hand. "You don't have to explain to me. I'm just shocked to know that Uncle Horace ever had the nerve to kiss a woman, let alone . . ." She waved her hand.

"It was a long time ago, and we lost touch." Prudence took several deep breaths. "When I found out I was pregnant, he had been called back to India, and . . . well, I was alone and with child. Chester had always been kind, and when he asked me to marry him, I did." She took several more breaths. "He knew Lavender wasn't his daughter, but he didn't mind."

I glanced at Lavender, who was still seated at the table, and saw that this revelation was as much of a shock to her as it had been to the rest of us sitting in the pub.

"So, you see, you aren't Horace's only heir. Lavender is his daughter, and I'm going to make sure that she gets everything that she deserves."

The reality of Prudence's words hit Debra full force. Her face contorted. She leaned forward and pointed a finger in the woman's face. "If you think you can come in here after my uncle is dead and make outrageous accusations about him and steal my inheritance, then you'd better think again." She turned and marched out of the pub.

Sebastian glanced at Prudence and then hurried after his fiancée.

Prudence stood in the middle of the pub. She glanced around and saw that all of the noise and commotion had stopped. The realization hit her that everyone had not only seen the altercation but also heard everything. She turned bright red from the roots of her hair to the bottom of her neck. She seemed frozen for several seconds. Then, she burst into tears and ran out the door.

Prudence's departure broke the spell, and the pub patrons returned to their conversations and drinks. Only Lavender seemed to still be trapped. Like a statue, she stared at the door where her mother had just escaped. After a few seconds, she collected all of the bags and made her own hasty retreat.

Nana Jo watched Lavender's departure and then spun around and returned to our table. "Well, well, well, wasn't this a fine bit of drama?"

No one knew what to make of it. Normally, a display of this type would have tongues wagging and would provide a good bit of fodder for conversation. However, this was different. It wasn't the juicy fodder that nosy gossips could feast upon. This exchange had cast a dark cloud over the pub. We tried to push away the foul atmosphere, but the jaunty banter and high spirits were gone. So, we finished our drinks and made our way back to the bus. Something about this entire situation seemed off somehow. I questioned whether Nana Jo could have been right about Major Peabody's death not being natural. I tried to shake the feeling that the major had been murdered, but there was definitely something about his death that seemed . . . off somehow. I just couldn't put my finger on it. All the while, Prudence Habersham's words echoed through my head: *"She gets everything that she deserves."*

Debra Holt and her fiancé, Sebastian, were already seated at the front of the bus when we arrived. When Prudence Habersham got on board, she kept her head high and carefully avoided making eye contact with anyone as she made her way to the last seat at the back of the bus. Lavender wasn't as careful as she struggled with bags and purses, but she too made her way to the back of the bus. The ride back to London was long and somber. Most people slept. I decided to occupy my mind by writing.

⁓

Lady Elizabeth Marsh entered the kitchen and stopped at the sight of all of the servants standing with puzzled looks. At the sight of Lady Elizabeth, everyone, including Jim and Frank, snapped to attention.

"Did I interrupt something?" Lady Elizabeth said.

"No, m'lady." Thompkins stood even straighter than normal and coughed. "It's just that Captain Jessup was just here."

"Oh, really?" Lady Elizabeth waited patiently. "Was there anything in particular the captain wanted?"

Gladys sniffed, while Jim and Frank exchanged glances. Thompkins coughed again. "I believe the captain wanted to discuss concerns about his shirt, but he changed his mind."

Mrs. McDuffie snorted.

Lady Elizabeth turned to the housekeeper.

Mrs. McDuffie flushed, which made her freckled complexion and thin red hair appear even redder. "I beg your ladyship's pardon. It's just that . . . jackanapes gets under me skin . . . upsetting poor Gladys and then coming down 'ere and talkin' like 'e owns the place."

Jim and Frank exchanged glances and snickered.

Thompkins gasped. "That will be enough," he snapped at the footmen. He turned to Lady Elizabeth. "I apologize for—"

Lady Elizabeth waved away his apologies. She was well aware of the butler's attitude about propriety and high moral standards when it came to etiquette. "I quite agree with Mrs. McDuffie's assessment of the situation in this case." She smiled at the housekeeper and then turned back to the butler. "Perhaps we could go into your office?"

"Of course, your ladyship." Thompkins dismissed the other staff and waited for Lady Elizabeth and the housekeeper to precede him into the small room that he used whenever he needed a quiet place to work on the books or to have a private conversation with one of the staff.

Once inside the room, Lady Elizabeth took a seat at the table and invited the housekeeper and butler to sit, even though she knew Thompkins would never sit in her presence. Mrs. McDuffie took the other chair, and Thompkins closed the door and took a staunch stand nearby and waited.

"I know Captain Jessup has been rather trying," Lady Elizabeth said.

"Trying?" Mrs. McDuffie snorted. A cough from Thompkins reminded her of her place, and she said, "I beg your pardon."

Lady Elizabeth smiled. "It's quite all right. I completely agree. He's been extremely difficult, and I have to admit that I don't like the way he treats the children."

"Ah, you've noticed that too?"

"It's obvious that he objects to them because they're Jewish."

"I didn't want to believe it," Thompkins said, "but I have to say that my son-in-law, Joseph, did mention that the captain has made some rude and unpleasant remarks to him as well as the children."

"That's not acceptable," Lady Elizabeth said. "I'm afraid I shall have to have a talk with Captain Jessup."

Thompkins cleared his throat. "Was there something in particular that your ladyship wanted to discuss?"

"Oh dear, yes." She smiled. "I want to have a small dinner party."

Mrs. McDuffie took out a small notepad and a pencil she kept in her apron pocket and prepared to take notes.

"Well, to be completely honest," Lady Elizabeth said, "I hoped that having more people in the house would dilute some of the captain's personality a bit. I hope that it won't be too much of an inconvenience to the staff."

Thompkins and Mrs. McDuffie reassured her they were well prepared for the dinner party.

"It'll be a small affair with the family, Penelope and Victor, Lady Clara and Detective Inspector Covington." She paused at how natural it seemed to include Detective Inspector Covington amongst the family, but then she hurried to add, "Of course, Captain Jessup." She waited while Mrs. McDuffie caught up on the list before adding, "I think Reverend Baker and his wife would be good. I think Mrs. Baker's father fought in the last war, and maybe she would be able to talk to him. Besides, Captain Jessup could hardly be rude to a minister or his wife." She thought a moment. "I was going to invite Lady Dallyripple, but sadly, I'm afraid Amelia may share too many of the captain's views."

"Gawd," Mrs. McDuffie said. "I never did care much for that one."

Thompkins bristled but said nothing, and Lady Elizabeth hurried on with her list. "What about Miss Olivia and Miss Marjorie Wood?"

"Those two spinsters love gossip, but they're as 'armless as milk toast." Mrs. McDuffie added the names to her list.

"I think both of them nursed injured soldiers during and after the war. I think they'd be perfect."

Mrs. McDuffie looked up from her notepad. "Will that be all?"

Thompkins coughed. "If my math is accurate that would be eleven for dinner."

Mrs. McDuffie quickly counted the names on her list. "You don't want an odd number for dinner, your ladyship. That's bad luck."

Lady Elizabeth paused and thought for a few moments. "William received a note from an old friend . . . Nigel Greyson. They were in the service together. Plus, I think Nigel was good friends with Victor's uncle, so he should fit in beautifully."

"If I'm not mistaken," Thompkins said, "Lord

Greyson is the son of the rector of Copdock and the grandson of the fifth Lord Walsingham."

"Your memory is perfect, as always." Lady Elizabeth smiled at the butler. "Nigel is in London taking care of some family business. William was going to make a trip into town, but I think we'll invite him to spend a few days here."

"I'll get a room prepared and make sure everything is ready for the dinner party," Mrs. McDuffie said. "When do you want to have the party?"

"I think tonight." She looked up at the butler. "That is, if you think Mrs. Anderson can manage."

Thompkins stood straighter. "I assure you we will be ready."

"Perfect. Please, tell Mrs. Anderson I'll trust her to come up with the menu, but I'll come down later to discuss it with her." She stood. "For now, I'd better get busy. I've got quite a few invitations to get into the post."

Later, Lady Elizabeth tracked down Detective Inspector Covington in a corner of the library in a large-backed chair. Lady Clara sat on the sofa, gazing into the fireplace. "Perfect," Lady Elizabeth said. "Both of the people I've been looking for in one place."

Lady Clara looked up curiously at her cousin.

Detective Inspector Covington rose and faced Lady Elizabeth. "Your ladyship."

"First, I do wish you'd call me Elizabeth. It would make things so much easier. Plus, then I could call you Peter and wouldn't feel the need to keep calling you Detective Inspector Covington."

The detective inspector flushed slightly and glanced at Lady Clara, who merely shrugged. "Don't look at me. I had nothing to do with it." She turned to her cousin. "I've been trying to get him to call me Clara since we first met."

The detective frowned slightly. "Your ladyship is, of course, welcome to call me Peter. In fact, I would prefer it. However, I hope you'll forgive me if I say that I don't feel comfortable bypassing the protocol of referring to you in so . . . intimate of terms."

Lady Clara sighed. "Poppycock."

"Of course," Lady Elizabeth said. "Please use whatever makes you the most comfortable. Now, I was hoping I could impose upon you for a favor."

The detective bowed slightly. "I will be more than happy to assist."

"As I mentioned, I've decided to host a small dinner party tonight." She handed a stack of envelopes to Lady Clara. "Due to the short notice, the servants are going to have their hands full getting ready, and I've still got quite a few errands. I was hoping that I could prevail upon you and Clara for assistance."

"Of course," they both said at the same time.

"Wonderful." Lady Elizabeth handed a list to Lady Clara.

The detective moved closer so he could look over her shoulder. The two asked a few questions, received their last-minute instructions, and then headed off.

Lady Elizabeth watched the two leave and smiled to herself.

*   *   *

The doorbell rang as the clock struck seven. Thompkins escorted not only the reverend and Mrs. Baker into the parlor but also Miss Marjorie and Miss Olivia Wood.

One of the instructions Lady Elizabeth had given her cousin was to make sure when she notified the reverend and Mrs. Baker of the invitation that she managed to casually mention the Wood sisters were also invited. She knew Reverend Baker would offer to drive the women.

Having called Nigel Greyson to invite him, Lady Elizabeth was able to provide the detective inspector with the information about which train Greyson planned to take so they could pick him up from the station. So, when the others arrived, Greyson was already comfortably ensconced and rested from his trip.

Victor and Lady Penelope, along with the Marsh family, Lady Clara, and Detective Inspector Covington, were all present when their guests arrived. Everyone except Captain Jessup was having a pleasant time enjoying cocktails in a jovial atmosphere.

After thirty minutes, Lady Elizabeth was just about to send Thompkins to check on the captain when the door opened and he stood in the doorway.

Like a model, the captain stood for several moments, gazing around the room with a smug look on his face.

Miss Marjorie Wood gasped and stared at Captain Jessup with a shocked expression.

Miss Olivia Wood's face turned pale, and she looked as though she would faint.

Detective Inspector Covington clasped her arm. "Are you okay? Do you need to sit down?"

Miss Olivia rocked on her feet but recovered herself and waved away his concerns. "I'm sorry. I just took a sudden turn, but I'm fine now."

The detective looked concerned but accepted the woman's response.

Lady Clara sipped her champagne. "Ah, there you are. I was afraid you'd gotten lost finding your way downstairs."

The captain said, "I'm touched that you were concerned."

Lady Elizabeth sat near Lady Clara and heard her mumble, "Don't be."

Captain Jessup strutted into the room and stood with his elbow on the mantle of the fireplace as though he were the lord of the manor.

Lady Elizabeth forced a smile and then rose, taking Captain Jessup by the arm and escorting him over to meet the other guests. "Let me introduce you to our minister. Reverend Baker, may I present Captain Jessup."

Lady Elizabeth was well versed on proper etiquette, which dictated that individuals of lower rank are presented to the higher-ranking or more prominent person. By her choice to present Captain Jessup to Reverend Baker, she established that Reverend Baker was considered of higher importance than the captain.

Her gesture wasn't lost on Captain Jessup, who colored slightly but gave a slight bow to the minister.

Lady Elizabeth continued this distinction, as she introduced Captain Jessup to Mrs. Baker, who flushed but stood surprisingly quiet.

When Lady Elizabeth introduced Captain Jessup to Miss Marjorie and Miss Olivia, she was slightly taken aback by the spinsters' cool response. Although, on closer inspection, both of the women looked pale. She hoped that neither was ill.

Finally, Lady Elizabeth guided the silent and now-seething captain over to Nigel Greyson.

Nigel Greyson was thin and tall with an unusual cowlick and piercing blue eyes. He was also extremely shy. He stood to greet Captain Jessup and extended his hand while barely making eye contact. Eventually, when the introductions were done, Nigel glanced at the captain and tilted his head. "Don't I know you?"

Captain Jessup smirked. "I feel confident that you don't. I doubt that we run in the same social circles." He walked away, picked up a drink from a tray that Thompkins offered, and stood in front of the fireplace with his back to the group.

The captain's quiet, surly behavior would normally have been a problem. However, Lady Penelope and Lady Clara were determined to make the evening a success and worked hard to engage their guests in conversation, which proved surprisingly difficult. The Wood sisters, who normally relished every opportunity to get out in society and could usually be counted upon to keep up a lively chatter, were uncharacteristically quiet. Mrs. Baker was slightly deaf in her right ear, and as people with hearing problems sometimes do, she tended to speak louder than was necessary; however, she was also very quiet. Lady Clara thrived on the captain's discomfort and worked to keep conversation flowing. She provided witty jokes, which generated what laughter and merriment existed in the group.

Thompkins announced that dinner was served, and the group wandered into the dining room. Lady Elizabeth glanced at the place card that Lady Penelope had put beside each setting and bit her cheek to keep from laughing. Lady Penelope had placed her uncle, Lord William, at the head of the table, while Nigel Greyson was given the position as guest of honor and placed at the opposite end of the table. As hostess, Lady Elizabeth was placed to the right of Nigel with Reverend Baker, Lady Clara, Victor, and Mrs. Baker completing that side of the table. To the right of Lord William was Lady Penelope, Detective Inspector Covington, Miss Olivia Wood, Captain Jessup, and Miss Marjorie Wood.

By the time Captain Jessup entered the dining room, he had consumed three drinks and was well on his way to becoming drunk. Seated between the Wood sisters, Captain Jessup barely spoke. In fact, surprisingly, neither of the Wood sisters seemed inclined to talk, and the captain sat and seethed while he glared across the table at Lady Clara.

When dinner was over, the group made their way back to the parlor, and Captain Jessup resumed his prior position in front of the fireplace, drink in hand.

Prepared to ignore his rude behavior, Lady Elizabeth sat on the sofa next to Mrs. Baker and the Wood sisters, while Victor, Lady Penelope, Lady Clara, and Detective Inspector Covington joked. Lord William, Nigel Greyson, and Reverend Baker quietly reminisced about the time spent in His Majesty's service during the Great War, although Nigel kept glancing over at Captain Jessup. In fact, everyone was stealing glances at the ill-behaved man.

Thompkins entered with coffee. He wheeled the cart to Lady Elizabeth and waited to distribute the cups. It was then that Captain Jessup burst into laughter. Everyone stopped talking and turned to gaze at the man who stood alone laughing hysterically. After a few moments, Victor rose and approached the man.

Victor whispered something and attempted to grab Captain Jessup by the arm, but the captain jerked away. "I'm not drunk, and I certainly don't need your help."

Victor colored but persisted. "I think maybe you've had enough to drink."

Captain Jessup sneered. "Oh, you do? Well, I don't. I haven't had nearly enough to drink. It would take more than a couple of glasses of cheap whiskey." He glared at Lord William, who bristled at the insult.

"Steady on, man," Victor said. "You're a guest in this house and—"

"Awww, now we're getting to the heart of the matter. I'm a guest." He waved his drink in the air, and the liquid sloshed onto the floor. "I'm a guest here, but it's you who's the guest."

Victor shook his head. "You're drunk."

"You're a thief." He leaned forward and glared. "You've stolen my birthright, but I'm the Earl of Lochloren."

Victor stared at the man in stunned silence for several moments. "What are you talking about?"

Captain Jessup laughed. "Your father wasn't the earl. He was the younger son, not the elder. The title, the house, and the lands all belonged to his older brother, Percival, who was the true heir and Earl of Lochloren."

Victor frowned. "That's true, but Percival died in the Crimean War, so the title fell to my father, Nevil."

Lord William said, "This is hardly the time or the place—"

"Time or the place? This is exactly the time and the place." Jessup waltzed around the room. "You all sit here like royalty and look down your noses at me. When I . . . the son of Percival Carlston, am the real Earl of Lochloren."

Victor's eyes grew large as he stared at his cousin. "What are you talking about? Percival had no children."

"None that you knew about." He tossed back the rest of his drink. "Or none that you acknowledged anyway. My mother was a nurse working with Florence Nightingale. She tended to wounded soldiers. She met Lord Percival when he was injured at the Battle of Alma."

"Uncle Percival got a flesh wound at the Battle of Alma but was patched up and returned to battle. He was killed later in the Battle of Balaclava."

Captain Jessup sneered. "Exactly, but not before he fathered a child . . . me."

"You? But I don't understand. Why didn't your mother come forward and tell the family? I'm sure my grandfather would have—"

"Would have what? Acknowledged that his son had fathered a child out of wedlock? Do you really think he would have wanted to admit that he had a grandson . . . from the wrong side of the blanket?"

"But, if that's true," Lady Penelope said, "then that would mean . . ."

Captain Jessup laughed. "Ah, I see you're finally starting to catch on. That would mean that I am the Earl of Lochloren, not you." He pointed at Victor. "That means I own Bidwell Cottage, and you two are mere interlopers. I appreciate the renovations you're making to my home, but I'll be claiming ownership, and you two can find someplace else to live. I intend to get everything I deserve." He slammed his glass down on the mantle and stumbled out of the room, leaving everyone staring after him in shock.

Chapter 9

The bus pulled in front of the hotel.

"We have a very busy day tomorrow," Clive said. "We will be leaving for the Cotswolds and staying overnight. We'll spend a morning exploring the racing world of mystery writer Dick Francis. In the morning, we'll get up close and personal with some of England's best race horses. At the stable, we'll witness the strength and discipline of these fine creatures as they go through their morning gallops. In the afternoon, we'll take a walking tour of Chipping Campden, where you'll be able to link aspects of village life to the world of Miss Marple and D. L. Sayers's books." He smiled. "So, be sure and get plenty of rest and be prepared for a vigorous day of fun."

I heard a groan from the back, which I suspected came from Prudence Habersham.

Rather than going inside the hotel after she got off the bus, Nana Jo waited. I turned to ask what was wrong, but she volunteered the information. "I still owe Prudence Habersham an apology." I nodded and waited alongside my grandmother.

When Prudence finally got off the bus, she glanced at Nana Jo, lifted her head, and prepared to walk by, but Nana Jo stopped her. "Prudence, I owe you an apology. I'm sorry. I was rude, and I'm very sorry for what I said earlier."

Prudence released a breath, and some of the tension in her shoulders relaxed. "Thank you," she said hesitantly. "I suppose I should have packed walking shoes."

"Mrs. Habersham, I bought an extra pair of tennis shoes . . . ah, I mean trainers." I glanced down at her feet. "I think they might fit you."

She smiled. "Well, that's really nice, but I don't want to inconvenience you."

I shook my head. "It's no inconvenience at all. I'll bring the shoes to your room."

She thanked me and then gave me her room number.

Lavender gave us a sincere smile, and the two women left. Nana Jo and I followed them, and that's when I got a whiff of tobacco. A wisp of smoke drifted by, and an orange glow attracted my attention. Leaning against the building and smoking a cigarette was Debra Holt, with Sebastian by her side. We nodded as we passed and entered the hotel. We stopped at the front desk to see if the airline had located our luggage but were disappointed to learn our bags were still MIA.

Nana Jo took a quick bath and then got into bed. She was sound asleep and snoring in record time. I went through my bag and pulled out the new sneakers I had bought at Harrods. For a brief second, I considered switching and giving Prudence the shoes I was wearing rather than the new pair of sneakers that still had the price tag attached but decided against it. Her need was greater than mine. I grabbed my key and cell phone and hurried downstairs. Prudence and her daughter were one floor below us. When I found the right room, I was just about to knock when I noticed the *DO NOT DISTURB* sign on the doorknob. Instead of knocking, I decided to simply leave the shoes outside the door. She'd find them in the morning.

It was after midnight, but I wasn't sleepy. So, instead of going back upstairs, I went downstairs to the lounge. I found a secluded corner and called Frank.

He greeted me the way he always did: "Hello, gorgeous."

I smiled, even though I knew he couldn't see me. "Are you crazy busy?"

"Yes, but I always have time to talk to you."

Frank always knew the right thing to say.

We squeezed a lot into a short timeframe. I told him about Major Peabody's death and Nana Jo's altercation with Prudence Habersham. Frank laughed. "That sounds like your grandmother."

We spent a few minutes talking about nothing, but I could feel the heat rising up my neck and found my heart racing anyway. When I heard the noise in the restaurant get louder, I knew this was Frank's busy time, and I ended the call.

Rather than going back upstairs, I went to the bar. I didn't care for wine, even though Frank was trying to change that. We had discovered that I was partial to sweet wines. So, I asked the bartender for a glass of the sweetest white wine he had. He poured a sparkling white wine, which he told me was from West Sussex.

It looked and tasted like champagne, but I knew from Frank that, technically, only wine grown in the Champagne region of France was really champagne.

The bar would be open for two more hours. I glanced around and saw Irma in a corner with the man I'd seen her with before. Their body language told me they would prefer to be alone, so I took my glass and returned to my quiet corner in the lounge.

I sat in a high-backed chair that looked out onto the street. It was nice to be secluded from the world. I enjoyed the peace and quiet and the time to reflect on the fact that I was in England. It wasn't my first trip, but when I'd gone before, I was on a much tighter budget and wasn't able to stay at nice hotels and take guided tours. A lot had changed in my world in the past couple of years, but I was about to realize a dream and become a published author. Despite all the ups and downs, life was good. I sipped my wine and enjoyed the moment.

The lounge was a wood-paneled room near the back of the hotel. There was a sofa and several comfortable chairs. Guests used the room to read the newspaper and a few old dusty books that were on a bookshelf that lined one wall of the room. My corner retreat wasn't visible to anyone walking down the hallway. I was just about to head upstairs when I heard voices.

"That old cow is crazy if she thinks she's going to waltz in here and pass that toad off as Uncle Horace's heir."

"Be careful, darling. Someone might hear you." There was a pause. "There's no one in there."

"I don't care if they do hear me," Debra hissed. "I've spent nearly thirty years of my life bowing to the whims and wishes of Uncle Horace. I'll not be pushed aside while someone else walks in and stakes claim to what's mine."

Sebastian chuckled. "Well, there's not much you can do about it."

"Just watch me."

I heard the click of heels on the marble floors and knew it was safe to leave. People often said things they didn't mean, especially when they were angry. Prudence Habersham had given Debra Holt a shock. I'm sure she didn't mean anything by her words.

That's what I told myself as I took the elevator back up to my room. When I got inside, Nana Jo was still sound asleep. Of course, now I was too worked up to sleep. So, I got out my laptop.

For about thirty seconds after Captain Jessup made his dramatic exit, you could have heard a pin drop. Then, the spell was broken and everyone started talking at once.

"He can't be serious," Lady Penelope whispered.

Lady Elizabeth glanced at her niece, who had suddenly gotten very pale. "Victor, I think Penelope needs to lie down."

Victor glanced at his wife and then hurried to help her up.

Clara assisted Victor in getting Penelope up to bed.

Reverend Baker stood. "I think it's time we started making our way home."

Lady Elizabeth smiled, grateful to the reverend for recognizing that the family would need some time alone after this devastating display.

Thompkins left to get coats, and Lady Elizabeth and Lord William said goodbyes to their guests. The Wood sisters looked reluctant to end their evening so soon, but good manners took over, and they thanked their hosts and hurried out.

Nigel Greyson announced that he too would be going to bed and went upstairs.

Detective Inspector Covington rose. "Perhaps it might be better if I returned to London tomorrow."

Lady Elizabeth looked at the detective. "Actually, I was hoping you would stay."

The Scotland Yard detective looked surprised but quickly acquiesced. "Of course, your ladyship."

When the guests were gone, Thompkins returned. "Would you like me to dispose of the coffee?"

"I think you better leave it," Lady Elizabeth said.

The butler bowed. "Very well." He turned to leave.

"Thompkins, I would very much appreciate it if you would stay."

"Of course, your ladyship." He bowed and went to stand in a corner.

After a few moments, Lady Clara returned. "Good. I thought you'd all still be here."

"How's Penelope?"

"She's upset, but I think she'll be okay. I do think we should have Dr. Haygood over to check her out in the morning."

The butler nodded. "I'll see to it."

"Thank you." Lady Clara sat on the sofa next to her cousin. "Now, what's the plan?"

Lady Elizabeth smiled. "Well, I don't know that I have one." She paused. "Not yet anyway, but I do think we'll need to look into these claims of Captain Jessup's."

"Dashed bad form," Lord William muttered as he filled his pipe, dropping tobacco on himself and the sofa.

"It wasn't the best timing, I'll admit." Lady Elizabeth reached down by her feet to the knitting bag she kept nearby and pulled out a ball of yarn and two needles. She took a few moments to find where she had left off and started knitting.

"Probably nothing but a pack of lies." Lord William puffed on his pipe as the embers glowed and the smoke wafted up from the bowl of the pipe. "Victor Carlston has lived at Bidwell Cottage his whole life. If there had been someone else, well . . . I'm sure his father or grandfather would have acknowledged it."

Lady Elizabeth sighed. "I tend to agree with you. However, that doesn't change the fact that Captain Jessup is here and claims to be the rightful owner."

Detective Inspector Covington leaned forward in his chair. "I'm not completely up to date on my understanding of primogeniture."

Lady Clara hopped up from her seat and paced. "That archaic practice should be abolished."

"I thought it was," Detective Inspector Covington added.

"It's a practice that has existed for hundreds of years," Lord William said. "I'll admit, it isn't exactly fair to the younger siblings, but the reason behind it is to protect the estate." He puffed on his pipe. "Splitting up the land, titles, and money amongst multiple children often meant that an estate became weakened. After a generation, the heirs can't afford to maintain the properties, and they end up getting sold off." He puffed. "Parliament abolished it as a governing rule when there was no valid will in place, but many of the old families have a will that supports the practice."

"So, if it turns out that snake Jessup is the son of Percival Carlston," Lady Clara said, "then he gets everything and Victor and Penelope are left with nothing?" She flopped back onto the sofa. "It's just not fair."

"Fair or not, that's the law."

Lady Elizabeth finished her stitch and then placed her knitting in her lap. "Penny and Victor will always be welcome here. That's not the problem."

"Victor is so proud," Lady Clara said. "Do you really think he'd agree to stay here?"

"He may not have much of a choice. Given Penny's delicate condition, he'll need to make sure that his wife and child have a roof over their heads." She looked out into the distance but then shook her head and glanced at her cousin. "You have to have seen how Victor has been acting lately."

"He's had his ears glued to the wireless."

Lady Elizabeth resumed knitting. "If England goes to war, he'll do his duty. Between the baby and the war, the last thing Penny needs is to have this to worry about too." She glanced from her cousin to the detective. "That's why I was hoping you two could help."

Lady Clara reached out and squeezed her cousin's hand. "Of course, Aunt Elizabeth. I'll do anything I can to help."

"That goes for me too," Detective Inspector Covington said.

Lady Elizabeth smiled. "Good. I was hoping you two might be able to do a little investigating. Perhaps you could check out the records at

Somerset House." She turned to the detective. "As a detective, I'm sure you have other resources that you can look into to determine if there's any validity in these claims."

"I'll be glad to do what I can."

Thompkins coughed discreetly.

"Ah, Thompkins. I haven't forgotten about you." Lady Elizabeth turned to the butler. "I was hoping you might be able to talk to some of the staff at Bidwell Cottage. I believe their butler and the cook have been with the family for many years."

"Yes, m'lady."

"I'm afraid the type of information I'm looking for might be considered *gossip*, but servants tend to know everything that's going on in a family. Perhaps Mrs. McDuffie might be enlisted to help."

The only indication that the butler felt any discomfort in asking another member of the staff to gossip came in a slight flush of color that rose from his neck. However, he maintained his composure. "Yes, m'lady."

"What about me?" Lord William said.

"I was hoping you might consider going back to town with Nigel tomorrow." She picked up her knitting and concentrated to finish a difficult stitch before continuing. "Isn't Sir Thomas Chadwick the Carlston family solicitor?"

"Yes, he is. He's also, as you well know, a member of my club."

Lady Elizabeth smiled. "Wonderful."

Clara stood to leave but stopped and turned back. "What will you be doing, Aunt Elizabeth?"

Lady Elizabeth continued to knit. "I'm going to invite Violet Merriweather to tea."

"Violet Merriweather?" Lord William sputtered. "That woman's the biggest gossip in the county."

Lady Elizabeth grinned. "Yes, dear, she certainly is, and if there's anyone in Britain who knows about the skeletons in the closets of old families like the Carlstons, it's Violet Merriweather. If there's a shred of truth to Captain Jessup's claims, she'll know."

Lady Elizabeth, Lord William, Clara, Victor, and Detective Inspector Covington sat in the dining room enjoying a hearty English breakfast when the peace and quiet was shattered when a loud crash and a high-pitched scream split the air.

Detective Inspector Covington leapt from his chair and dashed from the room. After a few moments, Thompkins entered.

"What on earth was that racket?" Lord William asked.

"I beg your pardon, m'lord. One of the maids, Flossie, had a fright."

Lord William buttered a piece of toast. "That noise would wake the dead."

"M'lord, it's Captain Jessup."

"What about him?"

"He's dead, m'lord."

Chapter 10

I wrote well into the morning and went to sleep around two. So, when I heard a loud crash and a blood-curdling scream at six, I was jolted awake. I sat up in bed and looked around the room to get my bearings.

Nana Jo came out of the bathroom with shampoo in her hair and a towel around her wet body. "What on earth was that?"

"You heard it too?"

"You'd have to be deaf not to have heard that."

"I hoped it was a dream."

Nana Jo rinsed the soap from her hair, and we quickly dressed and made it downstairs in record time.

The tour group all stood in the lobby, along with other guests I didn't recognize. The one person I did recognize was Clive Green. The normally immaculate Clive looked frazzled. His clothes were rumpled, and he hadn't shaved.

I was just about to ask him what happened when the elevator door opened to show Hannah Schneider holding a visibly shaken Lavender Habersham. Ruby Mae spotted the women and waved a knitting needle to catch Hannah's eye. When Hannah spotted Ruby Mae, she guided Lavender out of the elevator and maneuvered her toward the sofa and helped her sit.

Lavender's face was as white as snow. The woman sat shaking like a flag in the wind. Nana Jo and I walked over to her to see what had happened, and as I got closer, I could actually hear her teeth clattering.

Nana Jo yelled across to the manager. "Hey, this woman is in shock. I need blankets and hot tea or coffee and lots of sugar." She turned away with the confidence that her orders would be obeyed.

The manager picked up a phone, and within a few short minutes, several blankets and two large tea trolleys were rolled into the lobby.

Nana Jo took Lavender's hands and rubbed them between her own. "Now, dear. Don't worry. Everything will be okay." She talked in a low, soothing voice. "Do you want tea or coffee?"

Lavender stared at Nana Jo as though she were speaking a foreign language. Hannah Schneider poured a strong, extremely sweet brew and held the cup to Lavender's lips and made her drink.

After a few forced sips, Lavender shook her head and the ordeal was halted. "Mother is . . . I can't believe she's . . . dead."

Nana Jo kept trying to warm the young woman and continued her soothing talk. "Yes, dear. I'm sure it's horrible, but you're going to be just fine." She nodded to Hannah, who forced a few more sips of the tea down the poor woman's throat. After a few seconds, Lavender slumped down in a dead faint.

Dr. Vincent Blankenship and his wife stood next to the portly man that I recognized as the doctor who had examined Major Peabody.

"Hey, you're a doctor, aren't you?" Nana Jo yelled. "Get over here. This woman needs medical help."

Dr. Vincent Blankenship glanced at the other man, who looked frightened and merely stood against the wall shaking his head. Finally, Dr. Blankenship glanced from the man to Nana Jo and then quickly hurried over to the sofa. He knelt down and muttered, "For a few moments, I started to wonder if I was a doctor or not." He lifted Lavender's eyelids and looked at her pupils. Then, he took her pulse. He looked around. "She's in shock." He pushed Lavender's head down between her legs and after a few moments, the woman sat up, but she looked about as alert as a zombie.

Dr. Blankenship glanced around and spotted the German businessman and Professor Lavington standing nearby. He spoke loudly and accented the words with arm gestures. "We need to lift her. We need to take her someplace where she can lie down."

The doctor must have been a whiz at charades because both men seemed to catch on to what he wanted and positioned themselves to lift her. Between the two of them, they got Lavender up and started walking toward the elevators.

The manager hurried to their side. "There's a room around the corner. Follow me."

Just as they made their way through the lobby and were headed down the hall, the front door opened and an ambulance arrived.

Nana Jo hurried to the manager. "What's the number?" She extended her hand, and the manager gave her a key and rattled off a room number. Then, he went to direct the paramedics toward the elevator.

Dr. Blankenship had a quick word with the emergency medical technician, while Ruby Mae, Hannah, and I followed Nana Jo. Dorothy and Irma stayed in the lobby.

The room the manager provided was a handicapped-accessible room at the back of the hotel. It was small but functional, with a twin bed and a bathroom slightly bigger than the one Nana Jo and I shared.

Professor Lavington and the German businessman placed Lavender on the bed and then backed away. The room never intended to accommodate eight people comfortably. Ruby Mae and Hannah sat on the bed and spoke soothing words to Lavender and rubbed her hands and feet to try to keep her warm.

Dr. Blankenship gave Lavender a cursory examination. Nana Jo helped to unbutton her blouse and then laid her flat onto the bed.

"I wish I had my medical bag. The EMT is going to let me use their equipment once they . . ." The doctor glanced at Lavender and then took a few steps away and dropped his voice to a whisper. "Once they determine there's nothing to be done upstairs."

We knew he wanted to say once they determined that Prudence Habersham was dead, but no one wanted to send Lavender over the edge.

"For now, we just need to keep her warm. If you can get more of that sugared tea down her throat, that will be good."

Nana Jo nodded. Then she turned to the professor. "Go to the front desk and see if you can get a hot water bottle or an electric blanket. If they don't have either of those, then get some towels, take them to the kitchen, and get the chef to soak them in warm water. Then have him microwave the towels and put them in a Ziploc bag or whatever the British call them." The professor nodded and headed for the door. He halted when Nana Jo called. "Oh, and bring me a couple of T-shirts. I'll need something to wrap around the Ziploc bag."

The professor nodded and hurried out the door. To my surprise, I caught a glimpse of recognition in the eyes of the German businessman, who turned and followed him out.

Hannah reached down and got her purse and took out a

small bottle. She put a couple of tablets in her hand and then returned the bottle to her purse. She dropped the tablets in the teacup and gave it a stir. I was going to ask what she put in the tea when there was a short knock on the door. I hurried to open it. It was the hotel manager. "We were hoping you could come upstairs and . . ." He whispered to the doctor.

Dr. Blankenship glanced back at Nana Jo, who must have guessed the nature of the conversation because she merely said, "Go. We can handle this." He looked from Hannah to Ruby Mae and Nana Jo and then nodded and left.

Hannah lifted Lavender's head so she could drink the tea. Then, she gently placed her head back on the pillow. After a few moments, she repeated the steps, all the while muttering soothing phrases of comfort.

I stood by, watching for a few moments, and then backed myself to the door. "I should go and let you all take care of this."

"Samantha Marie Washington, if you leave this room, I'll put you over my knee and spank your bottom."

"You don't need me. I'm not the one with nursing experience and . . . wait." I scowled. "I'm a grown woman. You can't spank me."

She stood to her full height and glared. "Wanna bet?"

We stared at each other for several seconds, but I knew I was no match for my aikido-trained septuagenarian grandmother and backed down. "Fine."

There was a knock on the door, and Nana Jo glanced at me.

I hurried over and opened the door to find the professor pushing a cart with a teapot of hot water, Ziploc bags, steaming hot towels, and a bowl.

"Push that stuff over here," Nana Jo said. "Now, Sam, you're going to squeeze the water out of those towels, cram them into the Ziploc bags, and then—"

There was another knock.

I hurried to answer and found the German businessman with an armload of T-shirts with the hotel's logo. He handed me the shirts and then turned and left.

Nana Jo took one of the shirts and wrapped it around the Ziploc bag filled with the hot towel. She placed one blanket over the shaking woman and then placed the homemade hot water bottles around her, with two on her feet. When she was done, she placed another blanket over the top, and Hannah, Ruby Mae, and Nana Jo continued their efforts to keep Lavender warm.

Nana Jo had also increased the thermostat in the room so it was a tropical eighty-five degrees. I was soaked with sweat and wringing wet. I stood as far away from the bed as I could without incurring the wrath of my grandmother.

After a few minutes, Lavender's teeth chattering slowed down substantially. Then, nothing. I stared at the bed, afraid to breathe. When my curiosity grew too much, I whispered, "Is she all right?"

Nana Jo stood up and stretched. "She's asleep."

I released the breath I was holding. "Thank God."

Nana Jo turned to Hannah. "What did you put in that tea?"

Hannah smiled. "When my husband died, I had trouble sleeping, but I don't trust those new-fangled medications doctors push on people now."

Ruby Mae stretched and nodded. "I know what you mean. Every time I go to the doctor, all they want to do is give you a pill. Last time I went to the doctor, my blood pressure was a little high, and can you believe he tried to put me on blood pressure medications?"

Nana Jo glanced at Hannah. "I don't know about your national health care system, but in the United States, the pharmaceutical companies are running the whole country, and they've got a pill for everything."

Ruby Mae shook her head. "It's a crying shame. They

used to try to help people. Now, they just give you a pill and that's it." She put a hand on her hip and shook her finger in the air. "I told that man, he ain't giving me no blood pressure medication to treat something that he hasn't even tried to fix."

I should have known better than to interrupt, but I'm going to blame my poor decision on the fact that it was early and I hadn't had coffee. "But hypertension is dangerous and—"

Ruby Mae snapped around and pointed her finger in my direction. "And don't you start lecturing me either. I got enough of that from my own children."

I stared but said nothing.

"My point is that my blood pressure isn't high because of a lack of blood pressure medication. If my blood pressure is too high, then he needs to figure out the root cause of the problem and treat that."

"Good point," Nana Jo said.

"I mean, there used to be a time when doctors would put you on a diet and suggest exercise or more sleep, but now they don't even try. They just give you a pill and send you on your merry way." She pursed her lips and tapped her head. "Well, I told him he's going to need to put those brain cells to work before he puts me on some pills for the rest of my life."

"Doctors are the same everywhere," Hannah said. "Pills, pills, pills." She reached in her purse and pulled out the bottle I'd seen earlier. She held it up.

Nana Jo read the label. "Melatonin."

Usually, I zone out when Nana Jo and her friends start talking about medications, but I was familiar with melatonin. After my husband Leon died, I had trouble sleeping, and my doctor recommended melatonin. Then, a few months later, one of my dogs, Oreo, kept waking up in the middle of the night. So, when my vet suggested the same thing for my ten-pound poodle, I was able to use the same bottle, just in a smaller dose.

"Between the melatonin, strong tea with sugar, and all those hot water bottles, she should sleep like a log, at least for an hour."

Ruby Mae wiped her brow. "Do you think it's safe to leave her for a bit? If I don't get out of this oven, I'm going to pass out myself."

Nana Jo glanced back at Lavender. "I think she'll be okay. Let's just go out into the hallway. We'll keep the door propped open so we can hear if she wakes up."

We filed out of the room, and Nana Jo placed several of the towels in the doorway to keep the door from closing, and we were able to get out into the blissfully cool hallway.

Ruby Mae went to the lobby and came back with a maid and several folding chairs. We thanked the young woman and unfolded them and sat down in the hallway, making sure we had clear sight into the room.

Once we were settled, Nana Jo asked, "What do you think happened? Obviously, her mother is dead, but do you think it was natural causes?"

We shrugged.

Dorothy and Irma came around the corner. Dorothy stood in the center of the group. "Have you heard what happened?"

We shook our heads.

Dorothy leaned against the wall. "The police just arrived and went upstairs. Clive announced that we would have a free day this morning and he would pull everyone together this afternoon to tell us our next steps."

"The police?" Irma asked. "Is that normal?"

"They didn't call in the police for Major Peabody," Ruby Mae said.

Hannah shook her head. "No, it's not." She paused and glanced around at each of us. "You don't call the police unless there's been a murder."

Chapter 11

"So, someone murdered her?" Nana Jo said.

"Why are you looking at me? I didn't kill her!"

"Don't tell me you think it's a coincidence that Major Peabody *and* Prudence Habersham both died within days of each other on the same tour." Nana Jo tilted her head and stared.

I thought for a minute. "Something is definitely wrong. I just can't seem to put my finger on it right now."

"Good. I knew you didn't buy that horse poop that Clive has been shoveling us. You're much too smart for that."

"Are we going to investigate?" Irma said. "If so, then I need to go back to Harrods and buy a couple more dresses." She must have noticed the puzzled looks on our faces because she added, "I'm not going to be able to get any men to tell me their deepest, darkest secrets dressed like this, am I?" She waved her hands down her body. Normally, Irma's attire was extremely revealing, but apart from a few short, tight outfits and some lingerie, she had been dressing much more conservatively than normal. She extended her leg. "I had to search all over the entire store to find a pair of heels high enough."

Nana Jo swatted her leg. "Put that chicken leg down and listen up while Sam gives us our assignments."

Hannah looked puzzled. "Assignments? I don't think I understand."

Ruby Mae put down her knitting and turned to her friend. "Well, over the past few months, we've managed to solve a number of . . . murders."

Hannah's eyes widened. "Real murders?"

"It's not that many murders," I said.

"Actually, it turns out Samantha is a natural-born sleuth," Nana Jo said proudly.

Irma nodded. "She's another Miss Marple."

I tried to intervene but was cut off when Ruby Mae added, "She's the brains behind the operations, but we all help."

"It turns out we're pretty good at getting people to talk," Dorothy said. "I think people think of us as a bunch of harmless old ladies."

"We have a big network of friends," Nana Jo said.

Irma smiled. "And lovers."

Ruby Mae shook her head. "Between all of us, it turns out we know a lot of people."

"We all ask questions and investigate," Nana Jo said, "but it's Sam who manages to put the pieces together and figure out whodunit."

Something in the pit of my stomach made me want to puke, but I sat there and shook my head. "It's not that easy." I took a deep breath. "We've been lucky in North Harbor, Michigan. Detective Stinky Pitt couldn't investigate his way out of a brown paper bag. We're in an entirely different country. I doubt very seriously if the British police will allow a bunch of American tourists to nose their way into their investigation." I sensed Nana Jo was on the verge of speaking and rushed to intercept her. "Besides, we're on vacation. I'm on vacation. I'm supposed to be doing research for my book."

"Book?" Hannah said. "Are you an author?"

I could feel the heat rise up my neck. Writing was a dream that I'd kept hidden inside and only shared with a few people for so long. Even though I was now on the verge of realizing that dream, I still felt uncomfortable actually saying the words out loud. Thankfully, I didn't have to.

Nana Jo smiled. "Samantha just got an offer from a publisher to buy her first book."

"That's wonderful," Hannah said. "Congratulations. What type of books do you write?"

I swallowed the lump in my throat that always seemed to come when I had to talk to people about my books. "I write mysteries. Cozy mysteries. Cozies are—"

Hannah scooted to the front of her seat with a big grin on her face. "I love cozies. I read a ton of them every week."

I smiled, relieved that I didn't have to explain what a cozy mystery was, but also her enthusiasm for the genre was invigorating. "I love them too. I used to read at least four a week before I opened a mystery bookshop." I sighed. "Now, between the store, writing, and . . ." I glanced around at Nana Jo and the girls. "Having a life, I don't have as much time to read for pleasure as I used to."

"I can't believe I'm talking to a real-life cozy mystery author." Her eyes sparkled, and she smiled even bigger. She leaned close and whispered, "Who's your favorite author?"

"Agatha Christie."

She clapped and leaned back. "She's the reason I wanted to take this tour."

"Me too."

"When I heard this tour was going to Torquay, well—"

"I hate to interrupt this meeting of the Agatha Christie fan club," Nana Jo said, "but can we get back to the problem at hand?"

Hannah and I both sat up prim and proper with our hands in our laps and gave her our most innocent looks.

"I don't know what kind of cow dung Clive has been shoveling, but there's something fishy about Major Peabody's death. I can't put my finger on what's wrong, but I can feel it in my bones." She leaned down and gazed into my eyes. "Now, you look me in the eyes and tell me you still think that man died naturally."

As much as I didn't want to believe that Major Peabody's death was by anything other than natural causes, I had to admit the truth. "I will agree that something isn't right."

She smacked her hands together. "I knew it."

"Hold on a minute. I'm not saying I think he was murdered." I could tell she was about to interrupt, so I hurried on. "I'm not saying he was murdered, and I'm not saying he wasn't." I paused. "What I'm saying is that I agree that something is . . . odd." I tried to put my finger on exactly what was wrong, but I couldn't. "Something isn't right, but it's just a little too perfect to have a group of mystery fans on a 'mystery lovers tour' of England and to find themselves in the middle of a suspicious death." I shook my head. "That's just a little too much of a coincidence for me."

"But you do think we should investigate, right?" Nana Jo said.

"It probably wouldn't hurt if we asked a few . . . discreet questions."

"Hot diggity!"

I turned to Irma. "Maybe you could ask Professor Lavington a few questions. I assume that's who your date is with tonight."

"I'll definitely need to do some additional shopping," Irma said. "I think Albus is a leg man."

"Albus?" Nana Jo said.

I turned to Dorothy. "This may seem strange, but do you think you could talk to your German friend?"

"Well, I can talk, but I don't speak German, so I don't know how much he can really understand." She pulled out her cell phone. "But I downloaded an app that will translate conversations from English to German, so I'll definitely give it a shot. Is there anything in particular you want me to find out?"

I thought for a moment, unsure if I should tell her my suspicions. I wanted her to be unbiased. "Maybe you could ask him how he came to pick this tour. Did he know Major Peabody? Or, if he's a mystery fan, who's his favorite mystery author?"

She gave me a look that indicated she knew I was holding something back, but she merely nodded.

"Ruby Mae, do you think you could talk to Clive Green? Find out how he came to be in business with Major Peabody and . . . well, anything else you think will be helpful. You're so good at getting people to talk to you, so if you wouldn't mind asking some of your friends at the hotel, maybe they know something that might be helpful."

Ruby Mae smiled. "I'll be happy to help."

"What about me?" Nana Jo asked excitedly.

"I was hoping we could divide and conquer. One of us will take Debra, and the other one will tackle Sebastian, the demigod. Debra's going to be a hard nut to crack, so I'm not sure we'll be able to get much out of her, but . . . it's worth a try."

Nana Jo cracked her knuckles. "I'm pretty good at cracking nuts."

Hannah Schneider had been sitting quietly, but when I finished, she raised a hand. "Isn't there anything I could do to help?"

I smiled. "I didn't want to assume, but you've been excellent with Lavender Habersham. I think she trusts you. I was hoping you could see if she knew anything about her mother's claims that Major Peabody was her father."

Nana Jo nodded. "I got a look at her face when her mother dropped that bombshell in the pub and I can tell you, she was more surprised than anyone."

"I got the same impression." I looked at Hannah. "It's going to be a bit of a tricky situation since she's obviously had an emotional shock. I wouldn't want to upset her by asking too many questions, but . . ."

Hannah smiled eagerly. "I'll be the soul of discretion."

"I can't believe we're doing this again, but . . . it looks like 'the game's afoot.'"

Chapter 12

Dorothy left to get started sleuthing. Irma claimed she needed to go shopping before her date and headed off. Nana Jo glanced at her watch and then looked at Ruby Mae, Hannah, and me.

"No need in all four of us sitting here now, while she's sleeping."

We went in the heat box and watched while Nana Jo checked the Ziploc bags.

"This room is like a greenhouse." She removed the makeshift hot water bottles. Then, she checked Lavender's pulse. Everything must have been okay because she nodded and then pointed to the hallway.

Once we were back in the cool hallway, Nana Jo said, "What if we take one-hour shifts?"

Everyone agreed.

"She seems to be sleeping pretty soundly," I said, "so how about I take the first shift." Everyone nodded. I looked at my grandmother. "You can check on the doctor and get some lunch. If he comes back before then, I'll text you."

Ruby Mae volunteered for the second shift, followed by

Hannah and then Nana Jo. Once everyone had wandered off, I peeked in the room. Lavender was still sound asleep, so I sat in the chair in the hall, pulled out my notebook, and tried to sort things through in my head by writing.

Lady Elizabeth, Victor Carlston, and Detective Inspector Covington stood at a safe distance, while Dr. Haygood examined the body of Captain Jessup. The doctor felt for a pulse but found none. He opened the captain's eyelids and then did a very cursory examination. After a few minutes, he stood up.

"I'd say he's been dead somewhere between four and six hours." The doctor looked at his pocket watch and then pulled out a paper and began writing.

"Oh God," Victor said, running his fingers through his hair. "How?"

Dr. Haygood glanced at a bottle on the nightstand and picked it up. "We won't know for sure without an autopsy, but it looks like a heart attack. Although, there's an ugly rash on his chest, but it may be unrelated."

"You mean he wasn't murd—" Victor glanced around. "It was natural causes?"

"Like I said, we won't know for sure without an autopsy, but there are no signs of struggle or anything to indicate his death was anything other than natural causes." He turned to stare more closely at Victor. "Unless you have reason to believe—"

"No. No. I don't. It's just . . . I didn't know he had a bad heart."

Dr. Haygood showed him the medicine bottle. "This is digitalis." He squinted and looked closely. "And a pretty high dosage." He looked at the bottle of whiskey and the glass on the nightstand. "If he had a bad heart and was drinking alcohol . . ." He leaned down and sniffed the man's breath. "Which it appears he was."

Lady Elizabeth stepped forward. "Yes, doctor, Captain Jessup had quite a bit to drink last night."

Dr. Haygood shook his head. "He would have been warned of the risks of overexertion and excessive alcohol consumption." He wrote a few more things down. "I'll call his physician and find out what's what."

Lady Penelope appeared at the door, still wearing a robe and with her hair down, looking pale as a ghost. "Victor, what's happened?"

Victor hurried over to his wife's side. "You shouldn't be up. It's nothing to worry yourself about."

She glanced around her husband just as Dr. Haygood pulled the sheet up over Captain Jessup's face.

"He's dead?"

Victor hesitated for a moment, as though he was unsure what to say. "Yes, he died during the night."

"Thank God," Lady Penelope said. "Now everything will be okay."

Victor turned pale. "You're not well. Let me help you back to bed." He turned and glanced at Lady Elizabeth and then to Dr. Haygood and the policeman. "She's in shock. She doesn't know what she's saying."

Dr. Haygood looked up. "Perhaps I should give her a quick once-over since I'm here, and then I'll go downstairs and make my call."

Dr. Haygood and Victor helped Lady Penelope down the hall.

Detective Inspector Covington stared at the door. "I know what she meant, but I don't know that anyone else would believe this death was due to natural causes."

"I know," Lady Elizabeth said. "That's why I'm glad you're here."

"I can't ignore everything that happened last night. I don't believe any of you had anything to do with this, but I'm a policeman and I have to—"

She waved her hand. "I'm not asking you to sweep anything under the rug. In fact, I want you to investigate."

"Do you know what you're asking?"

"I do. I also know that Captain Jessup's death is very convenient. A few hours ago, he made claims that would have ruined Victor. When word of it gets out . . . and, we both know it will get out, regardless of what Dr. Haygood says, people will think Victor or one of us murdered him."

"That's about the size of it."

"That's why I'm glad you're here. You're a good detective. You have to get to the bottom of this murder."

Detective Inspector Covington shot a glance at Lady Elizabeth. "You believe it's murder then?"

"Of course. Did you notice the window?"

The detective smiled. "You noticed that too?"

"It was rather cold last night. Too cold to have the window open."

"Some people like a cool breeze, even in the winter," he said with very little enthusiasm.

She turned to the fireplace. "True, but they don't usually light a fire *and* have the window open at the same time. Plus, there are several bees in here."

The detective walked over to the nightstand and noticed several dead bees.

She looked around the room. "Captain Jessup had been drinking heavily since he arrived. He's never given any indication of a heart condition. Dying of a heart attack is just a little too . . . convenient. I need you to investigate and find out who killed him. We will, of course, help any way we can."

The detective smiled. "I had a feeling you would."

Chapter 13

"Sam." Nana Jo gave my shoulder a gentle shake, but the gesture startled me, and I jumped.

"You've got to stop sneaking up on me."

"I called you three times." She sat down in the chair next to me. "How's the patient?"

"Has it been an hour already?" I glanced at my cell phone for the time. I started to rise, but Nana Jo waved me back down.

"Don't bother. I'll go." She got up and went into the room. After a few moments, she came back out. "I turned down the heat in there. That room was like a sauna." She wiped a few beads of sweat off her brow. "Besides, she should be warm now."

"Did you get to talk to the doctor?"

"I tried, but those police wouldn't even let me off the elevator. I told them it was important, but they wouldn't listen."

Just then, we saw Dr. Vincent Blankenship walking toward us, closely followed by two emergency technicians.

"I'm sorry it's taken so long, but . . . things took longer than I thought."

Over the few hours since I'd last seen Dr. Blankenship, he looked older and more haggard.

"Have you had anything to eat?" Nana Jo asked.

Dr. Blankenship stopped and paused while he thought. "I don't think I have. I meant to, but . . . I'll get something as soon as I see to Lavender."

"Lavender is fine. She's still sound asleep. Why don't you grab yourself a sandwich and a cup of coffee first?"

Dr. Blankenship looked like a drowning man who'd just been tossed a life preserver, but the look quickly faded. "I'd better just see how she is and then I'll get something, but . . . thank you." He led the way into the room, and the two emergency techs followed him.

Inside, Dr. Blankenship took Lavender's pulse and used a stethoscope that he must have borrowed from the EMTs to listen to her heart. After a few moments, he stood up and stretched.

Nana Jo handed him a bottled water that she had brought with her.

"Thank you." He twisted the top off the water and took a sip. In a quiet voice he said, "She seems to be fine." He glanced from me to Nana Jo. "How'd you get her to sleep?"

"We drugged her," Nana Jo said.

Dr. Blankenship nearly choked as he spit out his water.

Nana Jo patted him on the back.

"You what?"

"Hannah Schneider had some melatonin in her purse. So, we put it in her tea."

Dr. Blankenship sighed. "Oh, well . . . as long as it was just melatonin."

Nana Jo squinted at the doctor. "If I was a betting woman, I'd say someone gave her mother something a heck of a lot stronger than melatonin."

Dr. Blankenship flushed. "I'm not at liberty to talk about it."

She nodded. "Poisoned."

"What's this about poison?" A short white male in a cheap, wrinkled coat over an equally cheap, brown wrinkled suit waltzed into the room. He was mostly bald, but what few hairs remained atop his freckled dome, he combed over to the side of his head. He was followed by a tall, thin woman.

The man barely reached Nana Jo's shoulder. He walked up to my grandmother and gazed up at her like a lovesick schoolboy. After an awkward pause, he slicked his hairs down and cleared his throat. "I'm D. I. Nelson." He grinned, revealing a mouth full of coffee-stained, crooked teeth. "That's Detective Inspector." He pushed his shoulders back. "And, your name is?" His voice bellowed through the room.

Dr. Blankenship hurried to make sure that Lavender hadn't woken up. "Perhaps we should continue this outside." He motioned toward the door, but the detective ignored him.

Nana Jo stared down at him. "Josephine Thomas."

"Josephine . . . well, what's this you're saying about poison?"

Nana Jo took one step forward and reached around the detective to extend her hand to the woman. "Josephine Thomas."

The woman's lips twitched as she fought back a smile. She shook Nana Jo's hand. "Detective Sergeant Moira Templeton." Moira Templeton was tall and thin. She was stunning, with light brown skin and wavy hair that she pulled back into a severe bun. She had large, gray, intelligent eyes and brilliant white, straight teeth.

D. I. Nelson didn't like being ignored. "Now that the introductions are over, Moira, you can take notes." He glared at the detective, who merely pulled a notepad out of her pocket and glanced up. "Now, what's that you were saying about poison?"

"I wasn't saying anything about poison," Nana Jo said. "I merely asked if that's how Mrs. Habersham was murdered."

Lavender Habersham's eyes fluttered open, and for a few seconds, she glanced around as though trying to remember where she was. Then, as recognition hit, her face crumbled, and she sobbed. "Mother's gone . . . what will Bella do? It's all my fault." She sat up and stared. "Oh my God! Bella!"

D. I. Nelson took two steps forward and glared down at the young woman. "What's that you're saying? Who's Bella? What's all your fault? Are you ready to confess to poisoning your mother?" He turned to Moira. "Templeton, get this down." He turned back to Lavender and leaned down. "I need to caution you that you do not have to say anything. But it may harm your defense if you do not mention something when questioned that you later rely on in court. Anything you do say may be given in evidence."

Lavender sobbed even harder.

Dr. Blankenship said, "Detective, I don't think this is the time or the place. My patient is under medical care and doesn't know what she's saying."

D. I. Nelson sneered. "Your patient is about to confess to murder. The last thing I need is some bloody American bleeding-heart doctor telling me how to do my job."

Dr. Blankenship shrank back as though he'd been smacked, but he dug deep and stood very erect. "I may be an American, but I'm still a medical doctor, and I have to do what is in the best interest of my patient." He stepped in between the detectives and Lavender and folded his arms.

As a show of support, Nana Jo moved next to him and folded her arms across her chest. I moved next to Nana Jo, arms folded, to further demonstrate our unity as we blocked Lavender Habersham from the detectives.

Nelson breathed heavily. "And who are you?"

"I'm her granddaughter, Samantha Washington."

He huffed. "Get those names down, Templeton. Looks like we'll need a wagon for all of these Americans."

If he thought the threat of arrest would scare us into moving, he was mistaken. In fact, I felt more angry than scared that he thought he could bully us.

Nana Jo scowled. "Sam, you better call the American Consulate. Looks like we're going to need some assistance."

I reached in my pocket and pulled out my cell phone. I maintained a stoic expression that belied the butterflies erupting in my stomach. I was angry, but I was also on vacation in another country with no luggage. For some reason, the lack of luggage made a bigger difference to my mental state now than it had previously. I also didn't have the American Consulate saved in my speed dial, so I would have to do an internet search, which would completely ruin the effect. I hoped he would back down as I swiped my phone in search of the number.

Nana Jo was a much better poker player than Detective Inspector Nelson, and after a few seconds of hard breathing, he plastered on a fake smile and tried a different tactic. "All right, I don't think any of us want an international incident." He sighed. "I'll take your word as a medical professional that she is not fit to answer questions . . . right now, but as soon as she's been treated, I will be talking to her."

"Now, if you'll kindly step outside," Dr. Blankenship said, "I can treat my patient. I'll be out in a few minutes."

Reluctantly, D. I. Nelson turned toward the door, but he yelled over his shoulder. "I'll be leaving a constable outside the door, so don't think you can spirit her away without me knowing." He marched outside.

"What an obnoxious, overbearing boor," Nana Jo mumbled just loud enough for the policeman to hear.

Once we were all outside, Dr. Blankenship closed the

door, leaving him alone with the EMTs and Lavender Habersham.

The hallway was crowded, but Nana Jo and I took the seats we'd used previously and posted ourselves like sentinels outside the door.

The Scotland Yard detectives faced us. Detective Sergeant Templeton's eyes sparkled as though she wanted to laugh, but she refrained.

Nelson rocked on the balls of his feet for a few moments. Then he grinned. "Maybe you two should tell me what you're doing here?"

As a former high school English teacher, I tried to refrain from correcting grammar when talking to friends. However, I wasn't feeling very friendly toward D. I. Nelson. "I assume by 'here' you're referring to England." I waited, but Nelson merely seethed quietly, so I continued. "We're on vacation. We're taking the Peabody Mystery Lovers Tour of England."

"You getting that down?" he said to Detective Sergeant Templeton.

"Yes, sir."

"Did you know the deceased well?"

We shook our heads.

"We met her for the first time the other day at the meet and greet," Nana Jo said.

Ruby Mae came around the corner. "Clive wants to meet with everyone from the tour group." She glanced at D. I. Nelson and Detective Sergeant Templeton but said nothing.

"What is this, some kind of bloody motorway?" He yelled to Templeton, "Get a constable to rope off this hallway and have him watch the ruddy door."

Templeton flipped her notebook closed and turned on her heels. "Yes, sir." She walked down the hall, but not before I noticed a faint glimmer of a smile.

Nelson said, "Who are you?"

Ruby Mae rubbed her ear. "Ruby Mae Stevenson. Who are you?"

Nelson had had enough of introducing himself and merely held up his identification card for her to read.

Ruby Mae squinted at the card and then looked up. "Rupert?"

Nelson grunted and hurriedly replaced his identification.

Nana Jo turned to me. "You better go to the meeting and find out what Clive needs to tell us. I'll stay here and make sure *no one* tries to violate Lavender's rights by bursting into this room before the doctor gives his permission."

"Bugger it all," Nelson said. He turned and marched down the hall, muttering something about overopinionated Americans.

When Nelson left, it was as though dark, heavy clouds had passed and the sun shone. I felt ten pounds lighter and much happier. I released a heavy breath.

Nana Jo shook her head. "That man sure knows how to ruin an otherwise good time. Talk about a wet blanket."

I smiled. "He seemed to be taken with you."

She shivered. "Now, that is a disgusting thought."

The door opened, and one of the EMTs came out. He walked down the hall and came back in a few minutes with a rolling stretcher. After a few moments longer, they came out wheeling Lavender Habersham. The woman looked on the verge of a drug-induced sleep, although this time, I suspected by the way her eyes were rolling back into her head, this drug was a lot stronger than melatonin. When she passed, Lavender reached out her hand and grabbed Nana Jo, forcing the EMTs to stop. She looked up at Nana Jo and worked her mouth. Nana Jo leaned down and turned her head so her ear was practically over her mouth in an effort to hear what the woman was trying to say. After a few seconds, Nana Jo stood up. She gave Lavender Habersham's hand a squeeze and said, "I'll take care of it."

With that, Lavender closed her eyes and drifted off, and the EMTs continued to wheel her down the hallway.

Dr. Blankenship came out of the room with a medical bag. "I'm going to ride with her to the hospital." He glanced at me. "Would you please let my wife know that I'll be back as soon as I can?"

"Certainly, Doctor."

With that, he followed the EMTs down the hall, leaving Nana Jo, Ruby Mae, and I standing in the hallway.

"You two go ahead to the meeting with Clive," Nana Jo said. "I've got a small matter to take care of." She marched down the hall.

Ruby Mae said, "We better head to the ballroom and hear what Mr. Green has to say."

I turned and stared at Ruby Mae. "What did you say?"

"Mr. Green. That's Clive's last name, remember?"

I stared at Ruby Mae for several seconds and then smiled. I knew something wasn't right with Major Peabody's death. Now, I knew what it was.

"Yes, let's go and meet with Mr. Green in the ballroom. I don't want to miss a thing."

Chapter 14

The members of the tour group assembled in the ballroom. The only ones missing, apart from Lavender Habersham, were Nana Jo and Dr. Blankenship. I stood near the door and looked around until I saw Tiffany standing against the wall, looking around nervously. I hurried to her side and whispered that her husband had gone to the hospital to see to Lavender Habersham, but that he wanted her to know he would be back as soon as possible.

"Once again I have to take a back seat to his patients." She tapped her foot in irritation. "Even the dead ones are more important than spending time with me. This vacation was a mistake."

I tried to think up some words of comfort, but I was at a loss. At least now I understood better why Dr. Blankenship kept emphasizing the fact that he was on vacation. "I'm sure it's got to be very difficult for you, but he really got dragged into this. He tried to get away, but—"

She raised a hand to halt my feeble explanation. "Don't think you have to explain. Trust me, I've heard all the explanations."

I was saved from having to think of a reply when Clive Green stood up, and I hurried to my seat.

Normally, Clive looked prim and proper and meticulously dressed. However, the events of the past few hours hung heavy on his shoulders, and he looked haggard. "Ladies and gentlemen, thank you all for coming." He glanced down at his sheet and then around the room as though quickly taking attendance.

Nana Jo snuck in the door. She had Lavender Habersham's bag and pushed it under the table and sat down in the chair I'd saved for her in between me and Ruby Mae.

Irma was on the same barstool she'd occupied a few days ago when we first gathered in this room. Had it only been a few days ago? She must have gone shopping because she was wearing a tight, short miniskirt with an even tighter top that showed off her cleavage to its best advantage. Professor Albus Lavington was enjoying the outfit in the seat next to Irma. Dorothy and our German businessman, Oberst, were also in their same seats.

I glanced around the room and saw Debra Holt sprawled on the sofa with a fur stole falling off her lap and her fiancé wrapped around her arm.

Hannah Schneider sat in a chair near Clive.

In addition to the tour participants, Detective Inspector Nelson and Detective Sergeant Templeton stood near the door.

Clive gave the detectives a glance but then hurried on. "I'm sure you've all heard the devastating news that one of our guests, Mrs. Prudence Habersham, has died."

Everyone muttered sympathetic comments.

Clive's voice dropped to a funeral home volume. "Sincerest sympathies to her family. Please keep the family in your thoughts and prayers, and especially her daughter, Lavender, who has taken the loss exceptionally hard."

D. I. Nelson snorted and then sucked his teeth.

"Yes, well, I'm sure many of you have questions about our tour, as we were scheduled to leave for the Cotswolds today. Obviously, we'll need to postpone our trip to allow the poli . . . ah, officials time to look into Mrs. Habersham's death."

"Wait, we paid our money to see the Cotswolds, Devon, and Torquay," Tiffany said. "Are you saying we aren't going?"

"No, not at all. You'll get to see all the places on the tour that you were promised in the brochure." Clive smiled. "In fact, I've spent the better part of the day talking to hotels and making the arrangements. I think I've managed to get everything rearranged. However, we won't be able to stay overnight in Devon, as the rooms at the pub are booked, so we'll make it a day-trip instead and keep our rooms here."

Hannah Schneider raised a tentative hand. "We've had two suspicious deaths since we started this tour. Are you sure this tour is safe?"

Clive shook off his tiredness and smiled broadly. "I assure all of you that you are safe. Major Peabody's death was . . . it has nothing to do with this unfortunate incident with Mrs. Habersham."

D. I. Nelson stepped forward. "I wouldn't be so sure."

Everyone turned to stare at the detective, and he walked to the center of the room. "I'm D. I. Nelson with the Yard." He stood with a cocky assurance. "I think in light of recent events, we'll need to look more closely into the death of Major Peabody. It seems to me undue haste was taken in an effort to cover up a death that may have been murder and connected to this Habersham murder."

The blood drained from Clive's face. He sputtered and stammered.

Debra Holt burst into laughter.

Nelson glanced from Clive Green to Debra Holt, unsure which one he should focus on first.

I didn't have a lot of affection for Debra Holt, and even though I didn't know Clive Green, I didn't think he deserved to be tormented. So, I stood up. "Clive, I think it's time you tell the truth about Major Peabody. Don't you?"

Clive glanced around the room and took out a handkerchief and wiped his neck. "Perhaps you're right."

Nelson squinted at me. "All right, Little Miss American Busybody, what do you know about Major Peabody's murder?"

"I know Major Peabody wasn't murdered."

Everyone gasped.

"What do you mean?" Nana Jo asked. "How do you know he wasn't murdered?"

"Major Peabody wasn't murdered because he's still alive." I turned to Clive Green. "Isn't that right, Clive?"

Clive Green nodded vigorously.

I turned to the other tour guests. "Don't you get it? This is a tour created *specifically* for lovers of murder mysteries, which promised a mysteriously good time with lots of surprises." I looked around. "Didn't anyone think it was just a little too convenient that a mysterious death occurred and that Clive refused to let Dr. Blankenship examine the body?"

Tiffany snorted. "Even I thought that was odd. Everyone is always looking for free medical advice or service as soon as they find out there's a doctor in their midst." She gave Irma a pointed glance, but if she intended to shame her, she was disappointed. It would take more than a vague comment and a targeted glance to shame Irma Starczewski.

I shook my head. "I didn't really connect the dots until Ruby Mae mentioned Clive's name." I glanced at my friend.

She looked at me. "Green?"

"Clive Green." I looked around. "Get it?"

Everyone still looked puzzled, so I continued, "It took me a bit to get it too. Then, I remembered what Debra Holt said when she met her uncle. She loved his 'games,' and she said the same thing to Clive when she got on the bus, remember?" I glanced at Debra, who merely waved her hand as though dismissing me. "Then, there's Professor Albus Lavington." I turned to look over at the professor in the corner.

"Albus, as in Dumbledor?" Tiffany asked.

"Albus also means white." I glanced at the professor, who nodded. Then I turned to Clive. "There were just too many colorful names. Clive Green, Lavender Habersham, Sebastian Rothchild-Black." I glanced at the handsome Sebastian, who flashed a dazzling white smile. "Although, I suspect Debra had you add Black to the end of your name in the hopes that her uncle would accept you for his nephew . . . in-law."

Sebastian grinned. "Guilty as charged."

I turned to the German businessman. "You were much more challenging because I truly believed that you didn't understand English, and I wondered how you could have been roped into this charade. That is until I put your name into the translation app on my phone. Oberst Senf in German is . . ." I walked over to Dorothy and held my cell phone up so she could read it.

"Colonel Mustard," she said slowly. "Colonel Mustard? Like in the Clue game?" She stood up with both hands on her hips. "You mean to tell me you speak and understand English, and you've had me googling and using hand gestures and . . . ooooh, I should have flipped you harder at the airport." She rolled up her sleeves as though she planned to do that exact thing, but I stopped her.

The German stood, held up both hands, and spoke in broken but very clear English. "I'm sorry. Please don't flip me again. I can explain."

"Please, let me explain," Clive Green said. "It's part of the tour. We got the idea a few years ago. Everyone on the tour is always a fan of mysteries. Peabody thought it would be a good thing if we staged a murder mystery of our own to add to the excitement."

There was a rumble of discord.

"We meant no harm. We've found that mystery fans tend to be very . . . suspicious." He smiled. "We stage a murder and leave a few clues."

Nana Jo frowned. "The glass that disappeared from the table."

He nodded.

"That's why you wouldn't let Vincent examine him," Tiffany added.

"I couldn't let a real doctor examine him. He'd know immediately that Horace wasn't dead."

I glanced down at Ruby Mae, who was sitting and knitting. "There was even Ruby Mae . . . your Miss Scarlet."

He nodded. "Yes. It was amazing to find so many people with names that matched the board game. Usually, we send out a letter to various members of the tour and ask them to play along. However, this group . . . well, we only had to enlist help from a couple of people."

Nana Jo frowned. "Was Lavender Habersham one of the enlistees?"

He nodded. "She loved murder mysteries. Her mother had her own reasons for wanting to come on this tour."

"So, that's what Lavender meant when she said it was all her fault." Nana Jo glared at D. I. Nelson. "She wasn't confessing to poisoning her mother. She blamed herself for suggesting the tour to her mom in the first place."

Nelson turned to Clive. "Let me get this straight. Are you saying that Major Peabody isn't dead?"

Clive nodded. "He's been hiding out in one of the hotel rooms."

I sat down, and Nana Jo looked across at me. "Well done, Sam."

I smiled. "I might not have put it together if it hadn't been for Ruby Mae." I patted her on the shoulder.

She chuckled. "Oh, you go on, now."

"Well, if Horace Peabody is still alive, then go get him. I'd like to have a few words with him."

Clive started to leave, but Sebastian hopped up. "I'll go." Sebastian hurried from the room.

"You mean to tell me this was all just one big game of Clue?" Hannah Schneider said. "How clever. I never put it together, Mr. Green in the ballroom with the wrench or the lead pipe."

Dorothy was still upset, as she moved a few seats farther away from the German businessman.

I wasn't sure if I was sympathetic toward the German or not, but I had some questions. "So, what's your real name?"

He glanced at Dorothy. "Oscar Hoffman. I own a small shop in Leipzig."

Dorothy scoffed.

We spent several more moments talking about the clues Clive and Major Peabody had set for us while we waited for Sebastian's return. The door opened, and we all turned to confront Major Peabody; however, the mood changed when we realized it was only Dr. Blankenship.

"Oh, it's just you," Dorothy muttered, fully prepared to give Major Peabody a piece of her mind.

Confusion passed across the doctor's face at his frosty reception.

"Don't take it personally," Nana Jo said. "We were expecting Major Peabody."

"Major Peabody?"

"It's a long story," Tiffany said. She pointed to the chair

next to her. "Come sit down, and I'll explain the whole thing to you."

Dr. Blankenship hurried to take his seat, and she filled him in. When she finished, the doctor stared at the door as anxiously as the rest of us. After what felt like a rather long time, the door opened and Sebastian stumbled in.

"All right, let's get this over with," D. I. Nelson growled. "I've had about as much of this as I can take. Where's Peabody?"

Sebastian paused and then glanced around the room. "He's . . . dead."

Chapter 15

"Dead?" I said. "What do you mean?"

Clive stared at Sebastian. "That's impossible. He can't be dead."

Detective Sergeant Templeton hurried toward the door. "Show me." She grabbed Sebastian by the arm and dragged him out.

"Don't anybody move," D. I. Nelson said. He took several steps and then stopped. He pointed to Dr. Blankenship. "Nobody except you." He beckoned for the doctor to accompany him.

"Look, I've helped you out multiple times today, but I'm on vacation, and I—"

"Oh, never mind," Tiffany said. "Just go."

Dr. Blankenship looked tired. Torn between his duty as a doctor and his wife, he was in a no-win situation. Eventually, he hoisted himself up and followed the detective.

D. I. Nelson led the way. When he got within a few feet of me, he stopped to sneer. "Amateurs." Then, he hurried to the back of the room, followed closely by Dr. Blankenship. At the doorway, the detective leaned out into the lobby. "Constable, stand by this door, and if anyone tries to leave . . . you have my permission to use your taser."

The two men left, and the constable closed the door behind him and stood there blocking the way.

I flopped down onto my seat. "I don't understand. He can't be dead."

However, after waiting in the electrically charged ballroom for over a half hour, Detective Sergeant Templeton returned. She whispered something to the constable and then announced, "Major Peabody is dead. We're going to need to get statements from all of you. Please, be patient and we will be with you shortly." She turned and whispered something else to the constable and then left.

Debra Holt had been anxiously pacing the floor ever since her fiancé had returned to deliver the news that her uncle was dead. The speed of her pacing increased as we waited. The only time she stopped was to glare at Clive Green. Eventually, she stopped, spun around, and pointed. "This is all your fault. You did this. I know you did. You knew my uncle intended to sell the tour company, and you were determined to stop him."

I hadn't thought Clive's pale face could have gotten any more ashen, but I was wrong. "I would never—"

Debra laughed. "You're a former policeman. You certainly know enough about crime to have killed Uncle Horace." She flung the words like daggers. "Face it. You never really cared about him. You knew he was allergic to bees, but you just had to have your bloody swarms. You had to have your honey, and you argued with him." She turned to Nana Jo and me. "You heard him."

I struggled to maintain eye contact and felt myself getting warm under her laser-focused gaze.

"Clive Green wasn't the only one who argued with Major Peabody," Nana Jo said.

Debra halted. "Uncle Horace and I argued all the time.

That was nothing." She waved her hand. "We're family." She scowled at Clive. "They should have handcuffed you."

"I've got handcuffs," Irma said. She reached into her purse and pulled out a pair. "I always keep a set in case of emergency." She twirled the cuffs and winked at Lavington.

"Put those away, you dingbat," Nana Jo said.

Debra Holt flopped down into a chair. "Uncle Horace would have come around eventually. He always did." She put her head in her hands and sobbed.

No one seemed to know what to do. Eventually, Tiffany walked over to Debra, slid a handkerchief into her hands, and gave her shoulder an awkward pat. Eventually, Debra's sobs subsided, and Tiffany returned to her seat.

I felt something move under the table and very nearly leapt out of my seat. I leaned down to take a look.

Nana Jo smacked my arm. "Be still."

"But . . . I felt something." I leaned down again and got another smack from Nana Jo.

"Stop. You're drawing attention to the . . . luggage." She lifted a flap that went down one side of the small bag she had brought down earlier, and I saw a pair of bright eyes and a muzzle. I glanced at Nana Jo.

"That's a d—"

"I know. Now, keep quiet. I'll explain later."

I glanced at my grandmother and tried not to keep glancing down at the bag, but it was a struggle.

It took several hours for the detectives to get through all our statements. I was afraid Clive Green would have a stroke. He looked dazed and pale and about thirty years older than when he had first entered the room.

Debra Holt was distraught. She kept mumbling, "It was the bees. It was Clive Green. I know it was." She was so agitated, she eventually had to lie down.

Her distress seemed genuine. I guess she really cared for Major Peabody. I knew from experience that families weren't perfect. They argued and behaved badly, but when the rubber hit the road, blood was thicker than water. I pushed my dislike of the woman aside.

Despite the serious nature of the events, I couldn't help being intrigued by the opportunity to see real detectives in action. I took a few notes and hoped that the basics hadn't changed much since 1939. I was one of the last to give my statement, and what I had to say was brief. I hadn't seen or talked to Major Peabody since the first night. The last time I'd actually seen him was when he faked his death. I didn't know much about the major, and I was still perplexed by what happened. Eventually, the constable gave up. I guess there's only so many times you can hear *I don't know* or *I have no idea*. I asked a few questions in the hope of gleaning a little information, but one thing British detectives shared with their counterparts in the United States was a repulsion for "amateur sleuths" meddling in their investigations. There must be a class that all policemen take, regardless of country, on how to avoid answering questions asked by potential suspects.

When I walked out of the ballroom, I found Nana Jo, Hannah Schneider, and the girls waiting in the lobby for me.

"I need a drink," Nana Jo said. "There's a pub down the street, and we're going." She no longer had Lavender Habersham's luggage with her.

Outside, I hurried to catch up to my grandmother. "Wait. Where's the dog?"

"One of Ruby Mae's new friends on staff is feeding her and agreed to watch her until we get back."

"But, how? I mean, why?"

Nana Jo shook her head. "Sam, I've had a long day, and I need food and a drink. If you care about me at all, you'll hold your questions until I get at least one of those things."

I smiled as I followed my grandmother down the street and into a pub called the Down Under.

The pub looked and smelled like every other bar I've ever been to. There were quite a few people, but we lucked out and managed to find a booth in a corner just big enough for the six of us. We slid in while Dorothy went to the bar and placed our orders. When the barmaid set our drinks on the table, Nana Jo decided to save time by immediately ordering two more and whatever snacks she could find.

The woman barely looked up from her notepad. She must have heard stranger requests. Her only question was, "Will this be separate or together?"

Hannah grabbed a dish of nuts from a nearby table, and when the barmaid returned with Nana Jo's next drink, she ordered fish and chips for us all and another round of drinks.

Once Nana Jo had two drinks in her system, she seemed a lot steadier. "We've been going since early this morning when Prudence Habersham was found murdered. Then, I was playing wet nurse to Lavender, only to find out that someone has now murdered Major Peabody, who we thought was already dead."

I glanced at my grandmother. "Wow. I guess all of that did happen today. It seems like it's been a lot longer."

"Now, I've got to hide that daft woman's dog." Nana Jo tossed some nuts in her mouth.

"How did you end up with her dog?" I asked.

Nana Jo swallowed her nuts. "Remember when they were about to wheel Lavender away and she whispered something to me?"

I nodded.

"That's when she told me she was worried about her dog. They couldn't leave the dog at home and snuck her on the tour."

"That explains why Lavender was carrying her luggage

everywhere she went." I wanted to smack myself for not thinking of this sooner.

Nana Jo nodded. "Bella is her Yorkshire terrier."

"How on earth did she hide a dog?" Dorothy asked.

Nana Jo chugged back her third drink. "It's a tiny little thing. It can't weigh more than five pounds."

Ruby Mae sipped a glass of wine. "Still, I can't believe no one heard the dog."

She shrugged. "Beats me, but she's a cute little thing and really doesn't bark much."

I stared at Nana Jo. "I'm surprised D. I. Nelson let you remove the dog from the room."

Nana Jo avoided eye contact and hummed.

I narrowed my eyes. "Nana Jo, how did you get the dog out of the room?"

She spent a few moments looking everywhere but at me, but eventually she gave in and slumped down. "All right, the police had that yellow and black crime scene tape roping off the door, and there was a constable stationed in the hallway." She tapped her fingers on the table. "So, I got the maid to let me into the adjourning room, and then I unlocked the connecting door and snuck in and got the bag with the dog, which, by the way, was under the bed."

I stared open-mouthed at my grandmother. "You removed evidence from a crime scene? You could go to jail for that."

"Look, the police had already been in the room." She sat up straight. "If Detective Inspector Nelson was such a great detective, then why didn't he find the dog?" She stared at me. "I mean, it was under the bed the entire time, and he didn't even know. Plus, I was doing a humanitarian service. That poor little dog needed to eat and go potty." She tilted her head to the side and gave me a sad expression. "If it were Snickers or Oreo who were left in a room all day with just a little food and water, wouldn't you want someone to do the same thing?"

When it came to manipulation and emotional blackmail, my family were experts. "Now I know where Mom gets it."

Nana Jo smiled. "If you can't beat them, make them feel guilty."

The barmaid brought our food and another round of drinks, and we stopped talking and took care of our gastronomical needs. When the hunger was satisfied, we got down to business.

Nana Jo pulled her iPad from her purse. "All right, let's get this meeting started."

Hannah Schneider looked puzzled. "Meeting?"

Ruby Mae pulled her knitting from her bag. "This is usually how all of our sleuthing meetings start."

Irma had spotted a single man at the bar and had turned in her seat so her legs were facing her prey, and she was making goo-goo eyes at her next victim.

Nana Jo reached across the table and smacked her on the arm. "Will you pay attention."

Irma swore at the interruption but turned her attention back to the meeting. "Fine, but can we hurry up? I'm about to hook a Brit, and you're cramping my style."

Nana Jo looked at her notes and then up at me. "Sam, you gave us assignments earlier, but with Major Peabody actually getting murdered, I'm not sure how you want to handle things."

"I suppose we should stick to our original assignments." I glanced around. "Does everyone remember what they were?"

Dorothy folded her arms. "I want a new assignment."

"Why?"

"I'm not sure I can look at Oberst . . . I mean, Oscar again, let alone flirt with him enough to get him to spill his guts."

Nana Jo stared down her nose at her friend. "Dorothy, I know you're upset, but this is serious business. This is murder."

Murder. The word tumbled around in my head. Someone had killed Major Horace Peabody *and* Prudence Habersham. I found it hard to believe that a few days ago I didn't even know either one of them existed, but now here I was, sitting at a pub in London, trying to figure out who killed them.

Nana Jo got my attention by waving a hand in front of my eyes. "Earth to Samantha."

I quickly returned to the here and now. "I'm sorry."

"What's the matter?"

"I don't know. I guess I'm just questioning why we're doing this."

Nana Jo put her iPad down. "What do you mean, why?"

"We got involved in solving a few murders back home in North Harbor, but there was always a compelling reason for getting involved. Let's face it, Stinky Pitt couldn't find a killer who was standing naked in the middle of the street with a neon sign over his head."

Nana Jo and the girls nodded.

Hannah looked confused. "Stinky Pitt?"

Ruby Mae looked up from her knitting. "He's the local detective in North Harbor, Michigan."

"Not the sharpest knife in the drawer?"

"I've got sharper spoons."

I took a moment and tried to collect my thoughts. "We all know that Stinky . . . ah, I mean, Detective Pitt is incompetent. Back home, we got involved to keep him from arresting some innocent person . . . like me or Nana Jo. We're in a different country, and no one is accusing any of us of killing Major Peabody or Prudence Habersham." I sighed. "Scotland Yard is known all over the world for their ability to solve crimes."

Nana Jo leaned forward. "Do you honestly believe that

Detective Inspector Rupert Nelson is capable of solving these murders?"

I gave the matter a moment's thought and then shook myself off. "I don't know. I do know that I don't really know Prudence Habersham *or* Major Peabody. I'm on vacation, and I want to enjoy it. I don't necessarily want to spend this entire trip trying to track down a killer." Even to my own ears, I sounded whiney. "Couldn't we leave this one to the professionals . . . just once?"

Nana Jo gave me a long stare. Then she closed her iPad and returned it to her purse. "Sam's right. We don't really know these people. Why should we care that they were cold-bloodedly murdered?"

I shrank back in my seat at the heartlessness of the remark.

Nana Jo reached out and squeezed my hand. "I didn't mean it the way that came out. I just meant that maybe you're right. D. I. Nelson looks about as bright as a burned-out light bulb, but that Detective Sergeant Templeton looks like one sharp cookie."

Ruby Mae nodded. "I'll bet not much slips past her."

Dorothy looked from Nana Jo to me. "So, what are you saying?"

Nana Jo patted my hand. "I'm saying, let's leave this murder to the professionals and enjoy our vacation."

Irma smacked her hand on the table. "Hot da—"

"Irma!"

Irma broke out into a coughing fit. She reached over and took the glass of white wine I had been nursing for an hour and chugged it. She then stood up and wiggled to slide her skirt down. "I'll catch you girls later. I'm going fishing." She marched over to the bar, placed an arm around the shoulders of the single man she'd been ogling, and turned on her charm.

Nana Jo shook her head. "That woman is man crazy."

We spent some time talking, drinking, and laughing. For the first time in days, I wasn't thinking about murder and was enjoying thinking ahead to a visit to Torquay and the home of Agatha Christie.

Murder was the furthest thing from my mind until Nana Jo nudged me. "Isn't that D. I. Nelson?"

I glanced at the door, and there stood Detective Inspector Nelson and Detective Sergeant Templeton. When they spotted us, they walked over to our table.

"Hello, detectives. What a surprise. We didn't expect—"

Nelson gave me an icy stare that froze the words on my lips. He then turned to Hannah. "Hannah Schneider, you are under arrest on suspicion of the murder of Prudence Habersham and Major Horace Peabody." He grabbed Hannah by the arm and pulled her to her feet. "You do not have to say anything, but it may harm your defense if you do not mention when questioned something which you later rely on in court."

"What are you doing?" Nana Jo yelled. "You can't be serious!"

Templeton avoided making eye contact, and the slump of her shoulders told me she wasn't happy about this, but Nelson was in charge.

He pulled Hannah's hands behind her back and handcuffed her. "Anything you do say may be given in evidence." He pulled her forward, and the three marched out of the bar.

To my dying day, I will never forget the stricken look on Hannah's face. All of the noise stopped, and everyone turned to watch our friend arrested and humiliated. However, the indictment that will forever wring my heart was the look on Ruby Mae's face as she turned to me. "Do you still think Scotland Yard will be able to catch the real killer?"

Chapter 16

We sat in shock for a few moments. It lasted until Nana Jo grabbed her purse. "Well, come on. We gotta go spring Hannah." Apparently, we weren't moving fast enough because she went into drill sergeant mode and started shouting orders. She tossed Ruby Mae a credit card. "Pay the bar tabs." She turned to me. "Call your sister." While heading for the door, she yelled, "Dorothy, grab Irma, and I'll get us a taxi."

I glanced at the time before I called my sister. I pushed the number on speed dial and waited. Eventually, I heard Jenna's voice. She spoke softly and quickly. I could tell this wasn't a great time.

"Sam, I can't talk. I'm just about to speak at the Southwestern Michigan Bar Association dinner."

"It's important."

"Are you dead?"

"Jenna, I—"

"I've got to give a speech in less than five minutes. So, unless someone's dead, I—"

"Actually, two people are dead."

That got her attention. "Is Nana Jo okay?"

"Nana Jo's fine, although she's a bit frazzled."

"Ruby Mae, Irma, and Dorothy?"

"We're all fine." I walked outside. "It's Major Peabody, he owned the tour, and Mrs. Prudence Habersham, but—"

"Did you kill them?"

I stared at the phone. "Of course I didn't kill them."

"Did Nana Jo kill them?"

"No! Nana Jo didn't kill them either."

"Then, why are you calling me?"

"I'm calling because—"

Nana Jo wrenched the phone from my hand. "Give me that." She put the phone to her ear. "Now, listen here, Jenna. She's calling you because we need legal advice. Neither Sam nor I killed anyone, and you know it. But the police just waltzed into a bar and arrested our friend, Hannah Schneider, who also didn't kill them, by the way. However, innocence doesn't seem to matter to Scotland Yard! They just hand-cuffed a poor recently widowed woman and marched her out of the pub and took her . . . well, I don't know where they took her, but she's alone and we can't let some overbearing, smelly detective inspector just whisk our friend away without doing something. Now, you turn on that brain and tell Sam what to do or who we should contact or I'll make the biggest international incident since the Boston Tea Party." Nana Jo spotted a taxi and shoved the phone back at me while she went to the corner and practically hurled herself in the street.

I put the phone to my ear. "Now you see what I'm deal-ing with."

The taxi didn't stop, and Nana Jo let fly a string of curse words that I didn't even know she knew.

"Was that Nana Jo?" Jenna asked.

"Yep. She was trying to hail a taxi. Look, Nana Jo's right. Hannah didn't murder those people either. I'm not sure what evidence they think they have, but . . . they're wrong."

Jenna sighed. "Is Hannah an American?"

"No. She's British."

"If she were an American, you could call the American Consulate. Since she's a British citizen, you'll need to try and get her a lawyer. Although, I think they're divided into two types. They have barristers and solicitors. She'll need a barrister." She sighed again. "Sam, you're going to need to talk to someone there who can advise you. Sorry."

"Thanks. I appreciate the help, and good luck with your speech."

"Only you and Nana Jo could go on vacation and have two people murdered on your tour group." Jenna chuckled. "Better you than me."

"Thanks." I hung up.

Nana Jo was still trying to hail a taxi and getting more upset.

Irma walked up to her. "Here, let me do it." She hiked up her skirt, slid her jacket off her shoulder, and stepped into the street.

Within seconds, a black taxi skidded to a halt.

Ruby Mae said, "You have got to be kidding me."

"We'll never hear the end of this," Nana Jo said.

We hurried to get into the taxi.

There was an awkward silence when the taxi driver asked, "Where to?"

Everyone looked at me, and I said, "New Scotland Yard."

The taxi driver set the meter and pulled away from the curb.

Under normal circumstances, I would have relished a trip to Scotland Yard. It would have provided a lot of useful information for my books. However, this wasn't a normal circumstance.

The name of Scotland Yard sent a shiver up my spine. However, when the taxi pulled up to the building, I felt a stab of disappointment. In my head, I knew my mental image of the famous Metropolitan Police Force was archaic. Policemen no longer walked around in Victorian uniforms, but the reality of modern day was still disappointing. Instead of the romanticized building visited by Hercule Poirot and Inspector Japp in the Agatha Christie novels I loved, I was confronted by glass . . . tons and tons of glass. New Scotland Yard was a glass-and-steel high-rise building. Apart from the sign, it could have fit into virtually any American city.

Inside, and as we'd prearranged on the car ride, rather than asking for Detective Inspector Nelson, we asked for Detective Sergeant Templeton.

Templeton didn't keep us waiting long. She looked surprised but friendly. "How may I help you ladies?"

"We're here to check on our friend," Nano Jo said. "Hannah Schneider didn't murder anyone, and we're not going to stand around and let that . . . that . . . lump of lard railroad our friend."

The corners of her lips twitched, but Templeton got them under control and didn't let the laughter we saw in her eyes escape from her mouth. Although, she did cough several times. "Ladies, I can assure you that your friend isn't being railroaded. In fact, she immediately requested legal advice and has refused to talk without it. Smart woman."

Nana Jo released a breath. "But, what does he have on her?"

Templeton looked around. "Would you ladies care for some coffee or tea?"

We were about to decline, but something in her manner made us realize that would be a mistake.

She glanced at her watch. "There's a diner not far from here that stays open pretty late to accommodate the Met. Why don't I meet you ladies there?" She quickly gave us the address and turned to leave.

We hurried outside and walked the short distance to the diner. We found a private table away from the window. After about fifteen minutes, Templeton hurried in and sat down at our table. "I could lose my job if Nelson knows I'm talking to you."

"Why?" I asked. "We're just concerned for our friend."

We waited while the waitress took our coffee orders. She came back quickly with six cups of steaming hot coffee, sugar, and cream. We waited for her to leave before continuing.

Templeton took a deep breath. "I'm sure you noticed that Nelson is a few sandwiches short of a picnic."

"Is that like saying a few fries short of a Happy Meal?" Nana Jo asked.

Templeton chuckled. "Basically."

"Then, how'd he get to be a detective inspector?" Irma said. She leaned forward. "Is he sleeping with someone high up?"

Templeton quickly put down her coffee and reached for her purse. "I shouldn't be here. I need to—"

Nana Jo reached out a hand to calm the policewoman. "Forgive my friend; she's an idiot. He's obviously like Stinky Pitt."

Templeton looked confused. "Who is Stinky Pitt?"

"He's a nincompoop police detective in our hometown who got promoted to detective because of family connections, but if your D. I. Nelson is a few sandwiches short of a picnic, then Stinky Pitt is missing the entire picnic basket."

Templeton smiled. "Nelson is connected to an influential MP. I graduated top of my class." She stared down into her coffee. "I was assigned to him to keep him from embarrassing himself or the Met, but he treats me like a glorified secretary."

I said, "You know Hannah Schneider didn't murder those people."

She gave me a hard stare. "Let's just say, I think it highly unlikely. I mean, her husband was a former copper. If nothing else, she would have enough knowledge to avoid getting caught."

"May I ask what evidence he has?"

She looked as though she was sizing me up. Then, she leaned back in her seat. "What's your interest?"

I glanced around, and Nana Jo gave me a slight nod. I took a deep breath and explained that I owned a mystery bookshop but that we had *unofficially* helped our local police solve several murders.

She squinted. "Detective Stinky Pitt allowed you to assist in his investigation?"

"Not officially, but as long as we allow him to take the credit for solving the murders, then he hasn't stopped us."

She glanced around the table and gave each of us a long glance.

Nana Jo folded her arms. "I hope you aren't one of those people who believe that just because we're older that we must be ready for a nursing home."

"The last person who underestimated us ended up flat on his back with my size-ten shoe on his throat," Dorothy said.

"Actually," I said, "Nana Jo and Dorothy are both black belts in two different martial arts."

"Plus, when I have my peacemaker with me," Nana Jo said, "I can still outshoot any young whippersnapper who's willing to put their money where their mouth is."

I pointed to Ruby Mae. "For some reason, people like to talk to Ruby Mae, and her extended family is huge."

Irma was making goo-goo eyes at a man sitting alone, who looked young enough to be her grandson.

The detective sergeant's eyes asked the question, *What about her?*

I shrugged. "She's got a way with men."

"Harrumph," Nana Jo said. "She's a floozy."

Templeton smiled and must have made up her mind to trust us because she leaned forward and spoke softly. "Several people heard Major Peabody make disparaging remarks about Jews in Hannah's presence. She was one of the last people in the ballroom the last night that the major was alive."

"But lots of people fought with the major," Nana Jo said.

"True, but she's the only one who argued with him who had digitalis in her room."

"Digitalis?" I said. "Is that what killed him?"

"That's what Dr. Blankenship guessed, but we won't know until there's an autopsy. But if anyone finds out I told you, I could lose my—"

Nana Jo waved her hand to silence the woman's fears. "We'll never tell."

Ruby Mae looked up from her knitting. "Hannah has a weak heart. I think the digitalis was her own medication."

"What's the evidence against her for killing Mrs. Habersham?" I asked.

She shook her head. "He doesn't really have anything other than the fact that she gave sedatives to the daughter."

"But that was just melatonin." I looked at Nana Jo. "We both saw the bottle."

"It's completely harmless," Nana Jo said. "Besides, Lavender isn't dead."

"Nelson's old-fashioned. He thinks he can intimidate her into confessing."

"Pshaw." Nana Jo snorted. "The man's a fool."

Ruby Mae said, "She's a tough woman, and she certainly won't confess to a crime she didn't commit."

"What are you going to do?" Templeton asked.

"First, we need to get Hannah out of jail," Ruby Mae said.

"I don't think that will be a problem. He doesn't have

much, and a good solicitor will have her out within hours."
She glanced at her watch. "She may already be out."

"What can we do to help?" I asked.

She gave me a hard look. "I'm supposed to say stay out of
it. This is dangerous. Someone has . . . up until now, gotten
away with murdering two people. They're dangerous. You
need to leave this to the professionals." She gave us all harsh
looks, but after we merely returned her glances, she shook her
head. "You're not going to listen to me, are you?"

We all shook our heads.

"How about this. Keep your ears to the ground, and if
you hear anything, you call me." She reached in her purse and
passed around her card. She sighed. "Look, martial arts black
belts or not, this person is dangerous."

Nana Jo patted her arm. "We'll be careful. Don't you
worry about us. American women are tough. We don't go
down without a fight."

The detective sighed again. "I knew you wouldn't listen.
American women are also stubborn."

"Not all American women are stubborn," I said, "but . . .
you're not entirely wrong."

"I need to have my head examined for sharing any of
this." She leaned forward and dropped her voice to a whisper.
"And, if this gets back to the Met, I'll shoot you myself."

Nana Jo crossed her heart and held up three fingers in the
Girl Scout salute.

"My money is on Professor Lavington. He—"

Irma sat up straight and stuck out her chest. "Bullsh—"

"Irma!"

She broke out in a coughing fit. She glanced around for
something to drink but was faced with only water or coffee.
She took a sip of coffee. "Albus wouldn't harm a fly."

Templeton gave Irma a hard glance. "Did you know

Albus Lavington was fired from the university when they learned he lied about his credentials?"

Irma gawked at the sergeant.

"What did he lie about?" I asked. "A lot of people overexaggerate or embellish their resumes."

"Albus Lavington never finished his doctorate. In fact, he never graduated from any college that we can find."

Nana Jo whistled.

Irma's shock wore off. "Well, that lying little weasel."

"Lying about his education and pretending to be a professor doesn't make him a murderer," Dorothy said.

"You're right, but the person who exposed his lies was Horace Peabody."

"Major Horace Peabody? Owner of Mystery Lovers Tours?"

"The one and only."

"So, you're thinking Lavington was so upset that he killed Horace Peabody and Prudence Habersham?" I asked.

Templeton shrugged. "I don't know. He should have told us about it when we questioned him, but he didn't. I'm not saying he murdered them, but it's a possibility. He knew one of the victims well, and when people don't volunteer information, I get suspicious."

"How did Major Peabody find out?" Ruby Mae asked. "The two men must have known each other pretty well?"

"The only connection we can find between the two men so far is that they were both in the military around the same time. However, that's not uncommon in men of that age."

"Anyone else?" I asked the detective.

She squirmed in her seat for a few moments, but we let her squirm. Eventually, she gave in to the silence. "Clive Green is retired CID, but he didn't exactly leave on good terms."

"You mean he was fired?" Dorothy asked.

"I haven't been able to find anything about his history, which is suspicious in itself. His records are sealed, and no one who worked with him is talking. I've been told to drop it."

"I wonder what dirty business Clive's been up to?" Nana Jo asked.

"What about Dr. Vincent Blankenship and his wife Tiffany?" Ruby Mae asked.

The detective shook her head. "Those two appear to be exactly what they seem, American tourists. Dr. Blankenship is a successful medical doctor, and his wife is a housewife. They have two small children. Tiffany filed for divorce about three months ago, but she never followed through." She glanced around. "Then there's you all."

"Us?" Nana Jo bristled. "You've been investigating us?"

I patted my grandmother's hand to calm her down. "Nana Jo, it's normal procedure. They don't know us."

She wasn't convinced but folded her arms across her chest and mumbled, "Wasting time and resources investigating us."

"Can I ask what you found out?" I asked.

"Detective Bradley Pitt of the North Harbor Police called you . . ."

Nana Jo glared. "Go ahead, spit it out."

Templeton took out her cell phone. She swiped a few times until she found what she was looking for. "He called you, and I quote, 'A bunch of nosey old broads who think they're Nancy Drew and who like to meddle in things that don't concern them.'"

Nana Jo smacked her hand down on the table. "Why that dirty little pip-squeak."

"After everything we've done to help him," Dorothy said.

Templeton held up a hand to quell the outrage. "He also said, 'Those old biddies have a knack for getting people to talk and a network that the FBI, CIA, and Interpol would envy. People trust them, so they tell them things they'd never say to the police.'" She looked up from her phone for a moment and then continued, "He said, 'I'd stake my reputation that none of those women killed anyone, but if someone was foolish enough to commit a murder within twenty miles of them, there's no way they'll keep out of it.'" She glanced at me. "'Samantha Washington is a pretty sharp cookie. If you need to sort things out, she's the one to do it, but if you tell them I said it, I'll deny every word.'"

I could feel everyone looking at me.

Nana Jo huffed. "Maybe Stinky Pitt isn't as worthless as I thought."

"Stinky Pitt?" Templeton asked.

Nana Jo explained the nickname was given when the detective was a boy and she was his math teacher. "I like to torment him by using it periodically."

Templeton finished her coffee and rose to leave. "I know you believe you're tough and invincible, but I want to caution you to be careful. There's a killer on the loose. If you have any information or an inkling of who could be responsible, please call me."

"I promise," I said. "We'll be careful." I extended a hand to shake. "American women are tough, but I suspect England has some pretty tough women too."

She shook my hand and gave me a slight smile and walked out.

We talked for a few moments and then paid our check. Rather than relying on Irma's assets to secure a taxi, I asked the waitress if she would ring one for us.

When we walked into the hotel lobby, Hannah Schneider was there waiting for us. We rushed up to her and hugged her. Everyone started firing questions at once, and Hannah looked overwhelmed.

Nana Jo held up a hand to halt the questions. "Do you feel up to talking?"

Hannah nodded.

We found a secluded area in the lobby and sat down and waited. Hannah got settled and took a deep breath. "I've never been so humiliated in my life." Tears started to stream down her cheeks.

Ruby Mae slipped a handkerchief into her hands and put an arm around the woman's shoulders. After a bit, Hannah sniffed, took a deep breath, and pulled herself together. "I'm sorry. It's just every time I think about it, I get so angry."

Nana Jo reached over and patted the woman's hand. "We can wait until tomorrow if you'd rather."

Hannah shook her head. "No, I'd like to get this out now. Then, I'm going to my room to take a long shower, make myself a cup of tea, and try to get some sleep and forget this horrible day ever happened."

"You might need something stronger than tea," Dorothy joked.

Hannah smiled and patted her purse. "Agreed." She dabbed at her eyes and took a deep breath. "After I was taken out of the pub like a . . . common criminal . . ." Her voice broke.

"Try not to dwell on that," Ruby Mae said. "What happened once you were at the police station?"

"Well, on the ride over, I got angry, but I remembered everything my husband and my daughter ever talked about with their jobs."

"Your daughter?" I asked. "We know your husband was a policeman, but your daughter . . ."

"My daughter's a barrister." Hannah smiled. "Didn't I mention it?"

"No, you never did."

"So, as soon as we got to the Yard, I demanded a solicitor and called my daughter. She got there in record time and demanded to know what evidence they had against me. Honestly, within an hour, I was released." She grinned. "She wanted me to go home with her, but . . . I told her I wanted to see this thing out." She looked at each of us. "We are going to investigate and find the real killer?"

Nana Jo and the girls all turned to me.

I reached across and squeezed Hannah's hand. "Absolutely."

Chapter 17

Hannah Schneider was wiped out, and after a few questions about her general well-being, we agreed to call it a day and meet for assignments early tomorrow morning after we'd all had a chance to get some sleep.

Irma spotted Professor Lavington in the bar and decided she would start gathering information tonight. The rest of us went up to our rooms.

Upstairs, Nana Jo was the first to go to bed. I tried to sleep but found myself tossing and turning. After about an hour, I gave up. I pulled a sweatshirt on top of my T-shirt that I'd bought to sleep in and slipped on my jeans. I grabbed my notepad, pen, and the key card for the room and slipped out the door. I had no clear direction in mind, but I found myself back in the quiet alcove where I'd written before. Maybe a bit of writing would help me sort through my thoughts.

Lady Elizabeth, Lord William, Lady Clara, and Victor Carlston sat in the library of Wickfield Lodge. Lady Elizabeth knitted, while Lady Clara gazed out the window. Lord William sat in a chair with one foot propped on an ottoman. His Cavalier King Charles spaniel, Cuddles, lay curled up in a ball near his master's foot.

There was a tap at the door and Thompkins entered.

"Good, now we can start," Lady Elizabeth said. "I wanted—"

The door opened again, and Lady Penelope entered. "I thought I'd find all of you here."

Victor hurried to his wife's side. "Penelope, you should be resting."

Lady Penelope became upset. "No, I won't go. I want to help. I'm not going to be able to rest until we find the murderer." She turned to her aunt. "Please, I want to help."

Lady Elizabeth stared at her niece. "You can help on one condition."

"Anything."

"You have to promise not to overexert yourself." Lady Elizabeth patted the sofa next to her.

Lady Penelope hurried to sit down. "I promise."

Lady Elizabeth gazed up at her nephew. "Victor?"

He stared at his wife's face for several seconds and then nodded.

Lady Clara, who had been pacing in front of the fireplace, turned to her aunt. "What about Peter . . . ah, I mean Detective Inspector Covington. Isn't he going to join us?" She colored slightly. "It might be handy to have a Scotland Yard detective helping us."

Thompkins coughed. "Detective Inspector Covington sends his apologies. He's been detained but will be here as soon as possible."

Lady Clara flushed.

"I'm not really sure where to begin," Lady Elizabeth said. She took a deep breath. "Dr. Haygood examined Captain Jessup, and as far as he's concerned, the death was due to a man with a weak heart overindulging in alcohol."

"Darned fool," Lord William said and puffed on his pipe. "Got to look after the ticker." He tapped his chest.

"If it's natural, that should be the end of it," Victor said. "There's nothing to investigate."

"People won't believe that," Lady Penelope said. "You know people will talk. They'll say you or I or one of the family did it so you would inherit." Her eyes pleaded. "You know I'm right."

"I know." Victor nodded and turned away.

Lady Clara flopped down into a chair. "So, we've got to prove that the odious captain wasn't murdered."

Detective Inspector Peter Covington opened the door and entered the study. He glanced at Lady Clara and then quickly turned away. "I'm sorry, but I was talking to Dr. Haygood and making arrangements with the Yard."

Lady Clara perched on the edge of her chair. "What arrangements?"

He took a deep breath. "Captain Jessup's doctor says he just filled Jessup a new prescription for digitalis."

"Digitalis is what they give people with bad hearts, isn't it?" Lady Clara said.

"It is, but the prescription was new."

"Ah . . . I see," Lady Elizabeth said. "The prescription was new, but the bottle on Captain Jessup's nightstand was empty."

"There's no way that bottle would have been empty unless . . ."

"Unless someone killed him," Victor finished the detective's thought and said aloud what everyone must have been thinking.

Lady Penelope turned to her aunt. "So, we need to figure out who murdered Captain Jessup."

Chapter 18

Sometime during the night, Clive Green sent emails and arranged for messages to be sent to all of the tour group, notifying us of a meeting in the ballroom at nine. In light of that development, we decided to hold off on our sleuthing meeting until after Clive's meeting.

At nine, the tour group made our way back into the ballroom. However, we weren't alone. This time, D. I. Nelson and D. S. Templeton were there.

If I thought Clive Green looked bad before, I was wrong. Today he looked worse. His eyes were sunken into his head, and he had dark circles and bags under his eyes. The already thin man looked as though he hadn't eaten or slept.

Clive stood in front of the group. "Ladies and gentlemen, first I'd like to say that Lavender Habersham is resting comfortably and is receiving the best care possible."

In all of the commotion around the murders, Lavender Habersham had gotten lost. I suspect that was her lot in life. The poor woman was a drudge for her mother and was often forgotten or overlooked. I made a mental note to arrange flowers be sent to her.

Clive cleared his throat. "Now, I must regretfully inform you that we will have to cancel the remainder of the trip."

There was a rumble as people complained about the waste of money and time.

Clive held up his hands to quiet the crowd. "You will all, of course, receive refunds for the portion of the trip that we were unable to complete."

Nana Jo stood. "Look, I realize there've been two murders, but some of us have traveled a long way, and it may be years before we can have the time to make a trip like this again."

Vincent and Tiffany Blankenship exchanged glances.

Nana Jo turned to me. "My granddaughter has been looking forward to this trip for a long time and was relying on this trip to help with the research for her next book."

I tried to hide my surprise at Nana Jo sharing something that was very dear to me and extremely private. One look in her eyes told me that she was up to something, so I forced myself to remain calm.

She turned to Clive. "The other day, you told us Major Peabody would have wanted us to finish our tour."

Clive started to speak, but Nana Jo wasn't done yet. "Look, I'm not trying to be disrespectful of the two people who have died. I know finding a murderer is important, but surely there's a way we can continue. I don't see how sitting around this hotel is going to make things better."

Nelson gave a snarky laugh. "Well, that's why a pretty little lady like yourself needs to leave matters like solving murders to the professionals."

Ruby Mae shook her head and mumbled, "Bless his heart."

I've known Ruby Mae long enough to know that rather than a prayer, she was using the phrase as it was used in the southern United States, which roughly translated to, *You poor pitiful fool.*

I was pleased to see that Nana Jo hadn't body-slammed the detective, although if the vein that was pulsing on the side of her head was any indication, it was taking a great deal of effort on her part to refrain. She gripped the side of the table and took a deep breath before turning back to face the detective. "Great. While D. I. Nelson focuses his mental energy on solving the murders, why can't we continue on our tour?"

Nelson rocked on the balls of his feet and stared at Hannah Schneider. "If you think I'm going to let a murderer go galivanting around the British countryside so she can make a run for it, then you'd better think again."

"Are you planning to arrest us?" Dorothy asked innocently. "Because if you are, then I need to contact the American Consulate."

"No one is under arrest . . . yet."

"If you aren't planning to arrest us, then what's to stop the murderer from simply walking away from the hotel?" Ruby Mae asked.

"You won't be prevented from leaving the hotel, but I will require all of your passports, and you will not be able to leave the country."

"So, what's the difference between us staying here in London or going on a bus tour?" Tiffany Blankenship asked. "It's a lot easier to get lost in a city the size of London than it would be in some place like the Cotswolds or Torquay." She glanced around. "Isn't it?"

Nelson sputtered, "Well . . . I . . . obviously I don't have the manpower to send officers all over the country. We're much too busy for that."

I saw a glimmer in Nana Jo's eye. She plastered on a fake smile. "Of course you are. Which is why we wouldn't dream of asking someone of your . . . stature to accompany us."

Unfortunately, I chose that exact moment to take a drink

of coffee. I nearly spit my coffee out and choked down the laughter that tried to escape, which started a coughing fit.

Nana Jo patted me on the back in an effort to help. Her back to the detective, she gave me a wink. "D. I. Nelson, you're obviously too important to babysit a bunch of tourists, but maybe you could have D. S. Templeton babysit us." Nana Jo hesitated. "Well, that is if you can spare her. I'm sure you find such a smart, young detective like her invaluable when it comes to handling some of the more . . . technical aspects of an investigation."

Templeton hadn't been expecting that maneuver, and her face mirrored her surprise.

Nelson gaped at Nana Jo, who smiled back and batted her eyelashes.

I stared at my grandmother in disbelief.

Nelson glanced from Templeton to Nana Jo. His face reflected his inner turmoil. If he refused, then he was acknowledging that he needed Templeton, but if he agreed, then he would be on his own. For a brief moment, a flash crossed his face. He smiled. "Well, that's a good idea. I can certainly spare D. S. Templeton." He smirked. "She'll accompany you on your tour, and of course, I'll hold her responsible for ensuring that no one makes a break for it."

Nana Jo clapped her hands. "That's great." She turned to our guide. "Clive, please tell me it isn't too late."

The tour guide looked baffled, but rallied quickly. "Let me make a few calls." He grabbed his papers, pulled out his cell phone, and hurried from the room.

Templeton's eyes asked, *What are you doing?*

Nana Jo merely winked. "I'm starving. Let's grab some breakfast."

We went to the dining room. We ate a hearty breakfast, and once everyone was finished, Nana Jo pulled out her iPad, and we got down to business.

"Now that we've managed to get rid of D. I. Bloody Nelson, we can get down to the serious task of catching a killer."

I looked hard at my grandmother. "What was all that balderdash really about?"

"What do you mean?"

I batted my eyelashes. "Oh, D. I. Nelson, you're so important." I batted faster and gave a sickeningly sweet smile. "Poor little ole me couldn't possibly solve a murder without someone like you."

Everyone laughed.

"Ugh," Nana Jo said. "Don't remind me. I nearly puked in my own mouth." She turned to Irma. "How do you manage to rattle off all that sickening tripe with a straight face?"

"Flirting and flattery is a dying art," Irma said. "They used to teach young girls how to flirt and entice men when I was in finishing school."

I said, "I didn't know you went to finishing school."

"Oh, yes. All well-bred young girls went to finishing school in my day. It's where they taught us how to land a husband."

I didn't realize my mouth was open until Nana Jo reached over and closed it. "They actually taught classes with the intent of 'landing a husband'?"

Irma nodded.

I looked around the table. "Am I the only one who didn't know this?"

Ruby Mae pulled her knitting out of her purse. "Well, I grew up in the South, and we were too poor for finishing school, but even in the Black community there were women who *informally* taught us how to put on makeup, dress, and walk in heels with a certain . . ." She smiled. "Oh, I don't know . . . sway, so as to attract attention."

Hannah Schneider nodded. "The upper-crust families of Britain sent their daughters to Switzerland for finishing before

they came out into society. Of course, my family couldn't afford to send me to Switzerland, but I did attend Lucie Clayton." She glanced around and noticed the blank looks. "Lucie
Clayton was one of the top finishing schools in Britain and
later became a modeling school. When I was there, they
taught cookery, flower arranging, makeup, deportment, fashion design, pattern cutting, and dressmaking. They've merged
with other schools now and offer secretarial courses. I think
they're considered a college these days."

"I had no idea," I said. I wondered, and not for the first
time, about the wealth of knowledge that my grandmother
and her friends possessed.

"Back to business," Nana Jo said. "D. S. Templeton got
me thinking last night. Whoever murdered Habersham and
Peabody thinks they've gotten away with it. It might be a
good idea to have police protection, especially since I don't
have my peacemaker." She turned to me. "Assignments?"

"Honestly, I think we just need to stick to the same ones
we had before when we were investigating Major Peabody's
suspicious death."

Hannah raised a tentative hand. "What about me? I was
supposed to tackle Lavender Habersham, but she's still in the
hospital."

"I still think we need to talk to her. She might have heard
or saw something the night her mother was murdered. But, I
don't think we can eliminate Dr. Vincent and Tiffany
Blankenship."

Hannah gave me a look. "You don't really think the doctor could have something to do with those murders."

I took a moment to collect my thoughts before I responded. "I'm not saying they murdered the major or Prudence Habersham, but this case is . . . different."

Nana Jo frowned. "Different how?"

"I think finding out *how* the murders were committed is going to be as important as figuring out whodunit. This murderer is cunning and brave. If we can't figure out how they did it, I think our murderer just might get away."

Nana Jo stared at me. "You know who it is. You know who murdered those people."

Chapter 19

I hesitated too long and everyone immediately started pumping me for the name. I held up a hand. "I *don't* know who murdered Major Peabody and Prudence Habersham. All I've got right now is a lot of questions and a feeling in the pit of my stomach that something is not right. I feel like I've been watching a magic show or a play. I feel like there's been sleight of hand or some type of misdirection, but I just can't figure out what. I also feel like I'm missing something . . . something to do with the Blankenships, but I just can't remember what it is."

"It's best to stop focusing on it," Nana Jo said, patting my hand. "Your subconscious will help sort things out. Now, let's get busy finding some answers."

We got a message that Clive wanted everyone to reassemble in the ballroom, and we hurried to find out if he'd been able to salvage any portion of our tour.

In the ballroom, we took the same seats we'd used earlier. Clive Green hurried into the room, and I could tell from his expression that he had good news.

"It wasn't easy, but with a few modifications, we should be able to see practically everything."

We clapped.

He hurriedly passed around handouts with our revised itinerary. When everyone had received a handout, Clive continued his explanation.

"This afternoon, we'll head to Cotswolds. We won't have time to do the racetrack today, but we can still take our walking tour of Chipping Campden, which demonstrates the village life that was integral to the world created by authors like Agatha Christie and Dorothy L. Sayers." He glanced around to catch our reaction. Satisfied, he continued on. "We'll come back here for the night. Then tomorrow, we'll go to Torquay."

I glanced at Hannah Schneider, and her face reflected the same joy that I felt inside.

"We'll spend one night in Torquay, and then it's back to London."

The room bristled with excitement. I could tell that I had a silly grin on my face by the way my cheeks hurt, but I honestly didn't care. For the life of me, I couldn't explain what going to the town where Agatha Christie lived and loved and wrote would do for me. The woman had been dead for decades, but more than anything else, I wanted to go to Torquay and now, I was going. Torquay was the major reason I'd selected this particular tour from all of the tour options available. I felt like a kid who just found out she was going to Disney World.

D. I. Nelson held up his hands and tried to get everyone's attention. "All right, settle down."

We fixed our attention on the detective.

Nelson stood next to Clive Green. "I've given my approval to the continuation of this tour, but there are going to be a few rules."

I raised an eyebrow and glanced at Nana Jo, who merely shrugged.

Dr. Blankenship asked, "What rules?"

Nelson rocked on the balls of his feet. "First, my sergeant goes along with you."

Templeton stood by the wall. She didn't look excited about a chance to visit the home of Agatha Christie, but then she lived in Britain, so maybe she'd been before.

"No one leaves the main tour group," Nelson said. "None of this . . . personal free time. You all stay together as a group."

There was a small rumble of opposition.

Nelson excitedly added, "Anyone who doesn't want to stick to the rules is more than welcome to stay here. Those are the conditions."

Not surprisingly, given the chance to continue the rest of our tour or stay with D. I. Nelson, everyone chose the tour.

Hannah Schneider raised her hand. "What about Lavender Habersham?"

Clive Green smiled. "In all of the excitement, I forgot to share. I got a call from Lavender, and she would like to continue the tour too."

Dr. Blankenship said, "Do you think that's wise? The poor woman's been through a lot with the shock of her mother's murder."

"Actually, the doctors think it might be good for her to be around people rather than sitting at home alone," Clive said. "Of course, if you feel it would be better if she didn't go, then I can certainly explain—"

Dr. Blankenship waved away the concerns. "No . . . no, as long as her doctor at the hospital feels she is up to it, then I have no objection."

"Great. I'm sure I'm not alone in saying that it makes me feel much better knowing we have a medical doctor on the tour."

Tiffany rolled her eyes, but neither she nor the doctor felt the need to remind us that *he was on vacation* again. For that, I was truly thankful.

Clive spent a few moments passing along last-minute details. "Then, let's meet on the bus in one hour."

I didn't realize D. S. Templeton was standing behind me until she spoke, and I nearly jumped out of my skin.

"I'm not sure what you're up to, but I sure hope it doesn't backfire," Templeton said.

The bus pulled in front of the hotel, and we all piled inside. D. S. Templeton and a uniformed constable were new additions. Most likely due to prearrangement, the constable sat upfront, while D. S. Templeton moved to the back of the bus. After a brief wait, Lavender Habersham arrived and climbed aboard.

I'm not sure how I expected the woman to look, but I was shocked to find that Lavender Habersham actually looked better than ever. She was still pale and thin, but her cheeks had more color, and her eyes looked excited rather than frightened.

Nana Jo leaned close and whispered, "Looks like her mother's death is wearing well on her."

I nudged Nana Jo to hush as Lavender made her way to our seat.

Nana Jo pulled the suitcase from under her seat and passed it to Lavender. "I suspect you've been looking for this."

At the sight of the bag, Lavender's eyes flashed and her face brightened. "I've missed Bella so much." She squeezed the bag to her chest. "Thank you for looking after her."

I glanced at Nana Jo, who had the decency to blush. "My pleasure."

Lavender and Bella headed to the back of the bus.

"You barely had anything to do with that dog!" I whispered.

"I've been busy trying to figure out who murdered the woman's mother. It was my pleasure to hand the responsibility of taking care of an illegal pet over to the hotel staff."

I chuckled and sat back to enjoy the ride.

The Cotswolds are a rural area that spans five counties in south central and southwest England. Clive sat at the front of the bus and got on his microphone as we approached the area. He explained that the nearly 800-mile area was designated as an *Area of Outstanding Natural Beauty* back in 1966.

"What's that mean?" Tiffany asked.

"It's designated for conservation." He paused for a moment. "It's similar to the protections from development given to national parks in the United Kingdom but with different governing bodies and limited recreation."

The bus traveled through rolling green hills dotted with sheep and through golden stone villages with slate- and thatched-roofed limestone cottages. Cotswolds was exactly what I imagined when I read historic cozy mysteries set in small English villages, like Agatha Christie's Miss Marple mysteries and Heron Carvic's Miss Seeton mysteries.

Chipping Campden was a small market town in the district of Gloucestershire. In the Middle Ages, it had been a rich wool trading center, but it was now more famous for the fact that it had been hosting its own "Olimpick Games" since 1612 and for the area's arts and crafts tradition.

Our bus stopped on the terraced high street, and we lined up to follow Clive on our walking tour. The area was a tourist's haven, so few looked twice as our group passed. The constable stayed on one side of the group, while D. S. Templeton, who had changed from her heels into a pair of sneakers, remained on the other. Given the short time she'd had to prepare, she must have had the shoes close at hand.

I took several pictures of the picturesque village, more for inspiration for my books than as a remembrance for sharing with family and friends. Clive was extremely knowledgeable about the area and stopped to point out landmarks of historic significance and to allow time for shopping in the marketplace. However, he had also fine-tuned his lecture to appeal to mystery lovers. After several hours, we stopped at the Noel Arms Hotel, one of the oldest Cotswold inns.

"Originally devised as a coaching inn for wool traders, the Noel Arms dates from the fourteenth century," Clive said. "While we weren't able to stay in this lovely inn this trip, we will still be able to enjoy dinner and drinks. Down a couple of stairs there's a lounge, a pub, and beyond that is the dining room."

We walked down the stone steps into the pub. The stone- and wood-paneled walls with dark beamed ceilings made the room cozy. Normally, Nana Jo, the girls, and I would have all sat together. However, when we were pumping suspects, we had adopted the policy of divide and conquer. Irma and Albus stopped in the pub. Despite being less than five feet tall, Irma climbed on a barstool as if she were six feet. Debra Holt and Sebastian secured a small table in the lounge in front of the fireplace. In the dining room, Dorothy and Oscar Hoffman secured a small table for two. She had, apparently, forgiven him and he had dropped the pretense of not understanding English. With Debra Holt and Sebastian temporarily out of reach, Nana Jo cozied up to Clive Green. Ruby Mae dined with Dr. Vincent and Tiffany Blankenship. Hannah Schneider and Lavender sat together, and I decided to join D. S. Templeton, who was seated alone by the window.

"Mind if I join you?"

D. S. Templeton looked up at me and shrugged.

"I'll take that as a no." I pulled out the chair across from her and sat.

We stared at each other for a few moments until the waitress came. I asked for a Diet Coke. Templeton held up two fingers, doubling the order. The waitress hurried to take care of our drinks. After a few more moments of silence, I asked, "Are you angry with the entire world or just me?"

"Not the whole world, just you and your grandmother."

"Why?"

She leaned forward and pointed her finger. "Because I didn't graduate top of my class and work my butt off to get stuck on babysitting duty for a bunch of spoiled American tourists." She breathed hard. "I'm a good cop, but I get stuck as a glorified secretary and babysitter for an old bugger who should have retired long ago."

"I'm sorry."

The waitress brought our drinks.

Templeton looked at her glass of Diet Coke and then said, "This isn't going to cut it. Bring me a bourbon."

The waitress hurried off, and we exchanged glances for a few seconds and then burst out laughing.

"I'm sorry," Templeton said. "I realize my plight isn't your fault."

"I understand your frustration. However, I do believe Nana Jo was only trying to help." I leaned forward. "Let's face it, the murderer is probably one of the people on this tour, so the closer you are to them, the more likely you are to catch the killer."

"I guess, but it just feels like babysitting."

The waitress brought the drink and took our orders. When she left, we talked. I learned that Moira Templeton was the only girl and the youngest of six children. Three of her brothers were doctors, one was a barrister, and one was an airline pilot.

"Sounds very prestigious."

The waitress brought our salads.

"All married with children," Templeton said. "So, the only girl who's single and a copper is the big disappointment."

"I doubt that. You graduated top of your class."

She stopped her fork halfway to her mouth and chuckled. "All right, I'm sorry I was snippy earlier."

"I'm serious. You've chosen a very important career. It's not many people who would choose a life of public service that requires so much of your time with so little thanks and money. That is, if being a policeman in the United Kingdom is similar to the United States."

"Long hours, crappy work with little pay . . . it's the same."

"Police have to deal with the worst society has to offer. It takes a special person to do that job."

"Thanks."

We chatted amiably throughout dinner. Nana Jo sauntered by the table. "Hey, when we get back to the hotel, we're going to get drinks and have our meeting." She glanced at Templeton. "You're welcome to join us, unless you have to get home."

Templeton took a sip of her bourbon. "I've got nothing better to do."

"Great."

We made our way back to the bus. The trip home was quiet. Most people slept, but I needed to think, so I turned on the light above my seat, pulled out my notepad, and wrote.

❦

The mood was somber, as the realization that Captain Jessup was murdered had settled in. Lady Elizabeth took a deep breath and picked up her knitting. "No matter how distasteful, the truth is the murderer has to be someone who is affiliated with the family." She glanced around.

"Thompkins, I know the staff were very upset about the captain's treatment of poor Gladys. Perhaps you could ask a few discreet questions and find out if anyone . . . took matters into their own hands."

Thompkins bowed. "Yes, m'lady."

Lady Elizabeth returned to her knitting. "William, I find it hard to believe that Nigel could be involved in this mess. His father is the rector of Copdock, but we certainly can't leave any stone unturned."

"Nigel's a fine chap," Lord William said.

"I agree with you, but we mustn't leave anyone out." She turned to Lady Penelope. "Penelope, dear, do you feel up to talking to the reverend and Mrs. Baker?"

"Of course." She glanced at her husband. "Actually, I suppose we'll need to make arrangements for the funeral, anyway. I don't know if he had any other family."

Victor shrugged and turned to the detective. "Any idea when we can . . . well, when your chaps will be done with the . . . well, with him?"

D. I. Covington said, "There'll need to be an autopsy, but I can ask for a rush and you should be able to make arrangements within a few days."

Lady Clara anxiously looked at her aunt. "What about me?"

Lady Elizabeth knitted for a few moments. "Actually, I was hoping that you and Peter could still check into Captain Jessup's claims." She looked at the detective. "I know you're now investigating a murder, but I do think we need to find out if there's any truth to his claims that he was the illegitimate heir of Lord Percival Carlston. That is, if you think you'll have the time."

Covington nodded. "Certainly, I can do that."

"What are you going to do?" Lady Clara asked.

Lady Elizabeth smiled. "I'm going to continue my plan to invite Violet Merriweather to tea, and then I'm going to have a nice long talk with the Wood sisters."

"Violet Merriweather I understand, but the Wood sisters?" Lady Penelope said. "You can't possibly believe those two old maids had anything to do with murdering Captain Jessup."

Lady Elizabeth stopped knitting and stared into space for several moments. "I'm not sure you can discount those two quite so easily. You have to admit, their behavior at the dinner party was unusual. They both looked like frightened birds, and they barely spoke the entire night."

"That *was* unusual."

"My grandmother used to say, 'Still waters run deep.'" She paused. "I think there's a lot more going on under the surface of the Wood sisters than people think." She frowned. "Yes. Much more indeed."

Chapter 20

The bus pulled up to the hotel. Everyone filed off with promises to return first thing tomorrow morning with luggage for an overnight stay in Torquay.

When I got off the bus, I joined my grandmother, who was waiting outside the hotel with the others. I wasn't sure D. S. Templeton would actually join us until she came up and stood nearby.

"Shall we head back to the same pub?" Nana Jo said. She turned to the detective. "That is, unless you can recommend another place."

D. S. Templeton shook her head.

So, we walked the few blocks back to the same pub from the previous night. When we got to the door, I saw Hannah Schneider hesitate before we entered. That was when I realized that she might feel uncomfortable after being removed in handcuffs the previous night. However, she took a deep breath and pushed through the door.

Inside, she stood tall, pulled her shoulders back, held her head high, and walked back to the same seat.

Once we were seated, I noticed Ruby Mae gave her friend's hand a squeeze of support.

We had the same waitress from the previous night. We ordered drinks and made small talk until they were delivered. When everyone had their drinks, Nana Jo pulled her iPad out of her purse and looked around. "Okay, who wants to go first?"

Irma glanced at her watch and then raised a hand. "I'm meeting Albus in an hour, so I better go first."

No one objected.

Irma pulled a compact out of her purse and touched up her makeup while she talked. "When Al was in school working on his doctorate, he got into trouble."

"What kind of trouble?" Templeton asked.

Irma rummaged in her purse and then dumped the contents on the table. "My handcuffs are missing."

Nana Jo sighed. "You probably left them in your bedroom. Now, focus."

Irma returned the items to her purse and pulled out a lipstick and puckered up and applied her lipstick. "Well, I don't know all of the details, but I think he stole some chemicals from a lab for one of his friends." She finished applying her lipstick and picked up a napkin to blot.

"Who was the friend?" Nana Jo asked.

"Horace Peabody."

"Why would Horace Peabody ask Albus to steal chemicals?" I asked.

She pulled a bottle of perfume from her purse. "He said Horace had some type of shopping-market thing going on."

"Spray that perfume at this table and I'll wring your neck," Nana Jo said.

Irma returned the perfume to her purse.

I mulled Irma's comments. "Do you mean the black market?"

She snapped her fingers. "That's it."

Templeton nearly choked on her drink. "He told you Horace Peabody was dealing in the black market?"

Irma nodded. "He said Horace had this black-market thing going on the side and a chap could always count on him if he needed things." She took a sip of her drink, careful not to ruin her lipstick. "That's all he would tell me, but I'm meeting him later and will see what else I can squeeze out of him."

Nana Jo shook her head and updated her notes.

"Well, I might as well go next," Dorothy said. "Oscar Hoffman really is a German businessman, but he's also a member of a group that hunts down Nazis and collaborators."

"Nazi hunters," Nana Jo said. "I saw a show about them on television."

Everyone started asking questions all at once, and Dorothy held up a hand. "I don't have all the details, but he was on the trail of Horace Peabody."

"Why?" I asked. "Wasn't Horace too young to have fought in World War Two?"

"He had reason to believe that Horace Peabody ran a black-market ring and sold everything, including weapons, to anyone with enough money to pay him." She shook her head. "The man was despicable."

"I don't see what the black market has to do with hunting down Nazi collaborators."

"I didn't either, but apparently there are still quite a few hate groups and people who either helped or are continuing to help advance and promote the Nazi ideology. Anyway, Oscar believed Horace's black-market dealings have helped fund these old geezers who are wanted for crimes against humanity."

"Wow!" I tried to find something much more profound to say, but the only thing that crossed my mind was, "Wow."

Templeton turned to Dorothy. "Did Hoffman confront Major Peabody with his suspicions?"

"He said he didn't, but . . . I'm not sure."

Nana Jo stared at her friend. "What's wrong? You're usually much more confident. Why are you doubting yourself?"

"I've been second-guessing myself since I got off that airplane. From the luggage mix-up to not seeing through the fact that Oscar understood more English than he was letting on. I don't know if I'm letting my anger at being deceived influence my feelings about him."

"What does your gut tell you?" Nana Jo asked.

Dorothy paused. "I don't think Oscar killed him."

"That will be for a court to decide," Templeton said with a surprising amount of compassion and softness in her voice. "However, I'll look into it."

Ruby Mae updated the row counter on the end of her knitting needle. "Well, I got a few minutes with Clive Green. It's not easy getting police to talk, and even retired police are close-lipped." She looked at D. S. Templeton. "Sorry."

Templeton smiled. "I think police everywhere are fairly good at hiding our feelings."

Ruby Mae gave me and Nana Jo a sideways glance before continuing her knitting. "I asked Clive what he meant when you heard him say that he knew where the skeletons were buried."

"What?" Templeton said, looking from Ruby Mae to Nana Jo to me.

Nana Jo looked sheepish. "Oops. I guess we forgot to mention that."

We quickly filled her in on the argument we had overheard between Clive and Major Peabody.

"You should have told us about this at once."

"Sorry, I guess we got distracted with the two murders," Nana Jo said. "What did he say, Ruby Mae?"

"He hemmed and hawed a bit, but finally, he said Major Horace Peabody wasn't a major. Apparently, Clive served in the military and knew someone in the British Armed Forces, and they said Peabody never made it beyond sergeant. After the military, he just started calling himself *major*."

"Interesting, although I think that might be more of a reason for Horace to murder Clive to keep his secret safe than the other way around," I said. "But you never can tell. I mean, Clive was furious when we saw him and Horace arguing in the hallway, so I could definitely see him killing Peabody over selling the business."

"Agreed," Nana Jo said, and she updated the information in her iPad.

Ruby Mae reached in her bag. "Clive seems like a nice man. He even gave me this honey. He's a beekeeper." She turned to me. "Do you think they'll let me take this through Customs?"

"I doubt it," I said.

"You're right. I better eat it before we leave." She returned to her knitting.

"Nice job, Ruby Mae," Nana Jo said.

Hannah glanced around and then raised her hand. "Is it okay if I go next?"

We all nodded.

"Well, I got a chance to talk to Lavender at dinner. The woman looks two hundred percent better than she did just twenty-four hours ago. I hate to say it, but I think her mother's death was really more of a relief than anything else."

"How do you mean?" I asked.

"Well, her mother was demanding and bossy."

Irma snorted. "We certainly saw that."

"The poor lass was bossed from pillar to post and never got to do anything she wanted to do," Hannah said. "She had to constantly be at her mum's beck and call. Seeing her mother dead was a big shock, but I think after she got a good night's sleep, she realized that she was finally free to do whatever she wanted." She glanced around the table at each of us. "She was free to wear what she wanted to wear."

"I noticed she had on makeup," Irma said. "She looked a lot better."

Hannah nodded. "The poor lass got excited about the idea of buying blue jeans. Apparently, her mum didn't think they were appropriate and never let her wear them."

"That explains the old dowdy dresses she's been wearing," Irma said.

"She wasn't even allowed to go to university. She's rather excited about the possibilities."

"The question is, did she kill her mother to provide that opportunity?" Templeton said.

"I don't think so." Hannah sat up excitedly. "Oh, I almost forgot the most important part. According to Lavender, her mother lied about Horace Peabody being her father."

That got all of our attention.

"What do you mean?" I said. "Is she sure? How did she know?"

"How did she think she could possibly get away with that?" Templeton said. "A DNA test would have quickly proven that Horace wasn't the father."

"According to Lavender, Prudence was upset by the way Horace had treated her that first day in the ballroom. So, when she saw Debra Holt, she came up with that crazy story about Lavender being his daughter. She figured maybe Debra would offer her a few quid to keep quiet, and then she'd have her revenge on both of them for being disrespectful."

"Why the conniving, little bit—"

"Irma!"

Irma broke into a coughing fit and gulped down her drink. "Sorry."

Nana Jo put down her iPad. "I didn't get a chance to talk to Debra or Sebastian, but I'll get them tomorrow. However, I did get a chance to chat with the Blankenships."

"What did you find out?" I asked.

"They're a young couple who have two small kids. Vincent works too many hours, and Tiffany's bored. I think they're holding back, but I did learn one interesting bit of information." She glanced at D. S. Templeton. "Dr. Blankenship noticed that Horace Peabody may have been poisoned by something other than digitalis."

"What?" Templeton said. "Why didn't he say anything? He's a ruddy doctor. He should have told the police."

"Don't shoot the messenger," Nana Jo said, holding up her hands. "Apparently, he's been working long hours and came on this trip for a vacation to rest up and try to salvage his marriage. He wasn't paying a lot of attention. He saw the pills in Peabody's room and made a call so he could get back to his wife. After thinking about it, he realized something wasn't right, and he tried to tell D. I. Nelson but was told to mind his own business and let the coroner make the diagnosis."

Templeton looked as though she might blow a gasket.

"He did manage to talk to the coroner and relayed his suspicions."

Templeton took several deep breaths and regained her composure. "Did he say what poison was used?"

"Not to me, but I think he has his suspicions."

We talked about poisons and murder for a bit longer. Irma stood up. "I've got a hot date, so I gotta go. Are we meeting tomorrow?" She smiled and patted her hair. "I might have more information tomorrow morning."

We decided to give ourselves the day to get more information and agreed that we would meet for dinner tomorrow.

D. S. Templeton looked at her watch. "I better get busy.

It looks like I've got a lot to investigate." She stood and gave us a sincere smile. "Thank you."

We chatted a bit longer and then headed back to the hotel. We had to get packed so we would be ready for our overnight excursion.

The good thing about not having luggage was that packing didn't take long. Both Nana Jo and I managed to get our bags packed in record time. Nana Jo picked up a book in the hotel gift store and sat up reading. I took my notepad and went downstairs to my writing cubby and tried to sort through the information I'd learned by focusing my conscious mind on other things.

Thompkins opened the door to the library and announced, "Mrs. Merriweather." He then stepped aside for the large, buxom woman to enter before he stepped back and closed the door. He went downstairs to get tea.

When he reached the door to the servants' dining room, he heard a wail that stopped him in his tracks. He got his composure and quickly flung open the door.

Gladys sat at the dining room table, sobbing. Mrs. Anderson, the cook, stood by, trying to comfort her, and Mrs. McDuffie looked as though she had just lost a fight with a flock of geese. Down feathers were stuck to her clothes and her hair.

"What's going on?" Thompkins said.

Gladys lifted her head, took one look at the

butler, and then dropped it back on the table and sobbed harder.

Thompkins glanced from the sobbing maid to the housekeeper, but no answers were forthcoming. So, he quickly closed the door and took charge. "Gladys, stop that noise this instant." He turned to Mrs. Anderson. "Mrs. Merriweather has just arrived. Please prepare tea for her ladyship and her guest."

Mrs. Anderson gazed from Thompkins to the maid, then hurried to the kitchen to prepare the tea tray.

Mrs. McDuffie looked at the butler. "Don't you dare start reprimanding me today. My nerves can't take it."

She looked on the verge of tears, something the butler never thought he would see. He turned to the maid. "Gladys, please go up to your room and collect yourself."

The maid lifted her red, tear-stained face from the table. She glanced from the butler to Mrs. McDuffie. After a nod from the housekeeper, she ran from the room.

Mrs. McDuffie looked up. "Before you start in on me, let me fill you in." She lifted her fingers and ticked off the items. "McTavish is missing. Frank said 'e didn't come 'ome last night. With Captain Jessup dead upstairs, 'es worried sick for 'is da'."

"What's wrong with Gladys?" Thompkins asked.

"She's worked 'erself up, believing Frank or one of 'is mates done the captain in on account of 'er."

Thompkins stared at the housekeeper. "And you?"

Mrs. McDuffie snorted. "I'm worn out. Flossie's mum wouldn't let her come in because there's a murderer on the loose. Gladys is . . ." She waved a hand. "Gladys is 'aving 'ysterics, and there's company in the 'ouse and work still needs done. Oh, and the police have traipsed mud throughout the 'ouse. I've barely had any sleep and . . ." She snapped her finger. "I'm this close to pushing Gladys out the way and wailing right beside 'er."

Thompkins stood straight and tugged on his waistcoat. "Why didn't you sleep?"

"With folks outside arguing all night, it's a wonder anyone got a moment's sleep."

"What are you talking about?"

"Don't tell me you didn't 'ear it either? Must 'ave been around two or three in the morning. I came downstairs for a cup of milk, and I 'eard Jessup arguing with that man."

"What man?"

"That other military man that was 'ere visiting his lordship."

Mrs. Anderson brought a tray loaded down with tea, scones, seed cake, and sandwiches and handed it to the butler.

Thompkins turned to Mrs. McDuffie. "Don't move. I'll take this tray upstairs and then I'll be right back."

Thompkins brought the tea cart into the library for the second time that day. Lady Elizabeth was in the same position on the sofa where she had sat earlier while visiting with Mrs. Merriweather. Her knitting was in the bag near her foot. However, this time, Lady Penelope sat across from her aunt. Lord William sat in his chair with his foot propped on the ottoman, with Cuddles curled up near the foot of his master's chair. Victor smoked near the fireplace.

Lady Elizabeth said, "I don't know if Clara and Peter—"

The door to the library flung open and Lady Clara rushed in, followed by Detective Inspector Peter Covington.

"Sorry we're late," Lady Clara said, hurrying to the sofa. "Glad we didn't miss tea. I'm starving."

Lady Elizabeth smiled at her young cousin. "You're just in time, dear. We were just getting started." She poured tea and passed the cups around, while the family helped themselves to sandwiches, scones, and pastries.

"Why don't I go first while you all have your tea," Lady Elizabeth said. "I invited Mrs. Merriweather over today."

Lord William grunted.

Lady Elizabeth grinned. "I know you're not a fan, but she really is a nice woman who does a lot of good charity work."

"Gossipy busybody," Lord William mumbled.

Lady Elizabeth picked up her knitting. "Violet's family has been in this area for centuries, and she knows a great many people, which is why I wanted to talk to her." She gave Victor a sympathetic look. "I didn't want to spread rumors about your family, but I just didn't think there was any other way but to ask."

Victor waved away her concerns. "It's bound to all come out now, anyway."

"I quite agree. Captain Jessup made his remarks in public, and we could hardly hush it up." Victor looked as though he was about to interrupt, but Lady Elizabeth hurried on. "Even if we wanted to, which of course, we don't."

"Let me guess what she had to say," Victor said. "My uncle was a cad who seduced young women and then abandoned them to raise their illegitimate children and fend for themselves."

"Actually, she didn't seem to know anything about Captain Jessup's claims. In fact, she seemed thoroughly surprised by them." She took a sip of her tea. "Her recollection of your uncle was that he was an honorable man. In fact, she spoke very highly of not only your uncle Percival but of your father and your grandfather. She felt very strongly that had your uncle fathered a child, whether it was covered by the veil of marriage or not, your family would have done the right thing."

Victor's eyes filled with water, and he turned away and fidgeted with items left on the mantle.

Lady Penelope wiped her eyes. "I knew it wasn't true."

"Unfortunately, just because Violet Merriweather hasn't heard it, doesn't mean it isn't true." Lady Elizabeth reached over and patted her niece's hand. "However, I do feel it's a good sign."

"Victor and I can go next," Lady Penelope said. "We went to visit Reverend and Mrs. Baker, and we decided to divide and conquer. Victor talked to the vicar, while I spoke to Mrs. Baker."

Victor, now fully recovered, turned back to face the group. "Once the police release the body, Reverend Baker will perform the ceremony. We'll add him to the family vault." He shrugged. "Not much more to talk about. He hadn't met Jessup before dinner the other night and didn't notice anything helpful."

Lady Penelope scooted to the edge of her seat with excitement. "Well, I got on much better with Mrs. Baker." She smiled at her husband. "It was so hard not telling Victor anything earlier, but I wanted to tell you all together. It turns out that Mrs. Baker *did* know Captain Jessup before the party."

"She did?" Lady Elizabeth asked. "I had no idea."

"Mrs. Baker was miserable. She seemed relieved to tell me about it. Mrs. Baker's father was German, and he belonged to an extremely conservative sect called . . ." She fumbled in her pocket and pulled out a scrap of paper. "Schwarzenau Brethren or Neue Täufer." She looked up. "I think I pronounced that properly."

Lord William pondered for a moment and then said, "If I recall my schoolbook German, that means New Baptist." He chuckled. "My German schoolmaster would be proud."

Penelope shrugged and sat back in her seat

on the sofa. "She said in the States, the New Baptists are sometimes called Dunkards. Anyway, her father was one of them. They're very conservative. They don't swear, won't go to war, and don't drink."

Lady Clara frowned. "Sounds boring but hardly criminal."

"The Kaiser didn't think much of Dunkards, and when Germany went to war, he made everyone participate or he shot them and their family. Her father was forced to join the military, but at least they made him a chaplain so he didn't have to actually fight. In the end, it didn't matter. She said just being there destroyed him. He saw so much death and devastation that he was . . . shell-shocked and ended up with an alcohol problem."

"How unfortunate for the poor man," Lady Elizabeth said.

"Yes, well, the thing is he couldn't just walk into a store and buy the alcohol, so he had to get it from someone." She leaned forward. "Guess who that someone was?"

Victor's eyes widened in shock. "Not Archibald?"

Lady Penelope nodded. "Archibald Jessup."

Covington sat quietly in a corner taking notes. "Where did Jessup get the alcohol?"

"That's the truly important thing. She said Jessup ran some type of underground market. He supplied whatever anyone wanted . . . for the right amount of money. Forget about ration books or shortages. It didn't matter if the items were legal or not. He had connections and could get anything."

"She knew for a fact that Captain Jessup got alcohol for her father?" Covington asked.

"Sometimes, her father was too bad to go himself, and she'd have to go. She was shocked through and through when she saw Jessup here."

"Did she confront him about it?" Lady Elizabeth asked.

"She said she didn't. She was too afraid that Captain Jessup would remember her and betray her father's secret, but she wasn't sure he recognized her." She smiled. "She said she used to be young and beautiful. I suppose Mrs. Baker could have come back and murdered Captain Jessup to keep her father's secret from getting out, but . . ."

Lady Elizabeth glanced at her niece. "But?"

"I don't believe it." She sighed. "I don't want to believe it. I like Mrs. Baker. I've known her my entire life, and I don't want to believe that she murdered that odious man."

"I know, dear. I like her too. However, we have a duty to find the truth and make sure that justice is served, regardless of who we discover committed the murder."

Lady Penelope flopped back in her seat. "I know, but I still can't see her sneaking back and poisoning the man."

Lady Clara said, "I can go next, if that's all right."

Everyone nodded.

"I went to Somerset House and there's no record of a marriage between Percival Carlston and anyone. Jessup must not have been born in England because I couldn't find a birth certificate either. All in all, a rather useless day. However, I'm going back tomorrow and will keep digging."

"I wouldn't say the day was completely useless," Covington said. "We learned there's no legitimate claim on the title, although . . . the legitimacy may not matter to Victor, but it might to the court." He flipped back a few pages in his notebook. "I swung by the Yard and had a chat with the coroner. It looks like Jessup died from an allergic reaction."

"Bees?" Lady Elizabeth asked.

"Yes. There was a rash where he was stung."

Lady Elizabeth looked up from her knitting. "Could a bee sting have killed him?"

"It could if he were allergic to bees. Apparently, some people are violently allergic."

"Amazing what medicine can do nowadays." She glanced up. "It's a bit cold for bees, but there could be a nest on the roof?"

"Modern medicine has come a long way. Maybe the bee got in through the window. Remember that open window in Jessup's bedroom you pointed out?"

"Did you find any fingerprints?"

"We didn't find fingerprints from our killer, but we did find imprints in the dirt below the window, indicating there had been a ladder there within the last few days."

"How do you know it was in the last few days?" Lady Clara asked.

"The weather's been dry. It rained the night before the dinner party, so it had to be within two days of the murder."

Lady Elizabeth glanced at her husband, who was very quiet. "How did your meeting go with Nigel?"

Lord William came out of his reverie. "I didn't get a chance to talk with him. He was off to see his solicitors. I'm going to try again tomorrow." He huffed on his pipe. "I did get to talk to Sir Thomas Chadwick."

Victor sat up. "The family solicitor?"

"He had never heard anything about Percival fathering a child and had a few choice words to say about the allegations."

"Anything else?" Lady Elizabeth asked.

Something in Lord William's face indicated he was bothered by something, but whatever it was, he kept it to himself. He shook his head.

Lady Elizabeth looked around. "Is that everyone?"

Thompkins coughed discreetly.

"How could I possibly forget, Thompkins." She smiled at the butler and waited.

Thompkins coughed again. "I'm sorry I didn't get a chance to interview more of the staff." He reluctantly explained about the missing groundskeeper. There was a slight flush to his skin when he talked about the upheaval belowstairs. He realized that the staff were his responsibility and didn't want anyone to get a bad impression of them. He took a deep breath and told of Mrs.

McDuffie's tale of going down for a glass of milk and overhearing an argument. "She wasn't eavesdropping." He quickly added, "But it was very difficult for her to avoid hearing the conversation."

Lady Elizabeth smiled. "I know Mrs. McDuffie would never deliberately listen to a private conversation that didn't concern her, but did she by chance hear what the argument was about or who was arguing?"

"She believed the gentlemen were Captain Jessup and Nigel Greyson."

"Nigel!" Lord William yelled. "Why, I wonder what he could have been arguing with Jessup about?"

Thompkins took a deep breath. "I'm afraid she didn't hear the nature of the argument, m'lord. The argument was ending by the time she stumbled upon them. However, she did hear one of the men say, 'You'll not ruin this. I'll make sure of that, if it's the last thing I ever do.'"

Chapter 21

The next morning, we loaded aboard the tour bus, and despite the fact I'd stayed up late writing and got very little sleep, I was excited. The ride to Torquay took almost four hours, but we eventually pulled up to the Grand Hotel, and I could barely contain myself.

Nana Jo chuckled. "You look like a kid who has just arrived at Disney World."

I smiled and whispered with the same reverence people generally reserved for church. "This is the hotel where Agatha Christie spent her honeymoon with Archibald Christie back in 1914."

Nana Jo smirked. "Yeah, her honeymoon with her husband, Archie, the cheater."

Agatha Christie's first marriage to Archibald Christie only lasted twelve years. In the twenty-first century, that is practically an eternity. In the twentieth century, or in my Nana Jo's mind, anything short of twenty years was merely a drop in the bucket.

The Grand Hotel was a striking Victorian building. Originally built in 1881, the hotel's seafront location made it popular during Christie's youth. The hotel website even mentioned the Agatha Christie room, which could hold five. However, our pockets weren't deep enough for that. Instead, we were housed in a nice, clean room. It wasn't expansive, but it was larger than our London hotel room and its closet-sized bathroom.

Our first order of business was lunch. We agreed to meet in the hotel's dining room. When Nana Jo and I got off the elevator, she spotted Sebastian sitting alone and made a beeline for him. I glanced around for Debra, but she was nowhere in sight. True to form, Ruby Mae was seated at a table near the window having a conversation with D. S. Templeton and someone who was dressed like a chef. Dorothy was seated with Oscar Hoffman, and Irma was with Professor Lavington. I glanced around and saw Lavender Habersham sitting alone and walked over.

"Mind if I join you?"

She looked up. "Not at all." I noticed the suitcase under the table and Bella in her lap.

She saw my look. "The Grand Hotel is pet friendly. Isn't it wonderful?" She petted the small sleeping dog.

Lavender leaned forward. "Do you mind if I ask you a personal question?"

"Not at all." I hoped she wasn't going to ask me about the birds and the bees.

"What do you do for a living?"

I couldn't believe this was the burning personal question she wanted to ask. "I own a mystery bookshop." I took a deep breath and hurried on. "And, I write cozy mysteries."

Lavender gasped and clapped her hands. "How wonderful. I love mysteries, but I don't know what differentiates them. What exactly is a cozy mystery?"

This was a question I was well prepared for, having answered it many times in my life. I went through the spiel I had fine-tuned over the years. "Cozy mysteries, or cozies, are mysteries that feature an amateur sleuth, which is usually a woman but doesn't have to be. They are often set in a small town, and they don't have excessive violence, sex, or bad language." I smiled. "It's all about the clues and figuring out whodunit."

Lavender Habersham hung on to every word, as though they were golden nuggets that would unlock a magic door to wealth and riches. "Oh gosh, that sounds wonderful."

"I enjoy them."

"How did you come to open your own bookstore? I love books, and I think that might be something that I can do to support myself."

I explained to her that it was something my husband, Leon, and I always dreamed about doing because we were such big mystery fans. "I think the idea of being surrounded by books and sharing that love of mysteries with other people who love mysteries too had a lot to do with it." I thought about Leon and smiled. "I remember one night Leon had just finished reading a mystery by Stuart Kaminsky. It was a Porfiry Rostnikov mystery. I think it was the fourth book in the series. Anyway, it was late, and he wanted the next book in the series. There was no local bookstore in North Harbor where we could get mysteries. The closest bookstore was in River Bend, Indiana, which was thirty minutes away." I looked across at her and smiled as the memory came back. "This was before you could just go online and download the books. It must have been ten o'clock at night, and he threw his clothes on over his pajamas and drove like a crazy man to get to the big-box bookstore before it closed." I chuckled. "He made it with ten minutes to spare and picked up the next three books in the series. On the drive home, all he talked about was how nice it would be to own a mystery bookshop where we could get any book we wanted whenever we wanted." I sat there and allowed the warmth of the memory to flood my being.

"How nice," Lavender whispered.

I laughed at her reverential tone. "Well, I think it was the spark that got us dreaming. When Leon died, he made me promise to take the insurance money, sell the house, and stop waiting."

"Waiting for what?"

"I think we let fear of failure hold us back. We were waiting for . . . our ship to come in, the planets to be perfectly aligned, and for everything to fall in our laps." I looked across at the eager woman, who was hanging on my every word. "Look, if you wait until everything is perfect before you take a chance and follow your dreams, then you'll be waiting for the rest of your life. Perfection doesn't exist. Life is much too short not to at least try."

"Weren't you afraid you'd fail?"

"Absolutely. I'm still afraid. Even the big-box bookstores are closing all the time. People either don't read or they're reading ebooks. Will anyone really want physical books? Do people still want mysteries? Maybe I should write other genres like fantasy or romance. I worry every single day, but then I get up and do what I love doing."

"Wow." Lavender stared. "You have to be the bravest person I know."

I smiled. "Have you met my grandmother?"

Lavender Habersham and I chatted through lunch, and then I felt the butterflies in my stomach as I realized it was time to go to the Torquay Museum.

The Torquay Museum had a large collection of photographs, letters, manuscripts, and memorabilia of their most distinguished resident, Dame Agatha Christie. In addition to Christie's personal belongings, the museum also included props used in the adaptations of some of her novels for television. Normally, I find things like this over the top, but I thoroughly enjoyed seeing Poirot's desk and the furniture from his London Art Deco apartment. There was even one of the outfits worn in a Miss Marple episode by Joan Hickson and the Hercule Poirot walking stick that actor David Suchet made famous.

After the museum, we took the bus through the Devon countryside to Agatha Christie's home, Greenway, which was where she wrote many of her famous books and plays. The house also served as the setting for three of her novels. Situated on the River Dart, the white Georgian home sits majestically in the landscape, with gardens that when in bloom must have been amazing. I took lots of pictures and fangirled over the first edition books in the house.

"You've taken pictures of every inch of this place," Nana Jo said.

I nearly jumped when she came up behind me. I was so intent on getting a picture of the frieze that encircled the four walls of the library that I hadn't noticed her until she spoke. Twelve of the thirteen murals were attributed to American Lt. Marshall Lee of the United States Coast Guard. According to the literature, Christie's house had been requisitioned by the Coast Guard during World War II.

"I have to figure out a way to incorporate this into one of my books." I turned to look at my grandmother. "Maybe Lady Elizabeth visits her good friend Agatha and comes to Greenway House." I had an epiphany. "Ooh, wouldn't it be great if they solved a mystery together?"

"The timing would be perfect. She and her second husband, Max, bought the house in 1938, which is right around the timeframe for your books."

My mind raced at the possibilities. Far too soon, our visit to Greenway was over. The bus took us back to the Grand

Hotel. Dinner was originally supposed to include a lecture by a local professor and Agatha Christie expert, but the changes in our schedule led to a revision to the plans. Nana Jo and the girls all wanted to hang out at a local pub.

Despite the name, the Hole in the Wall turned out to be a great experience. Opened around 1540, it held the distinction as the oldest pub in Torquay. Cobbled floors and low-beamed ceilings created an ambiance that would have been a perfect meeting place for smugglers, which it had been. Despite the pub's age and disreputable clientele from ages past, it was now a well-respected meeting place that featured live music and a world-class restaurant. I was pleasantly surprised to find the pub's restaurant offered everything from traditional pub food of bangers and mash and fish and chips to liver pâté and pan-seared scallops. The food was delicious, and the prices were reasonable. When we finished eating, we moved to the bar area to enjoy live music.

It wasn't long before Irma was flirting with a local at the bar. Dorothy, who had a deep sultry singing voice, was singing duets with tonight's featured musician, a guitarist and songwriter. Ruby Mae made friends with a waiter and was knitting by the fireplace and chatting with the staff like they were old friends. Nana Jo was getting a lesson on ales and was at the bar with about nine varieties in front of her. Even Hannah had run into a couple who were visiting Torquay from New Zealand. In the it's-a-small-world-after-all basket, the couple knew Hannah's sister.

I sat quietly nursing a glass of wine and soaking in the atmosphere. The pub was small, but I managed to find a quiet spot that was set back into an alcove. From there, I could hear and see, but unless someone stood up and looked around the corner, I couldn't be seen. It was private, and I imagined smugglers meeting to discuss their illegal cargo in just such a place. I overheard snatches of conversation from nearby tables when the music stopped. Once, I heard a voice I recognized as belonging to Debra Holt.

"Look, this farce is almost over. We've got two more days and then we can get out of this backwater and get married just as we planned, and no one can stop us."

"The police will—"

"The police can't stop me from selling the business. The bottom line is that I'm Uncle Horace's heir—his only heir. He wanted to sell the business, and so do I. There's nothing wrong in that."

The music started again, and I wasn't able to hear Sebastian's response. I sipped my wine, sat back, and allowed my mind to drift. I wondered if Agatha Christie had ever sat at the Hole in the Wall. Something about the very idea that the queen of the cozy mystery may have once dined here got my juices flowing. I couldn't wait to jot down my thoughts and pulled out my notepad.

Detective Inspector Covington walked around the outside of the house and examined the ground under the window of the guest room where Captain Jessup had slept. He stood up and found himself staring into the salon window and looking at Lady Clara. She opened the French door.

"What on earth are you looking for?"

Detective Inspector Covington took a moment to wipe his feet before stepping inside. "I was hoping for a footprint or some other type of evidence to the killer's identity."

"Any luck?"

"I found some pills." He held them out for her to see, but then put them in his pocket. He cupped his hands and blew on them.

"You're freezing. Go to the fire and warm yourself before you catch a cold." She walked to the wall and pushed the button to summon the butler. "I'll order hot tea."

The detective obeyed and walked over to the fireplace and extended his hands.

"What are you grinning about?" Lady Clara said.

"Have you noticed that you're always ordering me about?"

She flushed. "Apparently, you need looking after. It's a wonder you've survived this long. How on earth you've managed is beyond me."

"Looking after a policeman is a difficult job. Not many women would sign up for it."

She looked up. "I guess you must not have met the right woman."

The two gazed into each other's eyes. The warmth of the fireplace, their close proximity to each other, and a look that smoldered like the embers from the fireplace left them both flushed. As if by magic, the two were drawn into each other's arms by an invisible force. Within seconds, they were locked into a passionate embrace. Their lips hungrily sought each other, and they allowed their passion to wash over them like a flood.

The spell was broken when Thompkins opened the door. He stopped and turned to leave.

The two withdrew.

"Thompkins, could you bring tea and sandwiches, please?" Lady Clara's voice was husky with emotion.

"Yes, Lady Clara." Thompkins bowed and silently left, closing the door behind him.

The couple awkwardly avoided eye contact. Eventually, the detective inspector turned away from the fireplace. "Lady Clara, I'm sorry . . . I shouldn't have—"

"Don't ruin things by apologizing. You didn't force me. And stop calling me Lady Clara. Why can't we just be Clara and Peter?"

"Because that's not how things are. You're . . . an aristocrat, and I'm . . . not."

"I'm a daughter of an earl who, like many of England's *aristocracy*, is weighted down by a title but no money. Things are changing in England." She folded her arms across her chest. "The last war taught us that aristocrats can die just like butlers, footmen, and gardeners. And, if there's another war, which it seems like we're headed for, then earls like Victor and policemen like you . . ." She turned away as tears rolled down her cheeks.

He walked over to her and pulled her into his arms and held her close. He placed his head on hers and inhaled. "If there's another war, we'll have to go. It's our duty."

She sniffled. "I know, but that doesn't make it any easier."

There was a polite knock on the door. The couple stepped apart.

Thompkins entered, carrying a tray laden with tea, sandwiches, and scones. He placed the tray on a table, quietly turned, and walked out.

The detective inspector handed her a handkerchief.

She dried her eyes and wiped her face. "I must look an awful mess."

"You look beautiful."

"Liar." She glanced at the detective. After a few moments, she turned to the tea tray and began to pour. "I don't want to think about the war. Not today. Today, I just want to be a woman having tea with a man." She looked up at the detective. "Would you care for milk or honey, Peter?"

The detective shook his head and accepted the teacup. "Thank you, Clara." He sat down in a chair and sipped his tea.

Lady Clara stared for a moment, but then she poured herself tea and smiled.

Downstairs in the servants' hall, Thompkins was confronted by a flurry of activity. An inebriated Hyrum McTavish was stumbling about, barely able to stand.

"Da, let me take you home," Frank McTavish said, trying to steer his father toward the door.

"No, I gotta talk to his lordship." He pushed Frank aside and stumbled into a chair. "Gotta talk. His lordship."

"What's going on here?" Thompkins said.

The groundskeeper made another attempt to move toward the stairs but found the butler to be an immovable wall. "His lordship, gotta 'splain."

Thompkins stared down his nose. "You are in no shape to talk to anyone. Even if his lordship were home."

The groundskeeper stared at Thompkins and then crumpled to the floor.

Frank struggled to lift his father. "He's passed out."

Thompkins sighed and carefully removed his jacket and placed it on a hook on the wall. "You'll never be able to lift him alone." He turned to Jim, who was standing nearby. "Get the door." He then bent down and lifted the grounds-keeper's feet, while Frank reached under his father's shoulders and lifted him. Between the two of them, they carried him outside and across to the cottage.

The next morning, we boarded the Paignton and Dartmouth Steam Railway. The brochures promised a journey known to Hercule Poirot, Christie's Belgian detective. The tour followed the Devon coast, past the picturesque stations featured in the *ABC Murders*. We took time to explore the cobbled, winding streets of historic Dartmouth, then embarked on a cruise up the River Dart, where we caught another glimpse of Christie's house, Greenway. I couldn't help but think of *Dead Man's Folly*, which when depicted on television was set at Greenway and showed the boathouse where the first murder of a girl guide occurred. Clive was well versed in Christie lore and shared that notes were found demonstrating how she had been walking across her property when she first got the idea for the story. I was fascinated.

After the tour, we headed off for Dartmoor, the ancient moorland known for its enormous granite rock formations that the locals called "tors," wild ponies, mist, and rain. Clive explained this was where Sir Arthur Conan Doyle set his great story *The Hound of the Baskervilles*.

We walked along the moors, and I was surprised when I stumbled across a brightly painted smooth stone. I picked up the rock and smiled as I slipped it in my purse.

"What're you doing with rocks?" Nana Jo said. "We got plenty of those in Michigan."

"Who knows, I might need something to hurl at the murderer." I smiled. "After all, I used to be pretty good at fast-pitch in high school."

Hannah Schneider stared. "What's fast-pitch?"

"Softball," Nana Jo said. "Sam's team won the state championship in high school."

I rotated my arm as though I were pitching. "It's been a while, but I used to be pretty good."

We headed back to London for dinner. Tonight, we decided to try an Indian restaurant, Brigadiers, which Frank had recommended. Frank Patterson was a foodie through and through. He was not only a great cook but knew the best restaurants around the globe. We invited D. S. Templeton to join us, but she wanted to get home first. However, she did say she'd join us there later for drinks, and I suspected she wanted to get the latest news we'd managed to ferret out of our tour companions.

Brigadiers was a maze that seemed to go on forever. There were red leather seats, polished mahogany, and plenty of gold detail that supported the Indian theme. With a vending machine that dispensed whiskey and a pool room, there was definitely something for everyone in our group to enjoy. There was also a bar with at least ten televisions, which were all tuned in to sports. North Harbor, Michigan, was a small town with limited culinary options. These exotic-sounding dishes had my head spinning. So, I sent a quick text to Frank asking for suggestions. I wasn't surprised when, seconds later, my phone rang and his picture popped up. He asked a few questions about how many people were with me and if anyone had food allergies. Learning there were no restrictions, he then told me to hand the phone to the waiter.

Our waiter, Sunil, took the phone. After a tentative greeting, he listened for a few moments and then broke into a big grin and began speaking in another language. Sunil pulled out his order pad and wrote as quickly as he spoke. When he was done, he handed back my phone, bowed, and hurried away.

"What just happened here?"

Frank chuckled. "I just ordered you the most amazing dinner ever. I hope your friends will enjoy it."

"What language were you speaking?"

"Hindi."

"Hindi, Italian, Greek, what other surprises are you hiding?"

Even though I couldn't see his face, I knew he was smiling. "I'll be happy to show you all my secrets when you come back."

I could feel the heat rising up my neck, and I knew I had a silly grin on my face because I couldn't stop from smiling. "I can't wait."

We flirted for a few more minutes until Sunil returned with several dishes that smelled amazing and reminded me how hungry I was.

Sunil explained the dishes were pappadums and chutneys,

lotus root and puff chaat, and a double order of masala chicken skins. He also brought martinis, which he mentioned were on draft. Our next course included Amritsari fried fish pao, BBQ butter chicken wings, and Afghani lamb cannon kebab skewers. He then brought achari beef short ribs, Sikandari kid goat shoulder, tawa prawn biryani, and a full rack of tandoori lamb chops.

Afterward, Nana Jo leaned back in her seat and said, "I couldn't eat another bite."

Dorothy licked barbecue sauce from her fingers. "I have no idea what I just ate, but it was darned good."

D. S. Templeton walked to our table in jeans and a sweatshirt. She glanced at the dishes covering the table and raised an eyebrow but said nothing.

Sunil rushed over. D. S. Templeton glanced at my cocktail and then requested the same. Sunil hurried off, taking several of the empty platters with him. He quickly returned with the martini and took the remaining plates.

Irma was making goo-goo eyes at a man sitting at the bar and looked about ready to go join her new friend when Nana Jo pulled out her iPad.

"Before we split up and head out for our own vices, we should take care of business." She glanced at Irma, who pouted but sat silently.

"Who wants to go first?" Nana Jo asked.

Irma raised a hand. "I might as well go first. I don't have much to tell." She took her compact out of her purse and proceeded to refresh her makeup while she talked. "Al said he hadn't seen Horace in decades. He was just about to get promoted when the university ran an article in the newspaper about him. A day later, he got a note from Horace asking to meet him." She applied lipstick and then took a napkin and blotted her lips. "He thought it was . . . queer, but he went to the meeting. He said Horace was awful. He said if Al didn't start paying him regularly, the university would find out about his dirty little secret."

"Horace Peabody was blackmailing Lavington?" Templeton asked with steel in her voice.

"He tried to blackmail him, but Al said he didn't pay . . . well, he really couldn't pay. Apparently, college professors don't make a ton of money." She sighed. "Anyway, not long afterward, the university received an anonymous tip that Al wasn't who he claimed to be, and he was sacked." She looked at Nana Jo. "That means fired."

Nana Jo rolled her eyes. "I know what it means."

"That seems rather underhanded," I said.

Ruby Mae snorted. "That's nothing for Horace Peabody." She knitted and glanced over at Irma. "Are you done?"

"That's it. Al said he was angry, but he never touched Peabody."

"Well, if he'd killed him, he'd hardly admit to it, would he?" Nana Jo said.

Irma turned and batted her eyelashes at her friend at the bar.

"Ruby Mae, you might as well go next."

"I didn't get anything more from Clive, but I did get a chance to talk to the Blankenships." She completed a row before continuing. "They're a nice couple, but when Tiffany was in college—"

"Tiffany went to college?" Nana Jo asked. "She doesn't seem like the college type."

"You shouldn't judge a book by its cover, Josephine. Just because she's blond, tanned, and attractive doesn't mean she isn't smart."

"I agree. I shouldn't have assumed."

Ruby Mae knitted a few more stitches. "She spent a summer abroad. Unfortunately, her boyfriend took some nude photos of her."

"What's wrong with that?" Irma said. "I've got photos—"

"Irma!" Nana Jo smacked the table. "Trust me when I tell you that none of us want to know about any naked photos of you floating around the retirement village."

Irma stuck out her tongue.

I glanced at D. S. Templeton, who looked stricken, but she quickly took a sip of her martini to cover.

Ruby Mae smiled. "Well, like I said, her boyfriend at the time took these photos, which she thought were private, but when she broke up with him, he sold them to a magazine in Britain."

"Without her permission?" I asked.

Ruby Mae nodded.

"That's horrible," Hannah said. "I hope she sued him."

"She was devastated, but the damage had already been done. Taking him to court would have only brought additional publicity to something she hoped would die away." Ruby Mae halted to complete a complicated cable stitch. "Her year abroad was up, and she went home to the States. She met Vincent, and they fell in love."

"Let me guess," I said. "She never told Vincent about the photos."

"You got it. The magazine with the nude photos never made it to the United States, and his family was extremely conservative. Everything was fine until she came on this tour and ran into Horace Peabody."

"Horace looks like the seedy sort of chap that would buy girly magazines and then try to blackmail the poor lass into sleeping with him," Hannah said.

"You nailed it."

I thought back to the introduction at the hotel. "So, when he was talking to Sebastian about being a model . . ."

Ruby Mae nodded. "Poor Tiffany said she knew he meant her."

"I thought that was odd at the time, but I thought he was mocking Sebastian," Nana Jo said, tapping her pen on the table. "I should have caught that."

"Did she confront him?" Templeton asked.

"She said he tried to corner her in the elevator and demanded that she come to his room that night, but she didn't. The poor thing said she was scared out of her mind when she went down to breakfast, but was relieved when she learned that Horace was supposedly dead."

"Did he try again?" Dorothy asked.

"He couldn't," I said. "He was supposed to be dead. So, he certainly couldn't risk being seen by anyone, even Tiffany."

"Anyway, I told her she needed to tell her husband about the photos," Ruby Mae said. "Married couples shouldn't have any secrets."

"That's good advice," Hannah said. "Eli and I didn't have any secrets. We were happy together."

Ruby Mae patted her friend's hand. "She told him."

"How'd he take it?" Dorothy asked.

"He was furious that Horace Peabody tried to force himself on her. He said if he'd known about it before, he might have kil—"

"He might have killed him?" Templeton said. "How do we know he didn't?" She pulled out her phone.

"Wait," I said. "We don't know that Blankenship knew about Horace trying to seduce his wife."

"We have nobody's word that he didn't know except his and his wife's, which is hardly reliable. He had a motive. He's a bloody doctor, so he absolutely had the means, and he had the opportunity." She picked up her cell phone and tapped numbers as she got up and hurried out of the restaurant.

Ruby Mae looked as though she wanted to cry.

I reached across and patted her hand. "It's not your fault."

"She never would have found out if I hadn't opened my mouth." She raised a hand and caught Sunil's attention. When the waiter arrived, she said, "I'm going to need one of those martinis."

"You better do them all around," Nana Jo said.

Sunil smiled and hurried away. He came back moments later with a tray and six glasses. He passed them around and took the empty glasses and hurried away.

We took a few moments and downed our martinis.

Nana Jo picked up her iPad. "Who's next?"

I shared the conversation I overheard between Debra Holt and Sebastian at the Hole in the Wall, although I didn't see how there was anything useful that would help us. No one else had anything to add.

Irma hurried to the bar, while Dorothy and Nana Jo went in search of the whiskey vending machine. Ruby Mae and Hannah sat and talked about grandchildren, and I went in search of the ladies' room.

The restaurant really was a maze, but I eventually found my way. When I returned, Sunil and a woman who looked like his mother were seated talking to Ruby Mae and Hannah. I found Nana Jo and Dorothy playing pool, and Irma had made a new friend and had advanced from distant flirting to light petting.

I ran into D. S. Templeton, who was just finishing her telephone call.

"Can I ask you a question?"

She gave me a look that indicated she'd rather have a root canal.

"What did Major Peabody die from? Dr. Blankenship wouldn't tell me, but he did say it wasn't digitalis."

She stared at me for several moments, but I didn't relent. I'd learned long ago that silence was a great tool. Few people could stand it. Eventually, she said, "He died from an allergic reaction." She put her cell phone in her pocket. "Bee venom." She turned and walked out.

I found a secluded alcove, pulled out my notepad, and started to write. I tried to wrap my head around Dr. Vincent Blankenship as a murderer, but something just didn't fit. Time was running out. Tomorrow was the last day of the tour, and unless we could put the pieces of the puzzle together quickly, an innocent man would be arrested, and the guilty party could go free.

Lord William, in his favorite chair, sat in the library with Nigel Greyson. Lord William filled his pipe, while Nigel stared into the fireplace, nursing a glass of scotch.

"Penny for them?"

Nigel turned. "Excuse me?"

"Your thoughts, man. What's bothering you." He held up a hand. "Now, don't pretend nothing's bothering you because it's obvious that something's wrong."

Nigel stared at his old friend. Eventually, he nodded and took a drink from his glass. "You're right. I should have come clean the other night, but . . . well, one doesn't always know what to do."

Lord William leaned back and huffed on his pipe. "Why don't you start from the beginning and we'll see what we can make of it."

Nigel took a deep breath. "I guess it started back in the war." He stood up and paced. "I was in the Royal Naval Reserve in Belgium."

"I thought you were part of Naval Intelligences . . . hush, hush . . . Room 40." Lord William leaned forward and whispered, "Codebreaking."

"Yes, but that came later . . . around 1915. But before that, I was in the RNR. That's where I met Percival Carlston."

"Ah . . . Victor's uncle."

"Percy and I became good friends . . . real good friends."

Lord William frowned. "You know something about Jessup's claims, don't you?"

"I know Percival was honest and honorable." He hung his head. "More honorable than me."

"What do you mean?"

Nigel took a deep breath. "Percy wasn't the one who got Eileen Jessup pregnant." He turned to face Lord William. "I was. I'm the one that had a fling with a pretty nurse. Archibald Jessup was my son, not Percy's."

Chapter 22

The next day, I boarded the bus to Devon for the last leg of our tour. Normally, writing helped me sort through my problems, and I was able to solve mysteries, but this time, my subconscious had let me down. This morning, I wasn't feeling any closer to figuring out whodunit than I had been at the start.

Dr. Blankenship and Tiffany got on the bus. Both looked a lot older and more haggard than either one of them had looked yesterday. Based on the dark circles under their eyes, I'd say neither one of them had gotten much sleep. Given the cold look they gave Ruby Mae when they walked by her row, I suspected that D.S. Templeton had invited the couple to answer questions at the precinct and their lack of sleep was courtesy of D. I. Nelson and the Metropolitan Police Force.

Everyone climbed aboard, including D. S. Templeton. She barely spared me a glance as she moved to a seat in the back.

Today, we were headed back to the Cotswolds. Clive had managed to get us a quick tour of the racetrack that we'd missed. We would also get to spend some time traveling through the Forest of Dean. I had read a few Dick Francis novels but wasn't very knowledgeable about horses or racing. However, the horses were beautiful and powerful, and I enjoyed watching them run more than I thought I would.

The biggest surprise for me was the trip through the Forest of Dean. I erroneously assumed that the name meant a heavily wooded area with lots of wildlife and devoid of people. The Forest of Dean is an area that encompasses the three counties of Gloucestershire, Herefordshire, and Monmouthshire. It includes woodlands and game and has been a royal hunting retreat, but there are also villages, and the area is better known for ironworking and mining. The area's most recent claim to fame is *Harry Potter and the Deathly Hallows I* and *II*, as it was used as the filming location. The Cotswolds was also the setting for countless mysteries, including Andrew Taylor's Lydmouth series, Edward Marston's historical mystery *The Owls of Gloucester*, Rebecca Tope's Cotswold Mysteries, and M. C. Beaton's Agatha Raisin Mystery Series.

We stopped for lunch in Lydney at a pub called the Rising Sun. We realized that time was running out, but after an evening with D. I. Nelson, neither the Blakenships nor Clive Green seemed inclined to talk. Debra Holt and the handsome Sebastian maintained a good distance. Lavington and Hoffman sat together, and Lavender Habersham and Bella nibbled on cheese and bread in a corner.

I sat with Nana Jo, Hannah, and the girls. Lunch was fairly quiet as we faced the fact that this was the first case we weren't able to solve.

Nana Jo glanced at me. "Stop being so hard on yourself, Sam." She patted my hand. "Even Perry Mason had one loss in his career."

"I just feel like I'm missing something."

Ruby Mae pulled her honey out of her purse. "Well, we need to finish this honey today. I hate wasting food."

Nana Jo picked up the jar and poured a bit into her tea. "You say Clive made this?" She took a sip. "It's pretty good."

Irma shivered. "I don't know how anyone could stand being around bees."

"I like the honey, but I don't think I'd want to be the one to have to extract it," Dorothy said.

Hannah passed the jar to me. "I'm allergic to bees, so I certainly wouldn't be the one to extract the honey."

I stared at the jar and got a flash.

"I know that look," Nana Jo said, and she pulled out her iPad. "You've figured it out."

"I think I have."

"It was the honey, wasn't it?" Ruby Mae shook her head. "I hate to think of Clive killing that man."

"It wasn't Clive. At least, I'm pretty sure it wasn't." I looked around. "Where's D. S. Templeton?"

Clive Green rose and announced it was time to head back.

Everyone started making their way to the bus. I couldn't find D. S. Templeton anywhere. "I need to call D. I. Nelson." I took my cell phone from my purse and rushed outside. I climbed onto the bus and dialed the number for the Scotland Yard detective, but I got his voicemail. "Detective, this is Samantha Washington. I think I know who murdered Major Peabody and Mrs. Habersham. Please call me back, or better yet, send a car to meet us at the hotel."

"That's enough."

I hadn't noticed anyone was listening until I looked up and saw Debra Holt pointing a gun at me.

Chapter 23

"I knew you would be trouble." She smirked and extended her hand. "Now, give me that phone."

I made an elaborate gesture of pushing disconnect and dropped the phone into my purse. "What are you going to do now? Kill me like you killed your uncle?"

"Yes."

"You're not going to be able to frame Clive for my murder. I'm not allergic to bees." I prayed that was true. Actually, I'd never been stung by a bee, so I wasn't exactly sure if I was allergic or not.

"I'm sure I'll come up with something."

"Why'd you do it?"

"For the money, what else? He was loaded and planned on disinheriting me. I couldn't let that happen now, could I?"

"But why frame Clive? What'd he ever do you?"

"Nothing. Clive was just a useful fall guy. He raised bees, and Uncle Horace was allergic. Someone had to take the blame for the murder."

"And Mrs. Habersham?"

"That old woman was trying to take my inheritance for

herself and her crazy daughter. Battling a DNA case could have held things up for years, and Sebastian and I have plans." She glanced around. "Enough questions. Move."

She slid into a seat so I could pass and then pointed her gun to indicate she wanted me to move to the front.

"My grandmother and the others will notice if we're not on the bus."

The doors on the bus opened, and everyone climbed aboard and began taking their seats.

Debra glanced at the window and caught Sebastian's eye. He nodded and moved to the back of the queue.

I opened my mouth to scream when I saw Nana Jo climb aboard, but I quickly felt the gun muzzle in the small of my back. I felt the heat from Debra's breath as she whispered in my ear, "One word and you're a dead woman."

I clamped my mouth shut but tried to send my grandmother a mental message. Unfortunately, my mental telepathy wasn't working, and Nana Jo merely climbed aboard and took her seat.

I didn't see D. S. Templeton anywhere.

After a few moments, Sebastian climbed aboard. He looked back at Debra. "What do you want me to do?"

She pushed me aside onto the seat and then held her gun up so everyone could see. "Close the door before that detective comes back."

Sebastian did as he was told.

Debra walked to the front of the bus past all of the startled passengers. She pointed her gun at the driver. "Drive, and don't make any funny moves or you'll be the first to go."

The driver started the engine and pulled the bus into the street.

From a window, I saw D. S. Templeton. She stared after the bus in shocked surprise and then quickly took out her cell phone.

The bus drove at a slow, meandering pace through the narrow village streets back toward the forested area.

Debra turned to Sebastian. "Tie them up."

I stood to move back to my seat but was halted when Debra pointed her gun toward me. "Sit back down!"

I obeyed.

Debra turned to the bus driver and pointed. "Take that road."

The driver steered the bus down the narrow, rocky path.

"Hurry up!" Deborah yelled to Sebastian.

He turned and held up his hands. "It's bloody hard to tie people up without rope." He held up a necktie and two belts he'd confiscated from Clive Green, Oscar Hoffman, and Albus Lavington.

She pointed the gun at Ruby Mae. "That one's always knitting. Use the yarn."

Debra looked out of the window and then ordered the driver to stop the bus. "Keep your hands on the steering wheel where I can see them."

The bus driver did as he was told, and Debra reached in her purse and pulled out a pair of handcuffs. "I knew these would come in handy."

"Hey, those are mine," Irma yelled.

"I snagged them after you held them up in the ballroom the other day." Debra smirked. "This is a much better use, don't you think?" She cuffed the driver to the steering wheel.

Sebastian made faster progress with the yarn. He quickly tied my hands together and joined Debra at the front of the bus.

Ruby Mae was maneuvering, and I was sure she and Nana Jo were up to something. I also hoped that my phone was still recording.

"You never told me how you did it!" I yelled.

Debra looked up. "Did what?"

"How'd you use the bee venom to kill your uncle?"

Debra smiled. "I didn't." She turned to Sebastian. "That was all Sebastian."

Sebastian glared at Debra. "You told me to do it."

"So, when you went to tell Major Peabody that the game was up, he was still alive?" I asked.

"It was horrible," Sebastian said. "I had to plunge the needle into his chest, and he flopped around like a fish."

"What are you going to do with us?" Professor Lavington asked.

Debra smirked. "You're about to have an unfortunate bus accident." She pointed to the cliff.

Nana Jo moaned. "Oh my goodness. I think I'm going to be sick. Please, help me." She rose and took a few steps.

"Stay where you are," Debra ordered.

Sebastian bent down and began to work on something under the steering column.

Nana Jo moaned louder. "Please. Please help me."

Debra sighed and took a few steps forward. "I don't know why I'm doing this since you're just going to be dead in a few minutes anyway."

Just as Debra reached the seat, Nana Jo lunged.

Ruby Mae plunged a knitting needle into Debra's hand.

Debra screamed.

Nana Jo flipped Debra and held her on the ground and kicked the gun under the seats of the bus, out of reach.

Sebastian stood at the front of the bus, unsure what to do. He flipped the handle to open the door and took a step.

I slipped from my wool ties. I reached down and grabbed one of the rocks that I had picked up on the moors. Recalling my days from fast-pitch softball in high school, I wound up and sent the rock careening through the air. It hit its mark, striking Sebastian in the forehead. He was knocked out cold and crumpled like a deflated balloon.

The police sirens surrounding the bus drowned out the cheers from our fellow passengers.

"Still got your pitching arm," Nana Jo said, smiling at me. "That's my girl."

Chapter 24

We waited on the bus while Dr. Blankenship attended to Debra Holt's hand. Despite her cries to remove the knitting needle, he refused. Eventually, she passed out before the ambulance arrived.

Sebastian came to, and apart from a large red bump on the center of his head that looked like a doorknob, he seemed otherwise unharmed. He left in a separate ambulance.

The police brought strong coffee and blankets for the rest of us. After I gave a quick recap to D. S. Templeton, she allowed the bus driver to take us back to the pub at Lydney while she called for reinforcements.

If good news travels fast, bad news travels at the speed of sound. By the time we were settled back at the pub, the media had descended on the small town, and we were pressed for interviews. Most of us had had enough and just wanted a quiet place to recover. Irma looked at the attention as if she were the queen of England. She primped and wiggled and flirted with the reporters. When asked, "What was your role in solving this murder?" she smiled and said, "Well, it was my handcuffs the killer used to confine the driver."

Nana Jo merely shook her head. "If I had the strength, I'd get up and smack her."

When a reporter learned that I'd played a role in solving the murders and tried to interview me, I surprised my grandmother and my friends when I turned and faced the camera. "Actually, it was all Detective Sergeant Moira Templeton. She's the real hero. She knew the killer had to be on the bus, and she stayed with us, protecting the innocent while she hunted down the killer."

When I'd finished, the reporter tracked down D. S. Templeton to get the real story.

Templeton and I exchanged a brief glance before she was thrust into the limelight.

Nana Jo leaned over. "You laid it on pretty thick."

I gave her the most innocent look I could muster. "I have no idea what you're talking about."

Dorothy smiled. "You stopped just shy of inferring that D. S. Templeton was able to leap tall buildings in a single bound."

I chuckled. "Well, I think she deserved some credit. She did find us on that cliff."

"After we had already unmasked and disarmed the killers," Nana Jo added.

I waved my hand. "Pishposh."

D. I. Nelson arrived just as D. S. Templeton was in the middle of her interview, and his face grew as red as a beet.

Nana chuckled. "That sight alone was well worth letting D. S. Templeton take all of the credit."

Hannah turned to me. "I understand how you figured out that Major Peabody was killed by the bee venom, but how did you know it wasn't Clive Green?"

"Remember when Debra was having her hysterics?"

"Which time?" Ruby Mae asked.

"After they discovered that Major Peabody was *really* dead.

She mentioned how Clive kept his bees even though he knew that her uncle was allergic." I looked around. "Well, no one knew that Major Peabody was allergic to bees. When Dr. Blankenship diagnosed his death as digitalis, she was shocked. I wondered how she could be so sure and what difference it would make whether her uncle died from digitalis or not. That's what kept bothering me."

Nana Jo snapped her fingers. "She needed the death to be bee venom so she could frame Clive."

"But why did it have to be Clive?"

"Because she needed Clive out of the way so she could gain control of the business. She *said* she was her uncle's only heir and intended to sell the business, but she couldn't be sure *legally* that Clive wouldn't be able to stop her."

Hannah said, "Just like she needed to get rid of poor Mrs. Habersham."

"Exactly. Besides, there were several people who benefited from the death of Horace Peabody, but Debra Holt was the only person who benefited from the death of both of them."

We talked a bit further, but eventually the police allowed us to go back to our hotel. We got up and headed outside.

Clive Green was waiting at the steps of the bus.

Nana Jo whispered, "Clive looks like he's been through a few rounds with George Foreman."

As we prepared to board, he hugged me. "Thank you," he whispered. "If it wasn't for you . . . I . . ."

I gave him a squeeze. "It was my pleasure."

Everyone was worn out by the time the bus left, and we slept on the bus back to London. Unfortunately, sleep alluded me. Instead, I pulled out my notepad.

Lord William sat in his chair smoking and re-layed the story he had heard earlier from Nigel Greyson.

Lady Elizabeth knitted. "So, it was Nigel that Mrs. McDuffie heard arguing with Captain Jessup the night he was killed?"

"He tried to tell him the truth, but . . ."

"Jessup didn't believe him?" Lady Penelope asked.

"I suspect Captain Jessup knew the truth," Lady Elizabeth said, "but he didn't want Nigel ru-ining his chance to not only humiliate Victor but also get his hands on the title."

"But," Lady Clara said, "how could he possi-bly think he would be able to prove something that wasn't true?"

Lady Elizabeth gave Victor a quick glance and smiled. "I suspect he was counting on Victor being an honorable man. He knew Victor wouldn't want the title if he thought it didn't belong to him, and he gambled on the fact that Victor wouldn't fight him."

Victor stared from Lady Elizabeth to his wife. "I wouldn't have fought him. I never cared about the money or the title. I just never imagined he would lie."

Lady Elizabeth smiled. "That's because you're a good man."

Lord William puffed on his pipe. "That's not all. It turns out Jessup had another secret." He looked around. "This one's worse than trying to cheat Victor out of his title."

"Oh dear." Lady Penelope took out a handkerchief. "What else could possibly be worse?"

Lord William braced himself. "During the war, Nigel was involved in British intelligence. I can't talk about the details, but let's just say he had access to a lot of important documents. One of the documents he got his hands on was related to Jessup. At the time, he didn't know that Jessup was his son, mind you." Lord William bit on the stem of his pipe. "But he recognized his face."

"That must be why he asked if they'd met before the night of the party," Lady Clara said.

Lord William smiled at his cousin. "That's it. He recognized him, but he couldn't place him. It wasn't until later, much later, that he went back to London and . . . learned that Jessup, his son, was a traitor."

Lady Penelope gasped.

Victor was thrown for a loop and sat down and stared. "A traitor?"

"There was a horrible battle at Passchendaele." Lord William removed his pipe, and tobacco leaves scattered over his suit and onto the floor. "That's in Belgium. Jessup was in charge of a regiment, but when the battle took a turn for the worse, Jessup deserted his men."

"How is that possible?" Victor pounded his fist into his hand. "He should have been court-martialed."

"Most of the regiment was killed. There were rumors that they may have been betrayed, but there wasn't enough proof." Lord William paused a few moments. "It's believed only a few men survived, and . . . well, they were never the same afterward."

Thompkins had been standing silently near the wall. At this point, he coughed discreetly.

Lady Elizabeth turned to face the butler. "Yes, Thompkins?"

"I believe I know one of the survivors."

Everyone turned to stare.

For probably the first time since she'd met the butler, Thompkins seemed ruffled. He took a few deep breaths. "One of the few survivors at Passchendaele was a young private . . . Hyrum McTavish."

Lady Elizabeth nodded. "I suspected as much. How did you find out?"

"He told me himself." Thompkins gave her a hard stare. "He recognized Jessup immediately. I think when he saw him again, standing in the kitchen downstairs . . . something snapped."

"I can understand why," Lady Penelope whispered. "That's horrible."

Detective Inspector Covington asked Lady Elizabeth, "How did you guess?"

"You found ladder marks on the ground, but no ladder." She continued knitting. "I live here, but I doubt that even I would know where to find a ladder, let alone know where to put it back. It would have to be one of the servants. Thompkins told us about the encounter between McTavish and Captain Jessup, and more importantly, Jessup's reaction to McTavish." She paused. "Plus, there was the fact that the coroner found bee venom. The groundskeeper would know where to find bees at this time of year. He must have put some in the room. He wasn't aware of the captain's heart condition, but when he saw the digitalis . . . he must have gotten the idea he could make the death look like a heart attack." She sighed. "I'm terribly sorry for him and poor Frank."

Detective Inspector Covington stared at her for several moments, but then turned to Thompkins. "You'd better take me to him."

Lady Clara said, "Peter, you can't take him. He was driven to it. Can't you see? Jessup deserved exactly what he got. He was a horrible man."

"I have to take him in." He looked at Lady Clara and said softly, "It's my job, Lady Clara."

Lady Elizabeth accompanied Thompkins and the detective out to the groundskeeper's cottage.

Inside, she found Frank McTavish standing near the fireplace. His face was streaked with tears. He handed Lady Elizabeth a handwritten note.

She read the note and then passed it to Detective Inspector Covington, who read it.

Frank McTavish sobbed. "He confessed. Took his ladder and snuck into the room. Then he took some bees and put them in the room. The sergeant he knew in the war was allergic to bee venom." He sniffed. "But he couldn't live with what he'd done. So, he . . ." He sobbed uncontrollably.

Lady Elizabeth reached out her arms and pulled the young man into an embrace. He sobbed on her shoulder.

Detective Inspector Covington removed his hat and walked out.

Later, Lady Clara was waiting alone in the library. Detective Inspector Covington entered. The two gazed at each other, but there was something between them.

"So, he killed himself?"

He nodded.

"Poor Frank." She turned to the detective. "Does anyone have to know?"

"What do you mean?"

"McTavish was Catholic. If he killed himself, that's considered a mortal sin, and he can't be buried in the churchyard."

"But—"

"I know you're a policeman and you have a duty to perform, but he's dead now."

"But—"

"Doesn't poor Frank deserve some justice? He deserves to have his father buried properly alongside his mum."

"Listen, I just want—"

"What justice can be served by telling the world that McTavish killed himself? Can't you just—"

Peter Covington grabbed her and pulled her to him and kissed her. She flung her arms around his neck and kissed him back. After a few moments, he pushed away. "I'm sorry."

She raised a fist and shook it at him. "If you apologize one more time for kissing me, I'm going to hit you."

He smiled. "I'm sorr—"

She punched him in the arm.

"Ouch."

"I warned you." She glared. "Now, why did you stop me?"

"I just wanted to tell you that I agree. No one needs to know that Hyrum McTavish killed himself. As far as the police are concerned."

Her face lit up. "Really?"

He nodded.

She flung herself in his arms and kissed him hard. When she came up for air, she smiled and said, "I'm not the least bit sorry for that, either."

The detective pulled her close and kissed her slowly. "Neither am I."

Chapter 25

When the bus finally pulled up to the front of the hotel, it was dark. Everyone filed off and headed toward the elevators. The last evening of the trip featured a visit to the theatre. Everyone hurried to their rooms to get changed.

I was dead tired and probably would have skipped the theatre were it not for a chance to cap off my British adventure by seeing Agatha Christie's highly successful play, *The Mousetrap*. Even though I'd seen the play before, I went. It was great, and I enjoyed it more than the previous time I'd seen it, probably because this time I was seeing it in her native England. We arrived back from the theatre and were stopped by the hotel manager.

He spotted us and hurried around the counter. "I have some good news for you."

"I could use some good news," Nana Jo said. "What is it?"

He flung his hand around to indicate a pile of luggage. "The airline finally found your lost luggage."

We stared at the luggage stacked up next to the counter.

"I will have the bellmen take it up to your rooms."

"Don't bother," Nana Jo said. "They'll just need to bring it back down in a few hours anyway."

The manager looked confused. "What would you like me to do with it?"

"Tell the airlines to take these bags and shove them up their a—"

"Irma!"

She broke into a coughing fit.

I glanced at one of the tags. "Bangladesh?"

"Looks like our luggage has traveled more than we did," Nana Jo said. She went to catch the elevator, and when the doors opened, she said, "You coming?"

"I'll be up in a few minutes."

Nana Jo nodded and went upstairs with the girls.

I sat in the lobby of the hotel and thought about the trip. England had been exciting, dangerous, frustrating, and educational. I leaned back in the alcove where I'd sat many nights before. I had visited the native ground of one of my literary heroes, Dame Agatha Christie. I walked through her home and visited some of the same places where she was inspired to write so many amazing mysteries. I hoped that one day I could attain a fraction of her success. England was a wonderful place, but I was happy to be going home to my poodles and my bookshop, where all my British murders were contained in the pages of my books.

Made in United States
North Haven, CT
01 February 2023

31993620R00157